ADDITIONAL ATTENDEE

A PAULWHATSHISNAME MYSTERY

JOSH HARPER

PROPINQUITY PUBLISHES BOOKS

ADDITIONAL ATTENDEE

A PAUL WHATSHISNAME MYSTERY

Josh Harper

Propinquity Publishes Books

❀ Created with Vellum

PRAISE FOR ADDITIONAL ATTENDEE

"Harper's debut delivers a compelling mix of mystery and dark comedy... Harper's writing is crisp, witty, and conversational . . . The crime is layered and engaging, but not overly complex, and despite the wit, the suspense is consistent as Harper deftly blends mystery, satire, and Brooklyn character study, all with impeccable scene craft. Harper stages surprises, revelations, gags, and bursts of self-discovery with equal aplomb. Even readers steeped in the genre will find the ending a dazzling surprise with real emotional resonance." - *BookLife* (Editor's Pick)

"A wryly told mystery . . . Harper does a deft job of producing red herrings that will misdirect even the savviest of armchair sleuths . . . A diverting whodunit with an unconventional sleuth!" - *Kirkus Reviews*

"A smart, snarky, and satisfying high-rise mystery. Neurotic narration and a twisting plot make this first installment of the *Paul Whatshisname Mystery* series a refreshingly original and entertaining thriller." - *SPR*, ★★★★½

"If you like mysteries, if you like characters that are humorously self-deprecating, if you ever wondered about life in a condo microcosm, then this is the book for you. It's a who-done-it, missing-spouse, on-the-lamb, murder-in-the-building kind of read. I highly recommend it."- *Reedsy*

"Farce and introspection combine seamlessly in Josh Harper's fanciful send-up of the classic detective murder-mystery. More than a comic caper, it is also a study in self-delusion and loss." - *IndieReader 4.9 out of 5 stars*

"For readers looking for a blend of wit, satire, and mystery, Additional Attendee is a refreshing addition to the genre." - *A Look Inside*

"Evocative descriptions of the secretive, entitled residents and their jealousies and volatile relationships are riveting and bluntly presented. As Paul becomes a murder suspect, he and Alina begin a clandestine search of the building whenever residents are absent. Their partnership and Paul's inner dialogue and insecurity are frequently laugh-out-loud funny. Timely comments on inequality increase Paul's gravitas and appeal."- *Audiofile Magazine*

For Joel

CHAPTER 1
ORANGETHEORY

woke up thinking it hadn't been much of a spring, rainy and cold. I was hungry. For breakfast. Maybe bacon, egg, and cheese on a toasted sesame bagel? They don't make good bagels in New York City anymore. Other cities emulating New York make better bagels than New York. Isn't that disappointing? But before I allowed myself to fall into a food-related vortex of regret and anger, I groaned to a standing position, took two steps, my right heel hurting when I put weight on it, and peered around the side of the shade, out at our third-floor balcony and the gleaming blue city beyond.

Sunny. Huh.

I looked back at the bed where Laura lay smothered in our white comforter and her own black hair. She pretended to be asleep while I pulled on cargo shorts, a torn flannel, and a crusty cap, thus completing a look I call down-on-his-luck fisherman. Feet clad in flip-flops, I crept out the apartment door.

Wondering for no apparent reason whether Laura and I should have had children, I padded down the long hallway toward the center elevator, the dull sconces turning on as I passed. Yeah, my heel was still hurting. Bone spur? What exactly is a bone spur?

Maybe it's one of those things that's well enough left alone? Hitting the down button, I pondered my lifelong philosophy of leaving well enough alone. Had that been a mistake? But then in the elevator, a follow-up thought: no use fighting one's own nature—that's a losing battle.

The doors slid open onto the ivy-trellised lobby, and there she was: Alina, small behind the granite-topped front desk, reading a paperback with a library number on the spine. She looked up— oh, those large unfashionable glasses, her professional lacy white button-down, and that smile—and she said, "Good morning, Paul."

Yes, it is a good morning, Alina. It's sunny!

But I merely grumbled, "Morning," because I didn't want my sudden internal cheeriness at the sight of her to freak her out. Our tenant/front desk person relationship rested on a bedrock of apparent apathy.

"Did you forget someone?" she asked.

"Oh shit. The dog. Hopefully he's asleep on the couch?" I'd hear hell from Laura about not taking the dog out. "Unless it found a job and entered society. That would be a relief."

Alina didn't laugh. But why should she? It wasn't funny. She just stared at me, waiting for me to say something else stupid. She did that sometimes. That was our thing. No. We didn't have a thing. After all, I was a middle-aged man who knew his way around a muffin and looked it. And she was cute and smart and maybe thirty. I wasn't that deluded. Not yet.

"Want anything from outside?" I said because I had to say something.

"Where are you going?"

"Bagels, Bagels, Bagels."

"Their bagels are good."

"They're not. But I'm going there anyway."

I squinted down the sidewalk, leaning on my left foot to relieve the pain in my right. Next to me, traffic lazily loped in both directions on McGuinness Boulevard. I wondered whether there was anything in my repertoire with Alina that I hadn't covered that I could bring up on my way back. Ah yes, we did have one inside joke: I'd say, "Still trying to get fired?" And she'd say, "You know I am." Because she was trying to get fired, and I knew that she was. *Honestly,* I thought while waiting for my breakfast sandwich, *she isn't trying very hard.* I'd learned over months of idle chitchat that Alina had taken this job sitting at the front desk of a luxury building in Greenpoint, Brooklyn, because it gave her time to work on her chick-lit romance novel. Her home life was chaotic, so it was difficult for her to write there. She was Dominican or Puerto Rican or half of each or half of one? This should've been an easy thing to verify, but honestly, too many questions, they felt creepy, and who knows, I could do something stupid like . . . mispronounce Dominican?

"I'm seriously worried that inertia will keep me here my entire life," she once confided in me. "And that's okay, but it means I don't want to live a *long* life." And so she spent her days concerned she'd spend her days signing for packages and being nice to the rich tenants in the 190 or so units. Well, *I* wasn't rich, but we can get to that later.

I made my way home past the still-shuttered shops, attempting to drink my coffee, but the opening of the lid was aligned with the seam of the cup, and the coffee dribbled down my shirt. Shouldn't everyone in the hot drink biz know *not* to align the opening with the seam? And how come it happens so often? Like the opening and the seam are mysteriously drawn to each other. Looking forward to being distracted from the nonsense in my head, I pulled open the large glass door of the eight-floor, block-long, brick facade I called home, and there was Alina, still in her book but then looking up at me, her smile smaller now that she'd already seen me once today. I didn't take that personally for too long.

"Still trying to get fired?" I asked.

"You know I am."

I leaned on her desk with one elbow, heart thumping a bit in my ears. "I just think you're not trying hard enough."

"I'm open to suggestions," she said with a flat affect. "No perverted stuff."

"I'd never."

"You know, don't suggest I should have sex with someone in the mail room or—"

"Now I'm uncomfortable," I muttered.

"That's the best thing about you."

"That I'm uncomfortable?"

"Yes."

The way she was looking me in the eye, maybe she did like me a little. Or maybe she just wasn't afraid of eye contact. Either way it was hard for me to relate. She had said *sex* in my presence; that was a first. Without thinking about what I was saying, I let the following words tumble out: "The other day, I thought of one thing I could use your help with, and it would definitely get you fired."

"Intriguing." She sat back, arms crossed.

The floor was mine, but I lost my nerve. "It's personal. And um. I don't know if I could actually do it. I tend to get stuck."

"We have that in common."

"I guess we do."

She was still looking at me, and so I stumbled on with, "The plan I've formulated that you would help me with, the sort of action I'm thinking of taking, I'd have to be really angry. At my wife. You know, *moved* by my emotions in the *moment*."

"I'm game whenever."

"Oh, I don't think you will be."

"Oh, I will be."

This really was turning out to be a great day. But still, I felt relief when Alina's walkie-talkie squawked because what I wanted to suggest, what had been on my mind since I realized my wife was having an affair, was *extreme.*

From the walkie: "Helloooo, Alina. Can you come up to the roof, please?" The throaty voice of Stovan, the building's Serbian maintenance man.

"To the roof?" Alina asked.

"Something is happening on the roof," he said melodically.

"Jesus."

"Yes yes yes, and the woman, the same woman, she is crying, and she asks can *you* come up—"

"Of course."

"There's a ruckus on the roof?" I sympathized.

"Do you mind standing at the desk for a minute?" Alina crinkled her nose. She did that sometimes when she wanted to be cute. "It's nine thirty, so the UPS person should be here soon, and someone needs to physically be at the desk or they can't leave packages and all hell will break loose."

"Sure. But wouldn't it help you get fired if you left the desk unattended?"

"I'm a coward. And I hate when people are angry with me."

That was one thing we did not have in common. I had resigned myself to other people's anger a long time ago.

Alina shrugged, I shrugged, and then she jogged to the elevator. As I rotated my body behind the desk, I congratulated myself for not looking at her butt.

The first person to enter the Jax (the building has a name— why judge?) in Alina's absence was a skinny hipster with a hairstyle nodding toward the mullet, wearing a sleeveless undershirt and track pants. I said, "Hi, do you live here?" and he grimaced at me and kept swaying through space. Now it's true that Alina doesn't have to ask people if they live here; she just knows—a feat of genius.

That skinny hipster is indicative of a certain type of resident, the young dude who looks like he's come from the beach. Another type is the attractive professional in her thirties who still knows how to party. And then there's a contingent of less attractive young people who live with their dogs. My wife and I are forty, which makes us the oldest people to have ever set foot in this building.

Then the UPS guy came in with so many boxes that you wouldn't believe me, so why bother describing other than to say they were on the floor and on the desk in such a way as to partially block my view of the lobby and the glass-enclosed common area on the far side of the center elevator. Alina would have to enter all of these packages into the computer so that the tenants would get email notifications, a task the thought of which made me queasy.

The third and final person I saw enter during my time as front desk substitute was the one who would haunt me in the days to come. This leather-clad figure pulled the glass door open with one straight arm and strode across the lobby, head encased in a cherry-red motorcycle helmet, visor down. At first, I thought he was a delivery guy and would stop at the desk, but by the time I squeaked out an "Excuse me, sir?" he'd stalked down the parqueted hallway and was flinging open the stairwell door next to the northern elevator.

I sped-drank some coffee so that I'd be caffeinated enough to chastise him on his way out. And then I ate my breakfast sandwich. It wasn't bad: they actually cook the bacon there while you wait, rather than plucking it from a metal tin of premade meat. Which I do appreciate.

It was only after the first tenant died that I realized I never did see that visored stranger come back down.

Thirty minutes later, Alina was behind her desk, and I was in front of it, watching her anger-type on the keyboard, checking in packages. She seemed genuinely upset by whatever had transpired on the roof.

"The fucking tenants here," Alina said.

"Tell me about it."

"I mean it, Paul. I'm done. I might be angry enough to actually do whatever the thing is you want me to do that will get me fired."

"Excellent."

"So tell me what the thing is!" I think she meant to mock-shout, but it came out as a shout-shout.

"I'm not there yet," I said. "Sorry. It's . . . it's some next-level shit." And then, seeing that she was nearly in tears: "What happened up there?"

"On the roof?"

"Yeah."

"Fucking tenant in 705."

"The one you watch her dog?"

"I do all sorts of shit for that self-indulgent bitch. Every Saturday morning at nine, she's up on the roof, in the pool."

"The pool doesn't open until ten," I said, playing the part of well-behaved tenant.

"*Drunk,*" Alina mouthed.

"And inebriation in the pool area is forbidden." We have an outdoor pool and a landscaped garden on the roof. This building is a whole thing.

"So Stovan was trying to fish her ass out of the pool," Alina continued.

"And today is the day he has to change the air filters in all the eighth-floor apartments."

"How do you know that?"

"I pay attention to what you say."

"So he's already fed up. That's when he called me, 'cause she's being belligerent, refusing to get out of the pool, and me and her, we're like friends?"

"You're not friends," I said.

"I know. I coax her down to her apartment. She gets naked 'cause I don't know why, and so I left her there in her king-size bed, completely passed out, snoring, with *Ozark* playing on the TV." Alina let out a sob. "This can't be my life."

———

A few minutes later, I was back in my apartment, tugging at my beard, looking at the carnage on our bedroom balcony.

"I don't understand why you let this happen."

"What's to understand?" Laura said. "I let the dog shit on the balcony because you didn't take him out with you this morning."

I turned away from the glass door to where Laura was standing at the foot of our bed, the central air rippling through her silk robe. I still couldn't believe we had central air in New York City. Who did we think we were? We deserved any tragedy that might—and would—befall us. Well, any tragedy save one.

"I don't understand why *you* didn't take the dog out," I ventured.

"I *let* the dog out," she snapped.

"But Jesus, the neighbor upstairs hates it when Theo shits all over the balcony."

"Just answer a question for me," she said, employing a new tactic.

"Okay?"

"Our nicely proportioned balcony. Is that, or is that not, *outside*?"

"I prefer the dog to go to the bathroom outside. Like outside outside."

"Then *you* should have walked it!"

She had me there, so I scooted by her formidable figure and hurried into our open-plan kitchen, where I grabbed some paper towels and a trash bag. Then I scooted by her again and scurried out onto the balcony and tried to pick up all of the dog's half-liquid shit before the upstairs neighbor smelled it.

Laura often reminded me that our cockapoo has digestive

issues because I bought him from a pet store where he picked up a parasite. I *should* have gotten a dog from a rescue shelter. But Theo had looked so miserable, so hadn't I, in a sense, rescued him from the pet store? In any event, while I was picking up mushy turds, Theo, curly haired and russet colored, leaped down from his napping perch on our outdoor chair and joyfully jumped up, trying to nab the gloppy poop-towel in my hand. I gave him a pat-pat. I love that stupid dog.

Laura brought out her coffee and surveyed the parking lot below and the narrower luxury building behind ours. But I guess all that looking around got boring because she taunted me with, "I bet you were down there flirting with that front desk woman."

"I watched the desk for her because she needed to deal with the tenant in 705."

"You know she's paid to be nice to you. You know that, right? Like a hooker."

"Couldn't you at least say like a waitress?" I asked.

"If you want to sleep with her, go ahead. I just think it's going to be expensive."

"She's paid to be nice to me *like a waitress!*"

Shoving the paper towels in the trash bag, I huffed through the bedroom with the dog at my heels. Laura *was* making me angry, but not angry enough to implement my plan (the plan that would get Alina fired). There was only one thing Laura could say that would make me initiate that course of action: Orangetheory.

"What are you going to do with that trash bag?" Laura called, coming in from the balcony.

"I'm going to tie it *tightly* and throw it down the trash chute *immediately.*"

"Good boy."

"Don't patronize me," I groused as I picked up Theo before I opened the front door so that he couldn't make a run for it.

"You're so sensitive." Laura leaned on the bedroom doorframe and stared into the middle distance.

"What are you planning to do today anyway?" I asked, one foot in the apartment, one foot out.

"Maybe sit by the pool on the roof? Watch all the young people. Are you going to get rid of the trash, or do I have to do that too?"

I cast Theo back inside, made my way down the corridor, pulled open the small square metal door, and let the plastic bag spelunk into the darkness.

Ironically, Laura and I had moved to this building hoping it would restore some marital happiness. That living here would bring us back to the carefree attitude we used to enjoy at local bars or nice hotels. We'd been living in a tiny East Village walk-up that I'd bought in the early 2010s after a string of good-luck acting jobs. I'd been making decent money playing small roles on the blurry edges of your TV screen. Maybe I'd have a bit part where I found my fiancée dead on the stoop. Or I'd be a day-player begging a bookie for some extra time to repay a loan. Or I'd have a walk-on as a jersey-wearing sports fan who yelled *chug chug chug* before his buddy died of alcohol poisoning.

But ten years later, our East Village apartment had gone from dilapidated chic to actually dilapidated, and I couldn't think about auditioning without feeling existential vertigo. Was I really going to continue documenting my aging process by playing a consecutive string of "passersby" or "additional attendees" on shows you've never heard of? And that's if I was *lucky*? I was pretty sure I was one "Hey, any auditions?" email away from my agent suggesting I join an extra service where they pay you a hundred bucks to stand in the background. And meanwhile, in my marriage, Laura had lost all respect for me, or I had lost all respect for me (it was hard to tell the difference), and I was relegated to the person my wife complained to when things in the apartment broke, which was happening with precipitous frequency.

Happy day, then, when a real estate agent told us he could sell our East Village shithole for $1.2 million, netting me, us, $300,000 more than I'd paid for it when it was overpriced in 2011, so I said yes, please. And even though I wasn't acting much anymore (acting?), I still had a bit of passive income due to a couple of shows that were popular on the streamers. So, after a year of Covid-related isolation in our dank one-bedroom, we moved to Greenpoint in search of sunlight, an on-site maintenance man, and a pool on the roof.

Shuffling back into our apartment, I peered into the bedroom and saw Laura . . . *packing a gym bag*? She wouldn't dare . . . *would she*? Just because I hadn't taken the dog out? Warm anger filled my body. I made myself a Nespresso. *Maybe she'll just say she's going to the gym in our building. Right? She wouldn't dare say . . . Orangetheory.*

I sat at our table in the living room, tiny espresso cup nesting in my fingers. I gazed out through our wall of windows toward the water treatment plant (nicknamed "shit tits" for its eight giant metal breast-shaped cones heaving heavenward). *Goddamn it, was she really going to start this Orangetheory stuff again?*

When we'd moved to the Jax a year ago in 2021, Laura had seemed happy. We were exploring restaurants and even making some friends in the building. Sure, we were older than our neighbors, but because our jobs weren't in finance or digital marketing, we were *interesting*. In particular, we'd get together with Randy and Lisa, whom we'd dubbed the plant people because they had so many goddamn plants. And because their lack of enthusiasm in general made them seem . . . floral. But soon we realized that although *we* might be interesting, our new friends had nothing to say *at all*. So Laura and I would talk nonstop at get-togethers, and as you can imagine, that became tedious for all parties. I mean, these people must have discussed something when we weren't there, but I literally had no idea what that something might be. Soon we all just smiled at one another in the hallway, silently pleading, *Don't stop to say hi*, please. *I'm listening to a podcast.*

Laura dropped her gym bag on the counter, and my mind returned to the present moment. I saw her standing in the kitchen clad in gray and blue nylon. She was glaring at me, daring me to ask where she was going. I simply sipped my Nespresso and turned back to the window.

Around the time our social calendar dried up, Laura started going to fitness classes at Orangetheory on Saturday and Sunday mornings. At first, this solved our weekend ennui. She'd trot back into our apartment, flushed from her workout, and we could surf her endorphins to brunch or even take a bike ride by the river.

But then one Saturday I noticed something strange. See, our apartment is an end unit that runs the width of the building. So while our bedroom balcony overlooks the parking area, our living room windows look down onto the garage gate, the stairwell door, and the main entrance. *Those are the only ways in and out of the building.* That Saturday, I happened to be watching the people and their animals stroll by on the sidewalk when Laura bounded through our apartment door. But I couldn't remember having seen her reenter the building. And so, the following day, I peered down through our windows after she left for Orangetheory. And I never saw her exit the building. Let alone walk back in two hours later. Yet there she was back in our apartment. Sweaty.

So the next weekend, a moment after she left the apartment, I sprinted to the closest elevator and watched the electronic numbers go up to floor eight. The building's gym was on the eighth floor, but I checked and she wasn't there. I was certain in my bones that she was on the eighth floor visiting a . . . gentleman. To confirm my theory, all I had to do was stand in the gym and peer out of its glass door like a deranged maniac until Laura appeared from one of the apartments. And, goddamn it, that's just what I did.

Curling the smallest fucking weight I could find, I stared out onto the eighth-floor hallway for two full hours. (I couldn't care less what the lone Peloton rider thought of me; my eyes were so full of blood, I couldn't even tell you if that bike-riding son of a bitch was male or female.) Laura finally emerged from the second to last apartment at the other end of the hallway, nearly a full city block away. To confront her right then and there would have been ridiculous. Me running toward her, my heavy torso heaving up and down—that would have rendered me the cuckholdest cuckhold the world had ever seen. Not to mention I'd been lifting a two-pound weight for two hours—I was exhausted. So I watched her figure blissfully float into the far stairwell. I never even saw *him*, whoever *him* was.

Feeling murderous and hungry—a bad combination—I stalked down Manhattan Avenue and bought myself a honey-glazed donut at Peter Pan Bakery. Somewhat sedated by the carbs, I glowered back to our apartment, now feeling more pouty than angry.

Laura was in the glass-enclosed shower. I stood at the sink.

Me: "I know you were just in apartment 825."

Laura: "That's ridiculous."

Me: "I saw you come out. I was in the gym."

Laura: "That's on the other side of the hallway."

Me: "I have twenty-twenty vision!"

Laura: "I was at Orangetheory!"

She stepped out of the shower and grabbed her towel, but she didn't cover herself with it. She was mocking me with her magnificently tall nakedness.

Me: "You never exited the building!"

Laura: "What are you talking about?"

Me: "You're cheating on me!"

Laura: "And so what if I am!"

And then she cloaked herself in the towel and grabbed a second towel to dry her hair.

Me: "You don't even like sex!"

Laura: "I don't like sex with you!"

She pushed by me and shoved on her clothes.

Me: "Tell me you're not having an affair with the guy in 825, whoever that is!"

Laura: "Here I thought we could have a nice day today."

Me: "So you're not even going to deny it?"

Laura: "Exactly."

And, makeup-less, Laura strode out of our apartment. This time I saw her exit the building.

In the intervening two months, Laura had never mentioned, let alone gone to, Orangetheory, a tacit admission of her own guilt. But the threat of those two nonsensical words smushed together hovered over us when we bickered over banalities in bed or sat in silent contempt on either side of a meal. You might be wondering why we didn't explore divorce. Well, the cynical part of me knew that with her modest salary working for a not-for-profit, she couldn't afford to live in this building without me. And for my part? Divorce involves a lot of paperwork, and I have an irrational fear of paperwork. But honestly, I loved Laura. I admired her and knew that her head was a dark place from which to serve out a life sentence. And when we were in sync? It was us against the world. We knew it all, cigarettes and whiskeys in hand, everyone else be damned.

Sucking up the last foamy bits of Nespresso, my thoughts toward my wife were becoming kinder and warmer, when I realized she was standing over me. She was saying, probably repeating . . .

"Hey! Paul! Hey!"

"What?"

"I'm leaving now."

And then she said, almost apologetically . . .

"I'm going to Orangetheory."

CHAPTER 2
DEATH OF A HIPSTER

"I'm ready."

"For what?"

"Alina, this is your chance to get fired." I splayed my arms wide across her desk, hoping it looked like a power position, though I was actually trying to steady my quivering legs.

Whether she saw strength or desperation, I don't know, but she was instantly up for it. "What do I have to do?"

"You have the keys to every apartment, right?"

"I have access to the box that has those keys," she confirmed, taking a small gold key out of her desk drawer.

"You're going to give me the key to apartment 825, and I'm going to catch my wife having an affair."

Behind her large glasses, Alina's eyes widened. I don't know what she'd expected me to say, but I guess it wasn't that. Then with robot-like precision, she stood up and turned into the small room behind her desk. A moment later she returned with another small gold key and said in a quiet voice, "Let's go."

"Y-you don't need to come with me," I stuttered, following her quick, determined steps.

"I'm coming," she said as she let me into the elevator first. "I mean, we don't know each other well . . ."

That stung.

". . . and I don't want you to get . . . violent?"

"I wouldn't."

"Sure." She didn't sound sure.

Going up in the elevator, we were standing in an unusual position for us—next to each other. Boy, she was short.

"Why's it so important that you catch her in the act?" Alina asked, cracking her knuckles.

"Because she won't admit it. It's not the cheating that bothers me. It's the lying."

"I don't believe that."

"Besides, I mean, there's a chance she's just in there playing gin rummy."

"I don't believe that either."

The elevator doors opened and we crept down the hallway, Alina in front.

"Why are we moving so slowly?" I whispered.

She turned to me, took my arm, and asked, "Do you remember what I said when we first met?"

"Welcome to the Jax?"

"You were taking your dog out," she reminded me, "and he peed on the lobby floor. And as you were cleaning it up and apologizing, I said, 'Don't worry, dogs always get confused here. The lobby is a liminal space.' And you said . . ."

"'What does liminal space mean?'" I recited.

"And I said, 'It's an undefined place between two defined places.' The dogs don't know if the lobby is inside or outside, so they get disoriented. But, Paul, the more I think about it, this whole building is a liminal space."

"I can see that." I nodded. "The long hallways."

"And the fact that people are only permitted to rent here. And the rent is so high and the apartments are so small that no one stays for long."

"You yourself want to leave," I said.

"Because I'm not really anywhere."

"Me neither," I said.

"But," she concluded, "I feel now, with this key and that door, we're coming to some sort of destination. It's that anticipation that's making me walk so slowly." I liked it when she was literary. "But fuck it, let's get somewhere." Her tiny gold key pointing the way, Alina fast-walked to 825, me motoring behind.

"Wait." I touched her hand at the door.

"Don't. I'll lose my nerve," she protested.

"Do you happen to know who lives in this apartment?"

"You mean you don't?"

"It never really mattered to me *who* my wife was sleeping with," I said. "But does he have muscles?"

"His name is Ernest Whitaker. He's that guy, you know, with the tiny pompadour on the top of his head. He's a dog trainer— Really? Nothing?"

"Shit. Does he have a dog in there?" I asked.

"No, no, he doesn't have his own dog because he uses his apartment to train other people's dogs," Alina said. "I guess a dog trainer who loves dogs but can't have his own dog could be considered a tragic figure . . . Let's just go in. I'm spinning fiction because I'm nervous."

"Oh, I do that too," I said.

She put the key in the lock, turned it, shoved the door open, and called, "Maintenance!"

"Why maintenance?"

"I don't know."

The shades were drawn and the lights were off, but I could make out four animal training platforms dotting the living area and pictures of dogs lining the walls. The bedroom door, to our left, stood ajar and leaked light.

"It's quiet in here," I whispered. "And warm."

I pressed on toward the bedroom, tentatively nudging the door open with my foot. There in a sea of florescent and natural light, stretched out on a white bed, laid a skinny, naked man, his arms extended behind his head, hair shaven on the sides but long and amber on top. His armpit hair was also long and amber. His chest hair, long and amber. And then, my eyes working their way down, I saw his penis—also long but not amber (but not *not* amber). And oh Jesus, of course, I mean, I'm burying the lede, but his eyes were bugged open, and he was fucking dead.

When Alina said, "Holy shit," I realized she was right behind me.

I heard myself ask, "Should I check for a pulse?"

Alina shook her head. "Don't touch him." She was rubbing her hands on her pants, maybe to get the dead off her?

"As scared as I am of this body," I confessed, blood rushing through my ears, "part of me is interested in the layout of his apartment."

"Part of me is interested in his penis," Alina murmured.

"I noticed his penis before I noticed he was dead." Gesturing toward the balcony door at the far side of his bedroom, I asked, "Should we open that?"

"Why?" she asked.

"So his soul isn't trapped in here?"

"Do you believe his soul is trapped in here?" she asked.

"No."

Still looking at the closed balcony door, my attention was drawn to the adjacent picture window. The beaded cord was snapped in half and hung limply against the window jamb. This wasn't all that unusual. The steel ball chains in our apartment snapped all the time; the shades were too heavy for them. But not only was this chain broken, it was too short, like a segment was missing.

Alina had her hand on my arm and was leading me backward

out of the room, saying, "I think we should get out of this apartment." The feeling of her skin on my skin was still a great thrill.

Once we were in the cool air and neutral tones of the hallway, Alina called the police. But I heard my mind asking, *Could Laura still be in there?* And so, on impulse, I crept back into the apartment. "Laura?"

The concern, bordering on panic, I suddenly felt for my wayward wife wasn't something I'd planned. It just rose up within me and intensified as I threw open the closet door in the living room and then the closet door in the bedroom. I couldn't tell you what was in those closets, but it wasn't Laura.

Alina must have finished with 911 because I sensed her standing behind me in the bedroom again, exactly where we'd first seen Ernest's body.

"What are you doing back in here?" she asked.

"I thought Laura might still be in the apartment," I said, voice shaky.

"The police want us to wait in the hallway."

I nodded and turned to go, but Alina's eyes were now focused on the far side of the room.

"Did you open that?" she asked.

She was pointing at the balcony door, tapping gently against its frame in the breeze.

"No."

"I don't think his soul opened it," she said.

"What if Laura's on the balcony?"

I took long, quiet steps past the foot of the bed. I think part of me was expecting to smell the sickly-sweet stink of sex because I was surprised when I smelled nothing but . . . bleach. I snuck a glance at Ernest's body. There was almost something ritualistically clean about this death.

I pushed open the balcony door and ventured out onto the five-by-five concrete slab. No one. I held on to the metal railing and looked around. Ten feet to the next balcony over? The parking lot was eight stories down. Nine feet up to the roof? Possibly some sort of really athletic person could have vaulted from the rickety wooden table out here and used the metal trimming around the window and the grouting around the bricks to pull themselves up there . . .

"No one's out there," I reported to Alina, but now she was at the foot of the bed, transfixed by the corpse.

"Look at his neck." A magenta line streaked across Ernest's large Adam's apple. By itself the purplish band would have looked almost benign, even drawn on with a marker, but just below, his neck was mottled with angry red contusions, which I assumed were frustrated streams of blood.

"Looks like he was strangled," I said. "Such an old-fashioned way to die."

"I guess it's hard to kill someone with an app," Alina considered.

"You have to admire the murderer's hands-on approach."

"Too soon . . ."

I looked again at the broken chain by the window, but before I could say anything about it, a couple of uniformed officers had announced themselves and entered the apartment. Unamused that we were gawking at Ernest Whitaker's corpse, they instructed us to keep our hands where they could see them and escorted us into the hallway where we were told to wait for the on-duty detective to arrive. A third cop slouched against the wall a few feet down and kept a wary eye on us, like we were troublesome teens.

Alina and I stood blank and silent as the elevator deposited one batch of NYPD officers and then another. The first group taped off the area. The second wore white plastic suits and brought big black cases past us and into the apartment. Soon folks from the building's management company and the usual cadre of maintenance men were gathered in curious silence at the far end of the hallway. And then with impressive efficiency, six NYPD officers fanned out in twos and knocked on the couple dozen apartment doors on the eighth floor.

When I saw a compact young man with sharp cheekbones stride out of the elevator, I instinctually knew this was the on-duty detective. He blew past us in a fitted white button-down and beige suit pants, leaving the smell of minty chewing gum in his wake. I watched him glide effortlessly under the police tape and into the apartment.

A panicky energy overtook me. I leaned toward Alina and made an awful suggestion into her ear. "Follow my lead. I'm going to change the story of how we found the body."

"Why would you do that?"

"So I don't sound like some sort of deranged jealous husband."

Alina considered my face for a moment. And then she looked down at my hands.

"Why are you looking at my hands?"

"They're . . . just very large."

———

"This is simply us talking," Detective Kurlansky, the on-duty detective, said with the slightest hint of a Polish accent a few moments later, notepad in hand, sleeves half rolled up to tease his ropy forearms. He was giving us 100 percent of his generous, deep-water-blue eye attention while I was trying not to look at the just-visible neck tattoo under his partially unbuttoned collar. A flock of birds? "Once we get back to the station, you'll make an official statement. But this right now is just us talking."

"I, um, was in the gym on the treadmill," I lied. "On my way back to the elevator, this elevator here, the one closest to my apartment, which is um, five stories down, I heard some loud noises coming out of apartment 825, like struggling, so I went to the lobby and told Alina, the lobby person, and we decided the best thing to do was knock on the door, but we brought a key in case, and we used the key and there he was dead."

"Okay. Thank you, Paul." He made a few notes on a small spiral pad. "Alina Serrano." He clearly enjoyed saying her name. "Anything to add? No pressure. This isn't official yet."

"Nothing at this time, sir," she said quickly.

Did she look at my hands again, maybe in a way to indicate that Detective Kurlansky should also look at them? Nah, I was being paranoid because of all the lying.

And then Alina added, I thought unnecessarily, "Other than to say, sir, I understand that I will probably be fired because I didn't follow strict management protocol."

I opened my mouth, then closed it again.

"Paul, do you have something you want to add?" Kurlansky asked.

"Well, yes. But I was trying to leave space for Alina to speak more if she wanted to speak more. I've become aware in the past couple of years just how much white men talk, often at the expense of women or minorities who may be more . . . reluctant to speak themselves?"

"What else would you like to say?" Kurlansky asked me as if what I'd just said was totally appropriate.

"When we came back into the apartment, the balcony door was open."

"So you left and went back in?" Kurlansky asked.

"Yeah."

"Why?"

"I started to doubt whether he was really dead?" I said like a question.

"Why?"

"I doubt everything," I said more confidently.

"Including what you're telling me now?"

"Of course. But my point is that you probably want to get offi-cers on the roof because that's the only place the killer could have gone from the balcony. There's also a nice pool up there, if that's helpful."

Kurlansky snapped his pad shut. "Alina, this officer will take you to the precinct. And, Paul, this officer over here will take you. We'll get your statements separately, if you don't mind."

"May I go down to my apartment to check on my wife first?" I asked.

"Why are you worried about your wife?"

"Well, there's a deranged strangler in the building," I said.

"Oh." Kurlansky seemed surprised. "A deranged strangler escaped to the roof and is still in the building?"

"I think so?"

"You might just solve this case for me, Paul," he said with a surplus of kindness. "I'd appreciate that. It's summertime, after all." Kurlansky looked over at Alina and smiled at her. He *was* a good-looking man. His thinning hair? It somehow made him look tough. His modest stature? It only compressed his intensity. Alina, however, didn't smile back at him. But that might have had more to do with her nerves than his lack of charm. In fact, Alina had gone totally silent. I hoped it wasn't because I was taking up too much space.

———

A few moments later, when I opened the door to my apartment, Theo frantically jumped at me as if I'd been gone for a year. I scooped him into my arms and rubbed his fuzzy head and stroked his white goatee.

"Laura?"

No answer.

I looked behind me at the officer who had been tasked with escorting me down here on our way to the station. He stayed in the doorway and nodded at me, indicating that I could take a minute to look around.

The quiet whir of the AC, the gurgling of the refrigerator, the soft hum of outside traffic. But no lights. No Laura. No note from Laura. I padded into the bedroom. Her toothbrush was still in the bathroom.

I texted her. "Delivered" but not "Read." I called her. "Hi, you've reached Laura." But, of course, I hadn't.

Despite the officer's patience, I knew we had to get to the precinct, so I opened the balcony door and let Theo do his business out there, even though I'd been angry with Laura for doing the very same thing that morning.

After Theo waddled back in, I put some food out for him, and then the cop escorted me down the hallway and toward the elevator. I was mentally repeating the story I'd told Kurlansky so that I could replicate it at the station when the elevator doors slid open, revealing a surprising amount of sound and movement in the form of a happy family—the rare family that lived in this building. The boy, six or seven, was smacking at the elevator buttons with the palm of his hand, not quite hitting them, just daring his glowering dad to yell at him. The girl, two or three, sashayed her dress behind her mom's legs. The mom, pleasing to the eyes even without makeup, was whispering something into the dad's ear— probably bragging about her Wordle score—isn't that the sort of thing happily married couples talk about? The dad humored her with a smile, but his jaw remained clenched as he removed his son's hand from the elevator buttons.

I knew the dad a little, Patrick Backus. Patrick often sat in the glass-enclosed common area behind the lobby. Sometimes I'd see him there watching a movie on his iPad, always in a plaid shirt tightly tucked into his narrow khakis. We'd chitchat on occasion. Patrick had once told me that all four of them lived in a one-bedroom apartment, and that's why he sought refuge in the common area, called the Library, from time to time.

"Hey, Patrick," I said as my uniformed escort and I stepped into the elevator.

"Hi, Paul," Patrick responded. "Awful about what happened."

"Oh, you already know—"

"We live right underneath," Patrick's wife interjected, "so the police already talked to us."

"Um. Yeah. I'm the one who found the—" I almost said *body* but changed it to *situation* on account of the children. "This guy," I motioned to the cop behind me, "is taking me to the station so I can make a statement." As the doors closed us all in together, I prattled on. "I'd say you must have heard something, but we all know what these apartments are like. You know. With the luxury insulation? It's like we live in soundproof boxes. We don't hear anything."

Patrick paused for the slightest moment and then said, "Right, that's exactly right." His daughter then started to untuck her dad's plaid shirt. "No, thank you," he said to her in a falsetto that did little to belie his annoyance, but she didn't remove her hand from his waist. "No, thank you, Mable," he said to her again. That must be in a parenting advice book, to say, "No, thank you" when you feel like saying, "Get the fuck off me."

As I watched that giggling, bickering familial foursome skitter across the lobby, it was clear that Patrick had made some good choices, and I, practically being frog-marched outside by an officer of the law, had made some bad ones.

But what, exactly, were my bad choices? I'd always been so easygoing, so eager to please. I'd followed my heart in love and work. I'd only started flirting (if you could even call it that) with Alina once Laura had begun blatantly carrying on an affair. I couldn't for the life of me figure out where I'd gone wrong. (Don't worry, I'll figure it out soon enough.)

———

Eight long hours later, after I'd wasted away in the lobby of the sleepy police station, given my spurious statement in a claustrophobic interview room, and gone back to my apartment to take care of the dog, I found myself sitting in Temkin's on Greenpoint Avenue, in a black leather booth, steadily sipping bourbon. The dim red light, the checkered floor, the thick illogical silence, it was like a David Lynchian purgatory.

Tapping my wedding ring against my glass, I tried to keep my mind on the moment's most pressing question: Where the hell was Laura? Okay. I started with what I knew to be true: One, Laura had been sleeping with Ernest Whitaker. Two, Ernest Whitaker was dead. And three, Laura hadn't been home since she left for his apartment this morning. But I couldn't make any of these facts form connective tissue, let alone lead me to my wife.

I tried her cell again with predictable results.

Oh, why had I lied about the reason Alina and I entered Ernest's apartment? The detective I'd given my cockamamie statement to at the station wasn't even Kurlansky. It was some old white guy with a hearing aid. I just kept telling him (lying to him) about how we'd come to enter Ernest's apartment, and he kept saying, "What?"

Me: "I was in the gym, on the treadmill."

Elderly officer: "What?"

Me: "Treadmill! And then I went to the elevator."

Elderly officer: "What?"

Me: "I went to the elevator."

Elderly officer: "Okay, then what?"

Me: "I heard a noise."

Elderly officer: "What?"

After that baffling interview concluded, I received a text: I looked up your number in the computer. It's Alina. We need to meet. Feeling a prickle of excitement and no small amount of anxiety, I'd suggested the bar where I now sat. I assumed Alina wanted to get together to trade theories about what the fuck had happened to Ernest Whitaker and where the hell my wife could be.

But Alina was clearly running late because it was thirty minutes and three whiskeys past the agreed upon time. Since organizing my thoughts seemed to be a nonstarter, I moved on to texting Laura's few friends and coworkers (not her family, not yet) to see if anyone had heard from her today.

Pretty soon, Alina entered Temkin's, jolting me back to the here and now. Isn't that the great thing about attraction? It keeps you in the present? But honestly, watching her look uncertainly around the bar, she seemed so *average*. Without the novelty of her job and the dais of her desk, was she . . . uninteresting? And she still had her earbuds in when she ordered her drink. That put me on edge, it just seemed rude. And in off-brand jeans that looked too tight and a V-neck shirt that looked too pink, I wondered if, at thirty, she still wanted to be twenty-two.

Of note, she was lugging around a black plastic bag. What the hell was in it? She walked toward me, a drink in one hand and that rectangular bag swaying in the other. The bag was too big, too heavy, too out of place; I could hear it crinkling as she got closer. Why did its presence disturb me?

"This bar is the worst," she said loudly as she dropped the bag on the floor and plopped down into the booth. I could hear Latin music coming out of her earbuds.

"Is that music that you're listening to Dominican?" I asked.

She popped the earbuds in their case.

"Is it what?"

"Dominican," I said.

"That's not even how you pronounce it," she said.

"Listen, thanks for following my lead earlier," I said. "When I . . ."—leaning over and whispering—". . . when I made up that story about how we found the body."

"Yeah," she said, using her stirrer to play whack-a-mole with the ice in her drink. "That's why I asked you to meet me here. You see, I did not follow your lead."

"Excuse me?"

"When I went down to the station," she continued, "I told them the truth."

"Why would you do that?"

"Because they're police officers and I'm not an idiot." She raised her voice and looked me in the eye.

"Well . . . well, why?" I blustered. "Why didn't you tell me you were going to do that?"

"I don't know! I was nervous! You're like an older, established guy." Oh, it was clear that she did not see the real me. "And," she snapped, "I was stunned that you'd want to lie to cops." She downed the rest of her drink. "But it's cool."

"How is it cool?"

"I told Detective Kurlansky that you were just lying to protect your wife," Alina said.

"Well, *that's* a lie!" I spat childishly. "I wasn't protecting my wife! I was protecting myself!"

"Have you located your wife?"

"No. No."

"I need another drink," Alina said.

"I'll pay," I offered.

"Please don't."

I scampered behind her quick strides to the bar where she ordered a Midori Sour, and I asked for another bourbon, lamely paying only for myself.

I was kind of wondering if I hated Alina as we walked back to the table in a strange not-together formation. After all, I was in no way ready to leave my wife for someone who drank Midori Sour.

When I looked at her from across the table, her drink was already drained. "All right, I should go," she said.

"Don't you want to talk about today? About what happened?"

"Look, if this is some sort of fantasy about banging the front desk girl, forget it."

"What? No. Honestly."

"I don't mean to be a bitch," she said, pushing down on her

thick black hair for no reason I could think of. "This has been a real shitty day. Why is it so quiet in here?" Agitated, Alina looked behind her, as if to find the answer. And then she turned back to me. "I'm having trouble locating myself. I feel jittery."

"I think that's understandable," I said.

"And you want to know the worst part?" she asked.

"Sure."

"Merit Management didn't fire me!"

"You're kidding."

"I'm not. Despite this 'lapse in judgment,' they said I'm by far the most popular front desk person they have." Alina sighed again. It was a long, deep sigh.

"I like the night person, Leonard," I offered.

"Leonard is an idiot. I'm cute and intelligent, so I stay," she said.

"I'm sorry." And I really was. All Alina wanted from this deal was to lose her job. Instead, she'd been forced to spend time with a serial liar (me).

I watched Alina set her jaw and scoot herself closer to the table. She leaned toward me and, suddenly channeling Edward G. Robinson, she said, "Here's what you are going to do for me. As a thank-you for getting you into that apartment." She hoisted the plastic bag onto the table and shoved its crinkly dark mass in my direction. "You are going to read the novel I've written. The manuscript is in this bag. That's why I went home. To print it. People your age like to read from paper, right?" I resented the implication that I was old, but there was no discounting the fact that she was right.

"Why do you want *me* to read it?"

"You're, like, an actor, right?" she said. "You know famous people?"

"I've *met* famous people. Greg Kinnear was really nice. Vincent D'Onofrio and I had a couple of drinks together," I said. "What a crazy night that was."

"Give it to your agent then!" But then her face instantly lost all of its vitality. "I'm a good writer."

I've traveled a lot in my life between Los Angeles and New York. In LA, everyone wants you to pass their screenplay on so that they can sell it and get rich. In New York, people just want you to read their novel. So they can prove they exist.

———

Back home, after I'd taken Theo out for a proper walk, I closed the bedroom door and collapsed on my comforter. Theo bounded on top of me and licked my face as I lay motionless. I let him lick my lips, my eyes, I'd take it all. Then he curled up next to me and put his warm head on my bare arm. Thank God for dogs.

And then silence.

In our old East Village apartment, you could hear everything. That building had six units and no insulation, so everyone knew what everyone else was doing at all times: the people upstairs were having sex, the guy next door was yelling Republican nonsense at the TV, the woman below us was flushing the toilet, the two kids from the ground floor apartment were running up and down the stairs. And Laura and I were drinking and fighting and laughing and crying. There was life in that building.

But here? The concrete between the apartments was so thick, you heard nothing. We all lived in individual tombs where, if you were murdered, no one would hear your body die. Where, if your wife left you, no one would hear your heart cry.

CHAPTER 3
A POOL DAY, BRO

t's night, and I'm sitting at the table in our living room. The klieg lights from the gas station across the street glare through the bare windows and into my eyes. I hear a woman scream. And then I hear her scream again. The screams are coming from inside my apartment. I know that. But I don't get up. I don't even turn my head. The screams are coming from inside the wall, inside all the walls. They're traveling around like mice. Screams behind me, next to me, above me. But still, I don't turn my head. Maybe I can't turn my head? Now the screams are in the wall inches from my left ear, and they stay there. And now I know these screams are Laura's screams. And the screams turn to cries, to whimpers. "Paul, Paul, please, Paul." Then I'm suddenly across the table from myself. I'm watching myself do nothing. I'm watching myself sip from a tiny espresso cup. The cup's contents leave my lips a dark red. I'm watching myself drink blood from the cup. I'm watching the blood, the consistency of pudding, cling to my teeth and elongate in thick threads down from my mouth.

I startled awake, and it was morning.

I ambled down the hallway and into the elevator, carrying Theo so that he wouldn't pee until we got outside. Damn, my right heel still hurt. Should I replace my flip-flops with sneakers? Meaning I'd have to go to a store, try on, and buy sneakers? Or order them online and risk them being the wrong size and then live with the guilt of not returning them? No, everything about buying sneakers felt impossible.

Going down in the elevator, I couldn't shake myself free of that dream. Laura's screams in the walls. Me drinking from a blood-filled espresso cup. Apparently, dreams tell us what we already know but can't face. And they tell it to us dramatically to jar us into paying attention. At least that's what this one podcast said. I think.

I found myself in the lobby. Through the glass doors, the cloudy morning hung low over McGuinness Boulevard. I saw Alina, tired and drawn, at the front desk, hunched over the computer and whispering with Stovan, the maintenance man. Standing between the desk and the entrance, a couple of uniformed police officers drank coffee and chatted amiably.

I glanced at the back door and considered taking Theo out that way. I could just walk him around the patch of grass and the enclosed parking area. It felt awkward to see Alina, especially since I hadn't read her book yet. I mean, come on, what were the chances of that book being any good? What were the chances of me even reading it? As I mulled over how much of it I'd actually have to read to believably pretend I'd read the whole thing, I saw Patrick Backus watching his iPad at the long communal table in the Library.

I wandered past the glass partition, and Patrick looked up at me through thin-rimmed glasses. "Needed a moment's peace from the family?" I asked him. Patrick took his earphones off and smiled.

"Everything work out okay at the police station yesterday?" he asked. "I saw you in the elevator with that cop, remember?"

"Oh. I mean, sure. Worked out for me, I guess. Not so much for poor Ernest Whitaker."

"My wife is worried, of course." Patrick cleaned his glasses on a now untucked corner of his button-down. Without his glasses, his eyes looked tiny. In fact, all of his features looked a bit too small for his oblong head. "She thinks maybe we should move." Then, letting out a bit of barely repressed anger: "That's ridiculous, of course. I mean, for God's sake. The pool just opened."

"True," I said, the dog now squirming restlessly in my arms.

"That sounded terribly selfish, I guess. It's just the reason we pay this high rent all year long is so the kids have somewhere to swim in the summer." He sighed. "I need to get everyone ready. We're visiting Shaina's parents in Larchmont, and I'd like to beat the traffic."

As I watched Patrick gather his iPad and headphones, I remembered this one night when I'd come home at two or three in the morning and had seen him down here reading a book. I'd asked him what he was doing up so late, and he told me, "I can't sleep. I had this dream where my kids were stuck in the walls crying. But I couldn't find a way to get into the walls to help them." In *my* dream, I hadn't even tried to help Laura. I just let her scream. And whimper. And cry. While I drank espresso. What my dream had been telling me about myself . . . Yeah, I knew it, but I still wasn't ready to face it.

I decided against walking Theo behind the building, since we weren't really supposed to do that anyway, so I put on my big boy pants and trotted toward the front door, the dog now desperate to be free of my arms. Alina and Stovan were preoccupied with their whispering, but they both looked up as I passed. Stovan was old and overweight, but that boyish smile still contained a couple of teeth. "What's up, brother?" he sung in nasal tones. Fist pound.

Alina asked warily, "Did your wife come home last night?"

"No."

"Did you read my book?"

"Not yet. Want anything? I'm going to Bagels, Bagels, Bagels.

The bagels aren't water boiled like real bagels, but they have a pleasing sweetness."

"No," Alina said.

"You, Stovan?"

"No, thank you, brother. Good morning, pooch."

Alina and Stovan leaned back over the computer and resumed their conspiratorial whispering.

Feeling like I was still halfway in a dream, I passed the officers and went out the door. I noted a couple of TV vans parked in front of the building, put Theo down, and made my way beneath the moving gray sky. The dog bounced along next to me, amiable, tongue out. I thought about how we stick to our routines, even in crisis. Here, Laura was missing, and I was going to the bagel shop, just like I had the day before. Our brains practically beg us to walk the same paths, day in and day out. Must have something to do with evolution.

As I waited for my breakfast sandwich at Bagels, Bagels, Bagels, I saw that we'd made the front-page banner on the *Daily News*: "Mysterious Death at Luxury Building." I turned to page three. The article was tiny beneath a huge photograph of model-adjacent twentysomethings lounging on our rooftop. Though the article was cursory, it did contain a couple of interesting details. The police were calling this an unexplained death rather than a homicide. And an unidentified source claimed that the instrument of death had been a chain snapped from the bedroom's window shade. Ha! I noticed that—I noticed that Ernest's shade chain was broken and that it was too short! I held the paper up to brag to someone, anyone, but then realizing I was the only one in the shop, I allowed my paper-holding hand to wilt. This unidentified source also said the victim's death might have been a case of auto-erotic asphyxiation gone wrong. Huh. That didn't seem likely to me; Ernest Whitaker's body didn't look peaceful enough to have died in a masturbation accident. (May we all go so easily into the night.)

As I walked back into the Jax, the police asked which apartment I lived in. I answered and then noticed that Alina had been replaced by a sign: BACK IN FIVE.

Waiting for the elevator, I thought, *I have to call Laura's family today to see if they've heard from her*. Anxiety pinched the inside of my stomach. I really didn't want to alarm her parents, who always seemed to resent any intrusion into their happily isolated lives as reclusive academics. *Oh, and no doubt the police will be back in touch today*, my thoughts continued. I'll have to make another statement, you know, because Alina hadn't gone along with all my lying.

I stepped into the elevator and heard someone swish-swoosh in after me. I turned around and made eye contact with my elevator buddy, a neatly coifed man with coke-bottle sunglasses, a paisley shirt, and a solicitous smile. He said to me, "Even though it's cloudy, think we can make this a pool day, bro?" Theo licked the man's hairless leg.

"Maybe we can, bro," I answered. "Maybe we can."

———

An hour or so later, I was on the roof. I pressed my fingerprint onto the tiny trackpad, and the slatted wooden gate clicked loose. I pushed it open and signed in with the lifeguard. Then I eased down into a deck chair where the two concentric circles of the pool met. The water flowed outward into the surrounding grates, blurring the lines of pool and deck. No one up here yet, save me and the teenage lifeguard. I watched the wind try to uproot the scrawny trees unnaturally lining the roof. These gusts were also noisily bashing around the black plastic bag I'd brought up with me, so I tucked it under my legs.

I stared at my blank phone. There's this friend of Laura's, an artist named Alex. He says he has a clinically diagnosed fear of making phone calls. But that's bullshit. No one wants to make phone calls, ever. Nonetheless I dialed Laura's parents. No answer. Laura and I had gotten married at her family's remote home in New Hampshire. We transformed that scraggle into a fairy-tale land strewn with tiny starry lights . . . but that's another story. I tried to call Laura again. Right to voice mail. "Hey," I said after the beep, my voice sounding somehow far away from myself, "I know that something awful happened yesterday to your . . . friend. I'm not mad or anything. I just need to know that you're okay."

I'm embarrassed to confess that this wasn't the first time I'd left a message like this on Laura's phone. This past year Laura had occasionally disappeared after we'd had an argument or a particularly chilly day together. She would sometimes be gone overnight, and I never really knew where she went. I just put her secret sojourns on the tally of things that made her morally inferior to me. I'd like this pattern of behavior to explain why I didn't feel the urgency to find Laura that one might expect, but I must acknowledge that there were two key differences this time: In every other instance, Laura had texted me that she was fine and was just going to spend the night alone because she was feeling dark (not blue, not sad—dark). Also, an unexplained death had never before factored into her brief departures.

I put the phone down and, feeling eyes on me, turned to my left, and there was Robin Nash, the skinny brunette who Stovan and Alina had fished out of the pool yesterday morning. She was lying on her side on a deck chair, covered in goose bumps and the whisper of a black bikini. Her dark hair was cut boyishly short, parted on one side, her bangs swooshing above two permanently concerned creases in her forehead. She was closer to my age than most of the residents, and I'd thought at first that we might form a bond over that. But when I saw her one evening, walking her French bulldog outside the building, I'd asked how she felt, living among the young. Her response? To glare at me in silent contempt.

"I heard what happened yesterday," she said, her large green eyes now full of sympathy. "That you found Ernest Whitaker. How awful."

"Yeah." I surprised myself by feeling grateful for conversation or, at least, distraction. "Did you know Ernest?"

Robin shivered, and I looked again at her unnaturally large goose bumps.

"Are you cold?" I took off my sweatshirt.

With a suspicious squint, she sat up and accepted my offering. "We all knew Ernest," she said. "He trained our Covid dogs. And he was a fixture up here at the pool, always sneaking in alcohol, and, I mean, that guy was up for anything." Had she been sleeping with Ernest too? As if she'd read my thoughts: "It's no secret I'm a bit of a depressive, especially in the summertime, but Ernest was *fun* and he was nice to me. *At night*." She looked sad, sure, but perhaps sadder at her own loneliness than the loss of a specific lover?

"Did he ever talk to you about my wife, Laura?"

For a silent moment, Robin sat there holding her knees, watching the great gray mastheads swiftly fly by. "No. But I don't think I know your wife. Was she sleeping with him too? It's probable. Never has a *dog trainer* gotten so much pussy." She laughed. But it was a forced, dry laugh. "It was casual with us, with Ernest and me." She produced a vape from thin air and took a couple of pulls from it. "Did you see in the paper how he died? He always did like a little recreational asphyxiation." Then something on the other side of the pool captured her attention. She lifted her head. "Oh shit."

I followed her gaze.

"Alina, the front desk girl," she said.

Yep, there was Alina, stretched out on a recliner, eyes closed, professional shirt unbuttoned to reveal a pink bikini top.

"Are employees allowed to lounge by the pool?" Robin asked.

"I can't imagine."

"Well, good for her." She smirked. "I need to talk to her anyway." She stood and then turned to me, explaining, "I behaved like a real shit yesterday. Alina dragged my drunk ass off the roof and back down to my apartment. Then I took off all my clothes in front of her. But in my defense, I was just trying to prove to her that I'd stay put." She winked at me, but then after a moment's thought, she dropped the act and said, "I was pretty awful yesterday. But I haven't had a single drink today. Sunny days are hard for me. Cloudy days are easier. I don't know why." In that instant, she'd made herself vulnerable to me, and I liked her for it.

Huddled in my sweatshirt, Robin made her way against the wind and around the pool.

Watching Robin apologize to Alina made me realize that I needed to apologize to her too. I'd panicked and put her in a terrible position yesterday. I watched Alina sit up and hug Robin. I guess they'd reconciled. Alina was tiny in Robin's grasp, and not for the first time, Alina's small stature made me feel queasy. Was I really infatuated with this elfin person? Of course not. Talking to her, thinking about her, was just a way to escape into another life, into an imaginary life.

So I forced myself back to reality. *Where was Laura?* The facts, once again: Laura's lover was murdered, and Laura was missing. Okay. I didn't think Laura was dead—why would she be? But neither did I think she'd murdered Ernest. What would her motive have been? Nor could I imagine her being tangled up in some kinky asphyxiation nonsense gone wrong. Laura was more of a meat-and-potatoes-type lover. It had been a long time since I'd seen that side of her, but I knew her voluptuous intensity rendered ridiculous the idea of adding tiny cords or chains or any sort of plastic accoutrement to the sexual act. *Most likely*, I thought, *Laura saw Ernest get killed and then she fled.* Yes, finally a couple of synapses were firing in my brain, and I could feel myself making some potential sense of why she'd disappeared.

She could have witnessed Ernest being murdered and then run down the stairwell and through that exit while I had been chatting with Alina in the lobby. Laura was most likely scared and in hiding. Jesus, what had Laura seen? How awful had it been?

The rooftop was now full of tenants pretending the sun was out, and Alina was reclining solo once again, so I made my way toward her, bequeathing my seat to one of the skinny interlopers slinking around seeking an empty deck chair. As I got closer to Alina, I saw she was shading her bespectacled eyes with her hand and peering off to her right. I followed her gaze to the couple of outdoor tables and grills, surrounded by low-lying shrubs. Detective Kurlansky was sitting at one of those picnic tables, once again in beige suit pants and a white button-down, his back ramrod straight. Stovan, seated opposite him, slouched in his gray Jax coveralls, looking askance and shaking his head. Whatever Kurlansky was saying, Stovan didn't like it.

Now looking down at Alina, I tried to be cute. "Shouldn't you be down at the front desk?"

Unsurprised to hear my voice, her eyes still on Kurlansky, she said, "Starting on Wednesday, they want me to work in the corporate office."

"Who does?"

"Merit Management," she said. "Not only did they not fire me, but they're giving me a promotion. I showed composure, they said." She shook her head, disgusted at the fates that kept her gainfully employed. "If I can't get fired, I might as well enjoy the pool." But she didn't look like she was enjoying the pool. Nodding toward Kurlansky and Stovan, she said, "*That* worries me."

"What's Stovan got to do with this?"

Alina buttoned up her shirt. "He doesn't have anything to do with it. But between the dog training and the partying, Ernest Whitaker was an irritant to the staff."

"I thought maybe he was a charmer," I said.

"To the other tenants, sure. But to us?" Rather than laugh, Alina said, "Ha." And then she continued, "Stovan found Ernest to be so infuriatingly spoiled that he stopped replying to his requests for repairs, and there were a lot of them, what with the constant pets and the parade of women."

"That's what you two were looking at this morning, in the computer at the front desk? Ernest's repair requests?"

"Right," Alina said. "Stovan was worried about all the unanswered service calls. He was wondering if I could delete them or mark them as fulfilled."

"Could you?" I asked.

"Nope," Alina said. "Not without the time stamp looking suspicious."

"Oh shit." I suddenly remembered something and put my hand to my mouth.

"What?"

"Stovan was changing the eighth-floor AC filters yesterday."

"Correct," Alina affirmed. "And did you notice anything funny about Ernest's apartment?"

"It was really warm," I recalled. "So maybe Stovan didn't change that filter?"

"In any event, that puts him on the eighth floor yesterday morning," Alina said. "At least until he came up to the roof for a cigarette and found Robin in the pool." She must have seen the gears in my head turning because she said sharply, "Hey. Stovan didn't do this."

"I don't know," I said. "He's supersweet, but he's also a pretty big guy—"

"Stovan is a gentleman."

"Okay, okay."

"And besides," she said, "you don't kill someone just because they're a pain in the ass. If that were true, every tenant in this building would be dead."

Alina looked over once again at the two seated men. Stovan

was now dabbing his forehead with a handkerchief as Kurlansky leaned across the table, seemingly hissing something at him. Alina stood up, pursed her lips, and straightened her shirt and work shorts. "I need to go help him." Determined, she sidestepped the chair next to her and marched toward them.

"Before you go." I stood up and she turned to me. "I meant to apologize to you. For putting you in that position. Yesterday. Asking you to lie to the police. I'm sorry. Full stop." I'd learned from Laura's friend Alex, the one who's afraid of his phone, that when you apologize, you aren't supposed to make excuses. *He* learned that from therapy. I've gotten a lot of good advice from Alex's therapy.

Alina studied me. "I appreciate the apology. It's the second one I've received today." I can't say she looked pleased to have gotten these apologies. Rather, she looked annoyed that they were necessary in the first place.

"I'll come with you," I offered. "And I'll also vouch for Stovan." She cocked a skeptical eyebrow. "Or I'll just stand supportively at your side."

As we rounded the flower beds, I saw Kurlansky pound his fist on the table. Stovan, in return, sang uncomfortably, "What? Why is it I am angering you?"

Kurlansky growled in a low, steady tone, "You're being too nice."

Stovan shrugged and dabbed his forehead again. "I am a nice person—what can I say?"

But before Detective Kurlansky could respond, he saw Alina and me approaching. "Ah, hello there." Kurlansky, now warm and friendly, stood and greeted us like we were chums on a cruise ship. "Come, join us, please, please."

Prim and proper as ever, Alina stated, "I came to inform you that Stovan is a gentleman who could never be involved in this."

Kurlansky, his arms out wide, appealed to Alina, "I know that!

I keep telling him that! So he can stop being so careful about everything he says!"

Stovan shrugged and smiled. "I am a very careful person."

"Please sit, Alina," Kurlansky said, lifting the center of his eyebrows in a silent, amused plea. Then he looked over at me. "Ah, look who it is!" There was such joviality emanating from our detective's face. "It's Paul, the liar! Ha!"

"Y-yes, um, about that," I stuttered. "I apologize." But this time I couldn't come to a full stop. "I was only lying to protect my wife. To protect her reputation." But, of course, that was another lie.

"I know, I know," Kurlansky said, as if it were just a bit of confusion between old pals. "You were protecting her reputation because she had been having an affair with the deceased. I can only imagine how awkward you felt," he said, inexplicably pleased, putting an arm around me. And then in a conspiratorial tone: "I knew you were lying anyway." He turned to Alina and flashed a toothy smile. "The guy who took Paul's statement? He's the police station's janitor. Can't waste resources, after all!" Okay, now he was just showing off. "Let's let bygones be bygones. Come sit. We're all on the same team. The team of the living!" Kurlansky pumped his fist as punctuation. Stovan scooted over on the bench. I sat next to him, and Alina apprehensively sat next to Kurlansky.

Kurlansky extended his broad-gestured conviviality to Stovan. "Stovan, I just want to understand why you changed every air-conditioning filter on the eighth floor except for Ernest Whitaker's."

Stovan, all shrugging shoulders and bouncing knees, said, "Like I told you. No real reason. Ernest, I give him his privacy."

"But why?" Kurlansky pressed.

"Maybe," Stovan said, stretching out the vowels, "maybe Milos comes in and fixes on Monday. Ernest and Milos, better."

"Because you and Ernest didn't like each other," Kurlansky reasonably inferred.

Stovan shook his finger gently, reprimanding him. "No, no, I didn't say that. Just maybe Milos fixes that one."

"Okay, so you didn't go into Ernest's apartment at all that morning," Kurlansky said.

Stovan was pleased that he was finally able to give a straight answer. "Correct!"

"Did you see anybody come in or go out of any apartment while you were changing the other air-conditioning filters on the eighth floor?"

"Oh, I don't remember anything about who I saw," Stovan said too quickly.

Kurlansky went to slam his fist down again on the table, but remembering Alina and I were there, he stopped himself. "Do you see why I'm frustrated here?" he asked Alina.

"I knock. I say, Stovan is here. I go in, I change the filter, I leave, like a ghost. Ernest's apartment, you are correct, I do not even knock. Better for Milos on Monday."

"You remember nothing about who you saw on the eighth floor yesterday morning," Kurlansky said.

"Correct!"

Kurlansky stood up again and exclaimed with mock cheerfulness, "Okay!"

Stovan leaned down to his right and lit a tiny cigarette. I'm pretty sure I saw him smile victoriously. Kurlansky, meanwhile, was stretching his legs and gazing at the pool area. It was now full to the brim with beautiful young adults laughing, drinking, and ignoring the wind that was blowing their plastic cups across the deck. Mostly white people sure, but a few Black people. I recognized our Nigerian neighbor from down the hall—what was his name? Winston? Winiford? Is Winiford even a name? And there was one Black couple wading in the pool. They're cute and kinda nerdy and like to play Beyoncé on their JBL speaker. I like Beyoncé. Especially "Lemonade." Any Asians up here this morning? South Asians? I don't know why I was suddenly distracted searching for minorities. I do that sometimes.

"Look at all of these people," Kurlansky said, gesturing to the pool with his back to us. "They're all having a great time, despite the weather, despite that someone was murdered in this building yesterday."

"So it *was* murder. It wasn't masturbation experimentation," I ventured.

Kurlansky whipped his torso back toward me. "Certainly not. The building's management planted that rumor to tamp down hysteria. But he was definitely strangled with a steel beaded chain." Then to the pool at large, Kurlansky asked, "Why are none of you upset by Ernest Whitaker's passing?" No one looked over at him. "Is it because Ernest Whitaker was a hipster? Is that why no one cares about him? Because in Greenpoint one hipster more, one hipster less, what's the difference? Is it because his apartment is so easy to rent at a higher rate? Or is it because pool season in New York City is so brief, much like life?"

Kurlansky looked back at us, chewed the inside of his lip, and changed tactics. "Maybe you will all relax if I let you in on a little secret." He paused for emphasis. "I already know who murdered Ernest Whitaker."

"How can you know already?" Alina asked.

Kurlansky smiled like a mischievous child. "I love that question, Alina, because I have a terrific answer. Everyone tells me who they are the first time I meet them. The first time I met you, Paul, you told me you are a liar. And I mean that in a totally judgment-neutral way."

Could one really be called a liar in a totally judgment-neutral way?

"Alina, when I first met you," Kurlansky continued, "you told me you are studious and self-serving. Please don't be offended."

She looked offended anyway. "And, Stovan, my friend, when I first met you, you told me you're a people pleaser."

Stovan blushed. "Thank you, sir, thank you."

"I don't like being reduced to two adjectives," Alina groused.

"At least you got two," I muttered.

"Anyway," Alina said to Kurlansky, "you're just ripping off Maya Angelou. She's the one who said, 'When people show you who they are, believe them the first time.'"

Kurlansky shrugged. "Maya Angelou? I don't know who that is. What's important here is that the murderer has already revealed themselves to me."

"You mean you've already met . . . them?" I asked. I considered that Kurlansky had used a gender-neutral pronoun. Was that a hedge or just considerate policing?

"Yes," Kurlansky said, and his smile told us he had no shortage of good thoughts about himself. "But before we get to that," he continued with a wave of his hand, "what was your first impression of *me*?"

"Confident," I jumped in.

"Exactly," he said, snapping his fingers. I was starting to like this man. I had a vision of us . . . having brunch.

"So if you've found the murderer, then we're done here," Alina said.

"There is the small matter of evidence," Kurlansky said, tilting his head from side to side, as if weighing how small this matter really was. "And this is where I need you, Paul."

"Me?"

Kurlansky put his hand on my arm. His palm was dry and soothing. "Can you be focused on only one thing today, Paul?"

"That's hard for me. I was diagnosed with ADHD as a child," I confided.

"I need you to focus on finding your wife," Kurlansky continued, not dissuaded by my diagnosis (which, honestly, I couldn't remember if I had right).

"I *have* texted a few people," I defended myself, my voice cracking.

Kurlansky squeezed my forearm a little tighter. "Call local hotels. Better yet, go to them, show them pictures of your wife. Visit her favorite coffee shops. She is the missing piece here. I need to know what she saw, and I need to know it now."

"Okay. Can I say one thing?" I asked.

"I wish you would look for your wife, but of course," Kurlansky said.

"Thank you for not suspecting me of murder, even though I lied. That was stupid, and—"

"Paul!" Kurlansky shouted. "Your role here is clearly not murderer. Your role is . . . additional attendee. Here's my card. Call me when you find your wife. Now go!"

Additional attendee. How did he know that was my most famous part? God, he's a good detective.

Kurlansky then deputized Alina. "You better accompany him. Keep him on task."

"What about my job at the Jax?"

But Kurlansky, expert investigator, knew she didn't give a shit about her job. "What about it?"

"Good point," she conceded.

I strode across the deck (hoping Kurlansky didn't notice I was only putting pressure on my left foot). Alina power walked at my side.

Hitting the outdoor elevator button, shame unexpectedly flooded through me. I should have been out there, pounding the pavement looking for Laura, all morning. Not sitting here by the pool. What was wrong with me? I turned to the hedge maze and gardens that took up the northern half of the roof and considered that maybe my dream had been right. Maybe I didn't care enough about Laura to try to find her. Jesus, how awful. *Maybe I'm a sociopath,* I thought. Often, when I look at pictures of myself with old friends, I miss the clothing I was wearing more than I miss the people I was hanging out with. Isn't that a sign of sociopathy?

CHAPTER 4
TALKING, EATING, AND WALKING

The clarity of my new mission had me feeling focused for the first time in twenty-four hours. My wife had seen something horrible. We were going to find her and figure out what that horrible thing was. Then I would comfort her and most likely divorce her because of her terrible perfidy and maybe I would even marry Alina. I joke. I mean, who was this bespectacled person riding the elevator down from the roof at my side? In fact, it was difficult to even focus on her as we crossed the lobby. She was like a kaleidoscope, her image constantly shifting. She'd gone from my crush to my accomplice to my Judas. Who was she, now in her prim gray shirt, her tidy black shorts, and her shiny white sneakers? My reluctant assistant?

Alina brushed past the uniformed policeman at the front desk and grabbed her over-the-shoulder bag from beneath it. A middle-aged buxom blond woman in a business suit poked her head out of the back room. "*Why* aren't you at the desk?" she overenunciated as Alina jogged toward the front door.

"Sorry," Alina called back. "The police detective upstairs wants me to help Paul look for his wife in local hotels." The statement was so nonsensical it was impossible to rebut, and so suddenly we were outside, enveloped in the humid air ten degrees warmer than on the roof.

"That was Bonnie. She's the community manager," Alina told me as she led us down the sidewalk. Ten blocks ahead, the wide boulevard swooshed up toward the Pulaski Bridge and over to Queens, but we turned left on Greenpoint Avenue, the East River now visible, a mere half mile in front of us. The gray day glared, but we glared right back, set in our purpose.

As we rounded the corner onto Manhattan Avenue, passing the McDonald's, Alina said, "I don't know why I'm leading. I'm not sure where we're going."

"We'll go to the Box Hotel first," I said. "It's nearby and Laura and I stayed there before."

"I'm just glad to be away from that place," Alina said.

"The Jax?"

"Yeah."

"Popeyes on the way?" I suggested as the orange sign approached.

"I don't know. Isn't it my job to keep you on track?" she asked as I held the door open for her. "Then again, that's yet another job I don't really want." We ordered, this time she let me pay, and off we went, talking, eating, and walking.

"Oh shit," I said buoyantly enough that it wouldn't wreck our forward momentum as we continued north, bars and delis and pizza shops becoming sparser. "I forgot to tell Kurlansky something."

"What?"

"When I was in the lobby yesterday morning, I saw a delivery person enter with his helmet visor down, and I never saw him come back out," I said.

Alina considered this as she chewed. "I wonder if it's relevant . . ."

"Whenever I read mystery novels," I rambled on, "I have trouble keeping all the odds and ends straight. In a lot of detective books, I can't remember who is who, and often, at the end, like when the killer is revealed? I'm like, who is that again?"

Swallowing the last bite of her sandwich, Alina amiably contributed, "Mystery has never been my genre. The plot always feels really removed from the protagonist. Like nothing is personally at stake for the detective, so why should I care?"

"Totally," I agreed, throwing my wrapper in the trash. "Or I feel like I'm just following someone as they go from person to person, place to place, asking questions. A lot of it feels like killing time until some big reveal."

"Much like life." Alina sipped her soda.

Having sated our bellies and deconstructed a literary genre, we found ourselves standing across the street from the Box Hotel, charcoal gray with a glass banquet hall on the roof. The hotel's only neighbors were half-built luxury condos and a concrete stanchion supporting the Pulaski Bridge. As Bob Dylan sang, "Beyond here lies nothin'." Well, beyond here lies Queens. Same thing of course.

Once we were inside the cool, dark lobby, standing among illogically arranged plush red couches, Alina explained to the expressionless concierge that we were looking for a friend, and I showed him a picture of Laura. I thought I saw curiosity flicker across his face, but he quickly extinguished it. "I haven't seen her," he said. Maybe he was instructed to maintain a poker face. Maybe that's a necessary part of the job when you work at a hotel on the edge of Brooklyn.

Now outside again, we faced each other, a bit deflated. "Should we go shop to shop? Maybe head toward the couple of other hotels by the East River in Williamsburg?" Alina asked, skepticism shading her voice.

"Feels like a bit of a wild-goose chase," I admitted, hands on my hips. Stray trash blew down the empty street. The whole area stunk of garbage. Behind the hotel, pollution emanated in a nearly visible haze from the superfund site that is Newton Creek. "God knows why they're building so many residential skyscrapers out here," I said. "It's all auto repair shops and stench." My stomach turned over. The fast food sat heavy. The excess sodium pulsated through my veins.

Nevertheless, we trudged back the way we came, down Manhattan Avenue, showing Laura's picture in bodegas and bars she'd never even consider going into.

"I think there's a very real possibility," Alina said, "that Detective Kurlansky sent us on this errand to get us out of the way."

"Do you think we really *are* suspects?" I asked.

"Or Stovan is a suspect, and Kurlansky felt like we were interfering."

As we pushed against the flow of people, down the stairs into the Greenpoint Avenue subway station, I asked Alina, "Do you think Kurlansky actually knows who the murderer is already?"

"I doubt it."

"Damn," I said. "It made me feel secure to think we were in the presence of a crime-solving genius."

The MTA worker manning the underground kiosk shook his head when we showed him Laura's picture. He hadn't seen her either. Shocking.

Back on street level, Alina scanned the endless procession of banks and drugstores ahead of us, leading into the hipper, more commercial areas of Greenpoint and Williamsburg. She sighed. "Our hunt for Laura is feeling like a metaphor for all of life's pursuits," she said. "Pointless."

"Just because one thing feels pointless, doesn't mean everything is pointless," I posited, wanting to relieve her existential dread.

She looked at me quizzically, like she was surprised I could say anything half-intelligent. She kept studying me through her large glasses until I was forced to ask, "What?"

"I was just thinking," Alina said, "how you need to know someone for a really long time before you understand which of

their behaviors are defining and which ones are fleeting, inciden-
tal, ephemeral . . ."

I leaned into the role of motivator, as much for my benefit as
for hers, and pronounced, "Laura still needs to be found. And we
are going to find her."

Alina nodded, willing herself to believe. "So where to?"

"I already texted all of her friends, but she has this one friend
who is afraid of his phone. He lives in Bushwick. And his name is
Alex. Let's pay him a visit."

————

Alex shaded his eyes as he opened the front door. Behind his
slight, slouched figure, I could see a few half-finished canvases.
From his rumpled T-shirt and sweat shorts, I had the feeling we'd
woken him up, but he blinked a few times and waved us in
anyway. He didn't seem at all surprised by our visit.

The row house's exterior was all dirty blue vinyl siding, but
inside, his ground floor apartment was spotless and freshly
painted. Alex led us through his work area where four in-process
paintings reposed on easels at regular intervals and into the
kitchen where dull afternoon light filtered in from the back
windows.

Alex poured himself a cup of coffee as Alina and I sat on stools
at the long counter facing Alex's shiny new appliances. Even
though this was a rental, I knew that Alex had refurbished the
interior at his own expense.

After I introduced him to Alina, I asked Alex if he'd seen
Laura. Before he could answer, the shadow of a young man
peered up from the spiral basement stairs. Alex motioned for him
to go back down.

Laura had met Alex through her not-for-profit, which commissioned local artists to create new work in low-income neighborhoods. He painted a mural her company sponsored and then

introduced her to a cadre of New York–based painters, many of whom she went on to hire. Through these introductions, he became her entrée to a hip niche in the art world.

At first, I thought her only interest in him was those invitations to openings in deep-Brooklyn galleries and parties on abandoned boats in the Gowanus Canal. When their friendship extended to midday coffees and late-night drinks, I wondered if she liked him because he was Black, since having a Black friend is the white lady Holy Grail. I understand that's an unfair thought, but this is a safe space, right? Isn't it? Maybe it's not. Shit. Anyway, for the record, I was incorrect. After accompanying Laura to a few openings, I realized Alex was kind if taciturn, the type of person who was interested in the people around him but didn't impose himself upon them. I think Laura liked him because he respected her privacy and just let her hang around silently when she wanted to hang around silently.

Standing in front of me now, Alex took a drink of coffee. "Laura came by here yesterday. She seemed upset. I didn't press her. She sat in the backyard for a while. She looked at my paintings. Then she disappeared into the guest bedroom. We had dinner together. She asked me about my work. Then she went back down to the guest bedroom and went to sleep. I heard her sneak out early this morning."

"Did she mention an Ernest Whitaker?" I asked.

"No."

"Did she say anything about me?"

"No."

"Did she say why she was upset?"

"No."

"Or where she was going next?"

"No."

"Any hint at all?"

"No."

"Do you think," Alina asked, "that we could take a look in the spare bedroom where she spent the night? In case she left anything behind?"

Alex hesitated and then said unsmilingly, "That bedroom is currently occupied by another friend who had a tough night. I think it might make them uncomfortable."

The ensuing silence told me it was time to go. Passing back through his art studio on the way to the front door, I paused to look at a canvas filled with blurry two-dimensional shapes that gave me a pleasing sense of vertigo. Falling into the painting, I remembered a time, about a year ago, when Laura and I had been to a group show to see Alex's work. We were strolling through a low-ceilinged, overcrowded warren of rooms, face masks dangling from our wrists just in case, when we stopped to look at a painting like this one. That was the night Laura told me we were definitely not having children.

"I was a bad mother in a past life," Laura said with a red-lipped smile full of perfect white teeth.

"I don't know how to argue with that."

"Then don't."

"I just feel like," I said, "now is the time for us to start something new." I wish I had some other great reason to add one more person to this world, but I didn't. I didn't have a vision for the future to inspire her into procreation. I just knew that our conversations had started to feel tedious and that having kids seemed like the next natural step on our journey to death. "We wouldn't need to leave the city," I said in a voice thick with reassurance.

She took my arm, she in a slinky dress, me in a suit. I don't remember why we were dressed like that. Maybe the opening was fancy? Though we sometimes dressed up on a lark. She said to me with rehearsed finality, "I'm not cut out for it. Paul, there's a piece of me missing. I know that."

"I don't think that's true. You are extremely caring and loving to me."

"You're my teddy bear," she whispered in my ear, blushing.

"But I'm not nurturing. I'm not giving. I'm not. I like my life and my body. And besides. I don't believe in anything."

"People change with circumstances," I offered, trying to move us along to the next piece of art.

"They definitely don't," she said, planting her feet. "I'm the same way I've always been. Some circumstances perk me up, sure. But underneath I'm always the same."

One thing about Laura, she was beautiful when she cried. She cried silently, tragically, stoically.

An hour later, we were dancing at a party thrown in Alex's honor in the unlit courtyard of a restaurant, made even darker by tree cover. Laura was suddenly delightful, laughing and drinking. We were whispering jokes to each other about all the phonies around us. She was showing me what our life could be like, if I could just let go of what I thought I wanted.

But it's not enough to have a few fun nights on the town. Life, real life, is waking up, feeling fat, eating breakfast, cleaning up dog shit. Life is what we regret and resent as we fall asleep.

———

Alina and I said our goodbyes to Alex on his front stoop, but just as he was about to close the door, Alina thought to say, "Oh, and so you know, there was a murder in our apartment building yesterday."

I saw Alex's eyebrows crinkle a bit in the center. "Oh."

"It's possible the police will even stop by," Alina said.

"Okay. Good to know."

We turned away but Alex unexpectedly called to me, his gentle voice traveling without him having to raise it. "Paul? How are you? Are you okay?"

"Oh, I'm . . ." I tried to search my body for emotions, but I couldn't locate any. "I'm fine." And then I felt myself mirroring Alex's gentle voice. "How are you, Alex?"

"Concerned about Laura," Alex said.

"Oh, well, of course. Me too." And then because I didn't want to leave things on that admittedly defensive note: "Any tips for me today?" I explained to Alina, "Alex often gives me tips he learned in therapy."

"I do it under duress," Alex told Alina. And then to me, he said, "I always tell you, Paul, you can't just absorb other people's therapy. You have to go get your own."

"I don't know. I've picked up some useful things from you. Come on, give me something to mull over."

"How's this? All of your selves are always in the car. But *you* can decide who's driving."

Alex went to close his door, but I had one more question. "Are you still afraid of your phone?" I don't know why I felt the need to be a bit of a dick before we left, but I did.

"I'm not afraid of my phone," Alex said plainly. "I'm afraid of what it does to my mind." And with that, he shut the door.

As we walked past a car wash toward Graham Avenue, Alina told me she was going to catch a bus back home. "I have a date," she said with a shrug. I thanked her for her help and gave her a hug, which she returned without reservation.

"Did we get anywhere today?" she asked.

"At least we know Laura's okay," I said. "She'll probably even be back at the apartment when I get home."

"Yeah, of course." And then Alina jogged half a block to catch up to a lumbering blue bus. I wandered through low-income housing and back toward Greenpoint. My aching right foot aside, actually, you know what, I was feeling pretty good. For some reason, I was even glad Alina had a date. I couldn't really tell you why. Besides, Laura was alive—that had been confirmed. I didn't even realize I was worried about the alternative until the possibility had passed.

I put in my earbuds, pulled out Detective Kurlansky's card, and called his cell to update him on our progress.

"But where is Laura *now*?" he demanded.

"I don't know. Maybe home?"

"I think an officer would have alerted me," he murmured over a droning buzz. Was he shaving?

"Tomorrow I'll go by her work if she's still not back," I offered.

"Do that."

Before he could hang up, I rushed out, "Do you think after all of this is over, we could have brunch and you could give me career advice?"

"How old are you?" he asked.

"Forty."

Point made, Kurlansky hung up.

When I got home, the black plastic bag containing Alina's manuscript was hanging from the handle of my apartment door. I guess I'd left it by the pool. But who had known to return it? This thing was clearly not going to leave me alone. I sighed and brought it inside with me.

Laura wasn't there, which was beginning to feel disconcertingly normal.

I walked the dog and defrosted the fish, and, for entertainment, kicked around possible motives for Ernest's murder. Maybe he was the victim of a jilted lover? Perhaps another woman had seen him with Laura? Strangling *is* an act of passion. But then again, the bedroom didn't smell of sex. And the way Ernest was arranged with his arms spread out, Jesus-like on a pristine white sheet, made his death seem ritualistic.

Wait a minute. Where's my saltshaker?

I'd gone to season the salmon, and there was loyal pepper, but where was wayward salt? Weird.

And then there was the matter of the murder weapon. The chain from the window shade. That pointed to Stovan, didn't it? I mean, Stovan was constantly fixing those chains because they became tangled in the spool device and snapped. He'd mended ours twice in the last month. But the fact that those chains snapped all the time meant that they weren't very strong. Could you really strangle someone with one of them? Would the chain even hold? Maybe Ernest didn't fight it . . .

I cut up the salmon and added it to some pasta. Then I went to the bathroom. I always urinate before I eat. As a precaution. I don't like to be aware of my bladder at all when I'm putting food into my mouth.

As I opened the lid, there in the toilet bowl, bobbing up and down, I saw him, Mr. Saltshaker.

I considered calling Kurlansky as I gingerly fished out the glass receptacle. But what would I tell him? My wife didn't come home, but Mr. Saltshaker decided to go for an unsanitary swim?

I sat down and ate my unsalted fish. I gave a bit to the dog. Then as I was putting my plate into the dishwasher, so narrow that no one outside of New York would stand for such a thing, I noticed my phone charger was sitting inside of it, on the top rack, where the cups belong. What the fuck? Before I could reconsider, I called Kurlansky.

After one ring: "Have you *heard* from your wife?"

Me: "No."

Kurlansky: "Then you shouldn't be calling me."

Me: "Stuff has been moved around in my apartment."

Kurlansky: "Okay."

Me: "Isn't that strange?"

Kurlansky: "What sort of stuff?"

Me: "Saltshaker. Phone charger."

Pause.

Kurlansky: "I have to go. I'm on a date."

I took some ice cream from the freezer and ate it out of the carton. Kurlansky and Alina were both out on dates.

They weren't on dates with each other, were they?

I did the mental math: seven million people in this city. Let's say 1 percent of them are on dates on any given night. That's seventy thousand New Yorkers on dates. So, okay, mathematically they probably weren't on a date with each other. But wow. That seems like a lot of people on dates. Wouldn't restaurants be flooded with horny folks? Maybe some of them were at the movies? What was I thinking about? *Do* I have ADHD? It is hard for me to focus on one thing. I'm always all jittery inside.

I watched some TV with the dog, his head on my ankle, adorable, but after an hour or so, it was getting to be about bedtime. I turned the TV off and wandered into our shared office space. Paintings from emerging artists that Laura had commissioned covered half the walls. Rock and roll posters I'd collected from the sixties and seventies covered the other half. Standing between our two selves, I had an uncomfortable thought. Was I somehow culpable in Laura having had an affair? I didn't dare continue with this line of inquiry, so I grabbed the black plastic bag, opened the balcony door, and plopped down on the wrought iron chair under the dull wall light. The passing cars serving as white noise, I pulled out Alina's manuscript. The dog settled again at my feet.

I took a breath and attempted to focus my eyes on the first sentence. Starting a new book is like meeting a new person. In the beginning you're not sure if it's worth the effort. That's why I hate short story collections; it's like having to get to know a new person every twenty pages. And really, I'd just rather not.

As I was starting to settle into the book's unfamiliar syntax, I heard a knock at my front door. I scooped up Theo, mellow with sleepiness, and opened it. There stood Kurlansky, grimacing, square in the middle of the frame, hands in pockets, the same white collared shirt and suit pants he had on earlier that day. Maybe that's just what he wore.

"Is your date over?" I asked, moving aside to let him in.

"It became a bore." He wandered past me, through my bedroom, and onto the balcony.

I tried not to be offended on Alina's behalf, but he wasn't really out with Alina, I reminded myself. I'd just made that up. *I really need to stop making stuff up*, I thought. *It's confusing my mind.* I poured us two scotches, neat, and brought out the bottle in the crook of my armpit.

Kurlansky took his drink, downed it, and leaned over the balcony railing. He looked down into the walled-off parking lot and over at the luxury building behind ours, the back of which was cement gray, full of chips and cracks. Its windows small and unadorned. No attention had been paid to the rear of that building, as if it were the back of a film set.

"When you came home and discovered your things had been moved around," Kurlansky asked as he sat next to me, "was your balcony door locked or unlocked?"

"I didn't notice," I admitted and refilled his drink.

"Items moving around your apartment. That worries me." He crossed his legs.

"Why?"

"It doesn't fit my theory." But he wasn't forthcoming about this theory, and I didn't want to give him the satisfaction of asking.

"Hey," I said. "I've been thinking about motivations for the murder."

"I'd rather you didn't."

"Well, it seems to me," I said, the scotch having loosened my tongue, "that the killing didn't happen during sex because there were no sex odors in the room."

"I noticed that too." Kurlansky nodded, still looking straight out.

"And then," I continued, "I wonder how someone killed Ernest with one of those chains. They're not very strong."

Kurlansky nodded again. "A preliminary tox report indicates that Ernest Whitaker had an excess of antidepressants in his system. It's possible the high dosage repressed his breathing. But there were anomalies in the results that will take a few days to sort out."

"Here's another thing: I understand why Stovan would be a suspect." I fell into detective patter with surprising ease. "He hated that Ernest always had dogs and women in his apartment, and he refused to fix Ernest's broken appliances."

Now Kurlansky turned toward me, though he didn't quite look at me, the overhead light hanging long shadows on his face.

"You knew all that already, right?" I asked.

Kurlansky didn't answer, but he did refill my drink.

"Anyway, my point is," I said, trying to get back on track, "there's no reason to think that the murderer is someone who lives or works in the Jax because surely Ernest had a life outside of this building, right?"

Kurlansky made direct eye contact and said methodically, "On Friday afternoon, Ernest Whitaker was seen up at the pool and then down getting his mail. None of the front desk staff saw him leave the building after that. No guests were signed in or out. Someone in the building killed him."

"Are there any cameras in this place?" I asked.

"Nope. You live in a neighborhood with a very low crime rate."

"And DNA?"

Kurlansky grinned. "The bedroom was scrubbed clean. The living room, however, has so much DNA, canine and human, as to render any sample useless."

Kurlansky put his empty glass on the table. He rose and stretched. His shirt became briefly untucked, revealing faded tattoos on his midriff.

"Do you have a time of death?" I asked, looking up at him.

"Ernest's next-door neighbor was returning from the trash chute at nine thirty in the morning. He remembers the time because he was running late for a video chat with his mother. On the way into his apartment, he saw another neighbor with a Royal Poodle leaving Ernest's apartment. Ernest said goodbye to this woman. Coroner thinks he was killed before ten thirty," Kurlansky said as he tucked his shirt back in.

"Ten thirty. That's before my wife got to his apartment," I said.

"Only just."

"Which means Laura didn't see him get murdered. She just saw his body?"

"Possibly," Kurlansky said. "Curiously, you don't have an alibi."

He smiled at me and headed inside.

"But . . . of course I do," I bumbled, tripping after him through the bedroom. "I was down in the lobby until almost ten and then with my wife until ten thirty."

"So your wife is your alibi," Kurlansky said as he strode through the dark hallway toward my front door.

"For part of the time," I said, trailing behind.

"And yet she's still missing . . ." Kurlansky opened my front door and stepped into the hallway, the motion-activated sconces flickering on down the long corridor. He was teasing me, right? I laughed so that I seemed in on the joke. "I'm going to camp out in your lobby tonight," Kurlansky continued, leaving me alone, holding the door. "I'd like to get an idea of who comes and who goes."

"Do you really think you know who did this?" I asked.

"I know I know who did it, Paul," he said without turning around. "All that remains is evidence or confession."

"So who is it? Who's the murderer?" I couldn't help but shout after him.

I'm positive that I saw Kurlansky smirk before he disappeared into the elevator.

CHAPTER 5
ALINA'S NOVEL: THE CREST

"Trina, the front desk person at a luxury apartment building in Brooklyn, was having a tough day," Alina's novel began.

A few minutes after Kurlansky's departure, I'd settled back into an outdoor chair. The dog was passed out on his side in the middle of the concrete balcony floor. It was after midnight on a Sunday, and the city was quiet unless you listened hard.

I continued reading.

"Management had ordered Trina to send a preformulated email out to all residents, reminding them that smoking was prohibited in their units. Unfortunately, the wording of this email made it sound like management was reprimanding each tenant specifically, and so Trina spent the better part of the morning trapped behind her desk as indignant tenant after indignant tenant insisted that they had never so much as lit a match in their apartment! So Trina smiled, crinkled her nose, and assured each affluent white adult that they weren't being singled out for persecution."

Alina's book was good! It wasn't chick lit. Where had I gotten that idea from? Alina had written a semiautobiographical novel in crisp third-person prose about a young Dominican American woman who had lost her sense of self after her father died. And so with no career path and very few remaining relatives, she found herself trapped behind the front desk of a luxury apartment called the Crest. But I could see where this novel would be tough to get published. It was quirky and heartfelt and completely genre-less, a reflection of life experienced.

The story followed Trina over one week, conversing with various tenants while handling menial tasks. Intermittently, her thoughts would drift back to her early childhood in the Dominican Republic and then to her family's relocation to a relatively affluent neighborhood in North Jersey where her father worked as an emergency room doctor and her mother stayed at home with Trina and her sister. While her sister easily adapted to her surroundings and eventually followed her father's footsteps into medicine, Trina struggled to figure out how she fit into this multiethnic New Jersey town. She mostly kept to herself, hung out with the smart Asian girls, and spent her weekends reading. Her freshman year of college coincided with the death of her father from brain cancer. Having lost her great friend at the moment she'd entered the wider world was like "being in a tiny rowboat cut loose from its berth, suddenly overwhelmed by an unsteady sea."

As I got deeper into the novel, it seemed to me that Trina risked losing herself completely in the tenants' myriad needs. Sometimes it felt like her character *wanted* to lose herself; perhaps being lost was easier, more pleasurable, even, than trying to figure out what she wanted from the world.

I stood up and stretched. I moved the small table in front of me so that I could put my feet up and then I sat back down. The dog stirred and wrapped himself around the foot of my chair. I was maybe fifty pages in when I came upon a tenant who was clearly modeled after me. I didn't warrant a chapter or even a lengthy anecdote, but the passing description was unmistakable.

"Saul liked to hang around the lobby and chat," Alina had written about me. "Especially in the morning. He lived in the Crest while pretending he was nothing like the people who lived in the Crest. As far as Trina could tell, Saul was as lazy and over-privileged as the other tenants; he just had the misfortune of also being middle-aged. On this particular morning, Saul was once again complaining that his wife had allowed the dog to defecate on their balcony. It perplexed Trina how Saul could whine about the same things, day in and day out, and never recognize the repetition. And then he, like clockwork, started in again on the bagels at the shop down the street; they apparently weren't water boiled. Trina couldn't care less about bagels, but even she knew that if he walked only one block farther, there was a bakery that very clearly advertised water-boiled bagels. Many times, she'd considered sharing this information with Saul, but somehow keeping that petty knowledge a secret allowed her to hide a piece of herself away, even as the rest of her was constantly out on display."

Oh shit. Was this bagel place for real? What the fuck?

"Saul was between jobs. And seemed at loose ends. This kept him relatable, human even, to Trina, despite all of their other differences."

Well, I'd hold on to being "relatable, human even" and chock the rest up to being . . . true.

A few moments later, I read a beautiful section where Trina and another young woman who works at the front desk use the building's access keys to slip into residents' apartments, where they imagine these strangers' lives. They know which tenants aren't home because their doors have advertisements hanging from the knobs, flyers that were left by a food delivery service weeks earlier. I found the sequence fanciful and lovely and sad. Two young people inhabiting all of those possible spaces.

I looked up at a patch of black sky. A few faint stars struggled to reach me. I texted Alina: It is an amazing book.

Right away she texted back: You're not upset?

Me: Not at all.

Alina: I forgot that you're in there.

Me: There are so many voices in there.

Alina: I'm sorry.

Me: It's flattering to be written about regardless. I love it.

Alina: Thanks.

Me: I still have the last third to read.

Alina: So there's still time for me to fuck it up.

Me: Oh, sorry. One more thing. Your date tonight. I know this is crazy. But it wasn't with Detective Kurlansky, right?

Alina: Ha, ha, ha, ha.

Me: That wasn't an answer.

Shrug emoji.

She was teasing me.

Me: Did you have sex with Detective Kurlansky?

Alina: Of course not!

Then.

Alina: I did have sex tonight, though. It was fine. Eggplant emoji. Shrug emoji.

Me: Angry face emoji.

She hit the haha button on that.

Something in the universe was clicking into place. Like a small mystery had been solved. *Alina was my friend.*

Alina: Now stop texting and read!

I liked her text persona. It was cute.

And so I continued reading. And soon enough I came to a section that I indeed found very painful.

It's night, toward the end of Trina's shift. She's mopping the lobby when a tall woman named Sarah (a clear stand-in for Laura), wearing a black cocktail dress and heels, drunkenly skitters in from having had dinner with a friend, an artist in Bushwick. Sarah goes to hit the up button on the center elevator but stops herself.

"'I don't want to go back to my apartment,' Sarah said to Trina, both of them standing in the middle of the shiny lobby floor. 'Saul will be up there, watching TV in his underwear. Underemployed and overweight. Unashamed to pass gas and flirt with other women in my presence. Sometimes all at once.' Sarah let gravity pull her into a sitting position on a large unclaimed Amazon box, her knees together, ankles apart. 'Why is my husband punishing me for not wanting to be a mother?' Sarah asked. Trina was out of her depth here, but Sarah didn't seem to require a response. 'When I was a kid, I didn't give a shit about dolls. Honestly, Trina, to be perfectly honest with you, I give a shit about precious little. I love this city. I've always loved this city, and don't I try on a daily basis to make this city a more beautiful place?' Sarah worked with a not-for-profit that commissioned local artists to paint murals in low-income neighborhoods. 'And I love Saul. He used to be a lot of fun. He used to like to create things. He was a very funny actor, up for anything. He was the person I most enjoyed sharing this city with. But outside of New York and Saul, I don't know. I'm unmoved.' And then laughing and whispering, 'I barely care about the dog.' She took her shoes off and rubbed her feet. 'I know I'm not an easy person. I'm told I can be mean. But in my mind, I'm not mean; I just don't put up with any shit. And Saul? He used to love that person. He did. But since I've told him, I swear for the two hundredth time, that I don't want children, I think he's just ignoring me in the hope that I'll go away. I wish *I* were enough for him. I do. I wish I were worth more so he'd try harder. Though I'd settle for him just loving me enough to remember to take the goddamn dog out for a walk in the morning.'"

Oof.

My stomach turned into a dark chasm, swallowing me from the inside. Maybe I couldn't blame Laura for sleeping with another man. Maybe I couldn't blame her for anything. I even felt a wave of gratitude for Alina's clear-eyed third-person prose.

Every man should have an impartial observer write a description of him and how he treats his loved ones.

But the worst blow through literature was yet to come. It was an offhand passage, one of the last in Alina's novel. This passage would tear down so much of what I'd accepted as true.

There was no grand summation at the end of the manuscript. Rather the workweek is over, and Trina ponders whether the weekend will be all that different. "As Trina grabbed her over-the-shoulder bag, she thought about sitting in different rooms with the same thoughts. She walked past the elevator and out the back door."

At this point, I was curious as to why Trina would be exiting the building from the rear of the lobby. So far the layout of the Crest had exactly mirrored the layout of the Jax, and the back door of the Jax just led to the parking lot. Certainly, we weren't meant to believe that Trina paid the high monthly fee for a parking spot? I made a mental note to bring this constructive criticism up to Alina and continued reading.

"Trina traversed the small grassy knoll behind the building and followed the slate stone pathway beside a deteriorating partial brick wall, a wall from another building, from another time. She then jaunted across the parking lot . . ."

Yep, that all resembled the Jax, but where could Trina be going? You needed a car and a remote control to open the gate that led from the parking lot out to the street.

"She then jaunted across the parking lot to the backside of the apartment building behind the Crest. Trina pressed her finger into a trackpad and opened the now unlocked back door to this other building, simply called 350 Eckford. Tenants from her building often exited through this other building's lobby, which was managed by the same company, for the same reason that she did now. It was simply more pleasant to walk out onto tree-lined, humble Eckford Street."

I sat up, a cold sweat forming at my hairline. *There's not really an exit through the building behind ours,* I thought. Alina's just using that like a metaphor, how the character exits one lobby and enters another. Because if there really was a third way that residents left the Jax . . .

I staggered in from the balcony and right out my front door, not bothering to put on shoes and not noticing if the dog had woken. My heart was thumping in my ears. I was feeling more fear at the thought of this potential third exit than I'd felt when we discovered Ernest Whitaker's body. This was literary, I tried to assure myself as I rode down the elevator and then jogged by Kurlansky, who was playing solitaire in the Library. I didn't turn back as I pushed open the glass back door, registering the deep musty smell of the small patch of grass and moldy brick wall. I darted across the parking lot to the back of the building behind ours. And indeed, there was a small trackpad next to a glass door leading into their lobby. But the management company wouldn't let the residents of our building pass through this other building, right? I put my finger on the trackpad and prayed that it would reject my fingerprint. But no, the pad pinged agreeably, and the back door released. I opened it and peered into this other lobby that was more hallway-like than ours—our lobby but squished. A man I'd never seen before stood behind a desk I'd never seen before and craned his neck toward me. "Can I help you with anything?"

I passed by him as if in a trance and opened that lobby's front door out onto quiet, narrow, tree-lined Eckford Street. Pleasant, convenient Eckford Street. Eckford Street, which was closer to the shops on Manhattan Avenue. Eckford Street, which was closer to Orangetheory.

I texted Alina. Did you ever see Laura exit through the back door of our building?

After a moment—I'd probably woken her—she texted me back: She exited that way all the time. Why?

I sensed Kurlansky standing behind me. I turned. His stone-faced presence was somehow comforting. His body provided the bit of gravity I needed to keep from floating away.

For a minute neither of us said anything. Four in the morning felt surprisingly damp here on Eckford Street.

"What if my wife never had an affair?" I asked Kurlansky. "What if she was just going to Orangetheory?"

"I thought you were certain they were sleeping together."

"I didn't know you could exit out of our building this way," I said.

"Alina said that one morning you saw your wife come out of his apartment," Kurlansky said.

"Yeah." But I had to admit, "I *was* on the other end of the hallway."

"That's almost a city block," Kurlansky considered.

"I have twenty-twenty vision!" I claimed desperately.

"What does that say?" Kurlansky asked, pointing to a white sign under a streetlight farther down the block.

"It's a street cleaning sign."

"Read to me which days you can't park on this side of the street," he commanded in a quiet voice.

"I have no idea," I admitted. The words were fuzzy.

Kurlansky said, "You don't have twenty-twenty vision."

Clearly.

CHAPTER 6
A NEW BEGINNING

startled awake to a phone call from Kurlansky, asking me to get down to the precinct as soon as possible so that I could revise my earlier fallacious statement. Eager to have this whole business behind me, I dressed quickly, not even bothering to parse my dreams. Dog walked, oatmeal eaten, I speed-flip-flopped to the police station in the leafy heart of Greenpoint—damn my right heel to hell. On a quiet street across from a YMCA and next to Davy's Ice Cream, the station might as well have been in small-town America. Before I stepped up into the modest concrete building, my phone pinged. It was a text from my agent, telling me I had an audition later in the day for an independent film. Coincidentally, I was already planning to drop in on him to hand over the black plastic bag I was carrying. Busy day. Sometimes it feels like when the universe notices you for one thing, it notices you for everything. But first order of business, untangle myself from this murder, which Laura and I most likely had absolutely nothing to do with.

Three community officers sat at separate desks in the front room of the police station, one Polish, one Hispanic, and one

Hipster. I suppose each served their own segment of the population. Reductive but effective? The hipster community officer took me past a couple of uniformed cops chatting behind the tall intake desk and into a dim hallway, where she invited me to sit on a bench. I remembered very little from my first trip here just two days ago. I must have been too disoriented by Ernest's death and Laura's sudden absence.

While I waited on the bench, I opened the email from my agent and looked over the audition pages (or sides, as we in the industry call them). I'd be reading for a role in a horror movie, and this section of the script had me in a log cabin, fighting off a murderous gang of vicious Pineys (apparently Pineys are people who live in the Pine Barrens of New Jersey—*research*). Cool. I was going to act the shit out of this. I looked up from my phone, and as if on cue, my community officer appeared from around the corner and motioned for me to follow her into a low-ceilinged, institutional-green interrogation room. I guess I was only expecting Kurlansky, but instead, Kurlansky was one of four people who awaited me. At the metal table sat a squat man with a large mustache and pleasant smile, looking more like a middle manager than a protector of the people. Behind him, against the far wall, sat Kurlansky and two folks I'd never seen before.

The mustached man at the metal table rose to greet me, though it did little to improve his height. "I'm Investigative Chief Christopher Sanchez, the borough investigative chief for Brooklyn North." Jesus, what a mouthful. He shook my hand. "You know Kurlansky, the precinct detective." Kurlansky, legs crossed, nodded at me, a bit shrunken, perhaps with fatigue. "Kurlansky has been doing some fine work," Chief Sanchez continued, "but this is an unusual case with a lot of media attention. And frankly, this precinct doesn't deal with a lot of murders."

Kurlansky shifted in his seat.

"So that's why I'm up here today," Sanchez continued genially.

"Nice neighborhood, Greenpoint. Maybe if the hipsters start killing each other, it'll make it more affordable for the rest of us." He laughed too loudly at his own joke and then looked over at the uniformed woman to Kurlansky's left. "Am I right, Morales?" She grimaced. "This is Deputy Inspector Morales, the precinct's commanding officer." Morales grimaced again, this time in my direction.

"Oh, and this is Detective Stegley." A young Black man with a thin mustache and a neat navy-blue suit lifted his hand as if to say *present*. "Stegley has been focusing on the victim's family and friends."

Sanchez motioned for me to sit, and then I think he sat, but it was hard to tell. He took out his reading glasses and looked at the file in front of him. "According to your statement, Paul, you were on the treadmill when you heard a noise and—"

"Oh, let me stop you there, sir." And not wanting to offend him, I offered generously, "I'm sure there's a lot to catch up on, so you might still be unaware that everything in my statement is a bunch of lies."

"Ah. Kurlansky had said you wanted to update your statement, but—"

"You can just throw that file out." I laughed. "Bunch of lies."

"Well, you have our attention, Paul. Please." Sanchez turned on the pentagonal electronic recording device in the middle of the table.

"I'm just putting my phone on silent," I said, full of modest consideration.

Then I looked over at my audience of four. Sanchez had the premium seating, but it was a small house, so every seat was a good seat. Yes, all of the attention was making me feel important, I won't lie. And I had that jittery sensation in my stomach that's sometimes a precursor to me saying things I haven't thought through. *But* I had a story to tell, and these people wanted to hear it. And I was in a good mood—I had an audition coming up. I was also thinking that everything I was about to say would forever extricate me from this mess. This was to be my final performance for the NYPD, my encore. I was ready to wow them with my ability to be . . . honest. *After my final bow, they will turn to one another and say wow, that took courage to be so . . . honest.*

"I thought my wife was having an affair with um . . . um . . ." Okay, I guess I was nervous. After all, it had been a while since I'd performed for any sort of audience, and so I went up on my first line. "This guy . . . um . . ."

"Ernest Whitaker," Kurlansky prompted.

"Yes. Thanks. Sorry. Right," I said. "I thought my wife was sleeping with Ernest Whitaker, and so I asked Alina, the front desk girl—woman, *young* woman, young *woman*"—*yes, that was right*—"to let me into his apartment so we could catch him and my wife in the act of coitus, so I could prove once and for all that they were having an affair together, my wife and Ernest Whitaker. But instead of finding my wife engaged in sensuous intercourse, there was Ernest, as you surely know, rigor mortis. And now it turns out my wife wasn't even having an affair with him! How about them apples?"

"And how do you know that?" Sanchez asked. "Your wife *is* still missing, right?"

I tried to explain to Sanchez, as clearly as I could, how I had originally thought there were only two exits from our building, but I'd been made to realize there was an additional exit in the rear that my wife had most likely been using, unbeknownst to me. And how my vision wasn't nearly as good as I had supposed— the brunette coming out of Ernest's apartment could have been anyone. And while sure, I guess it was possible that my wife was sleeping with Ernest, it no longer looked at all likely. "In fact," I said in lawyerly summation, barely repressing the instinct to stand, "my wife and I most likely have nothing to do with this case at all!"

Sanchez squinted his eyes.

"So!" Now I did stand, for I could suppress the urge no longer. "All that is left for me to do is apologize for taking up so much of your time and let you get back to the work of protecting the good people of New York City." And with that, I was sure someone would say I was free to go, but they just continued to stare at me. And when people stare at me, I am compelled to speak. "I mean, I'm sure you're annoyed that Laura and I were merely red herrings! I can imagine that you must be *very* annoyed that the woman you thought would be a witness to murder in fact was at a fitness class! But imagine how *I* feel. I feel like an *asshole*. If my wife never had an affair, that means I've been a total jerk to her for no reason. Well, maybe not for no reason, but not for *that* reason. Sure, the sudden unlikeliness of her supposed infidelity doesn't change the fact that our lives were—are—going in different directions and that we really don't belong together because clearly we can't communicate. So maybe overall, okay, this is all okay!" And I lowered my voice, becoming vulnerable, showing off my range. "Just so you know, I do feel like an asshole. And I'm very much looking forward to seeing her, my wife, to her coming home, so I can apologize for being said asshole." And then I brought my energy back up to a crescendo with, "And then yes, maybe I will divorce her! But I don't know! Who knows? Life! It's crazy, am I right?"

"I want to be clear on one point," Sanchez said softly, the words further muffled by his voluminous mustache. "It's a coincidence that at the very moment you decided to confront Ernest Whitaker—"

"I don't know if I'd use the word *confront*."

"It's a coincidence that at the very moment you wanted to catch Ernest Whitaker making love to your wife, he was found dead?"

"Well, I don't know. Is that what you'd call a coincidence? Maybe it's an irony? Or maybe it's just a misfortunate happenstance! Would it have been a coincidence if Stovan had found him? I just mean to say, anyone could have found him. Someone was bound to find him! Why not me?"

"And why do you think your wife left you yesterday and hasn't returned yet?" Sanchez asked.

"Well, probably because I'm an asshole!" Hadn't this guy been listening? "I don't take the dog out, I flirt with other women, and I think the worst of my wife without substantial evidence!" Why was I feeling defensive? Why was I still talking? "But you know what the thing is about being an asshole? It's not illegal, contrary to popular opinion. Being an asshole is not breaking one of the ten commandments. No commandment says 'Thou shalt not be an asshole.' Being an asshole isn't going to keep you out of heaven. At worst, you'll end up living alone. And that's not so bad! And sometimes? Sometimes? Sometimes being an asshole doesn't even have any consequences at all!" Now I was laughing. Why was I laughing?

"Are you okay?" Sanchez asked.

"I'm fine." But I did sit back down. I couldn't deny I was sweating. "I guess I'm suddenly feeling a little manic," I admitted. "I haven't slept much. And like I said, I am racked with guilt." *Had* I said that? "About my wife," I clarified. "I feel guilty about my wife. *And* I was up all night reading a book by my new friend. You know, not getting a good night's sleep. I mean, that's enough to make you commit murder, right? You'd know better than I. Lack of sleep just puts you on edge, like quitting cigarettes. *And* I have an audition today." I looked at my phone. "Shit, I'm running late."

I stood up again, which didn't feel natural, but maybe my director would give me better blocking. Wait. What director? I reminded myself this was real life. God, I really did feel guilty about how I'd misunderstood Laura, how I'd falsely accused her, based on a lot of assumptions. And now that guilt was maybe making me look like I was guilty of something else, everything else. Time to make a speedy exit. "So you know where to find me," I said as I tried to confidently stride to the door but ended up tripping on my own feet. "And hey, I might not have solved the mystery of who killed Ernest Whitaker, but I think I solved the mystery of did my wife cheat on me. One mystery at a time, people, one mystery at a time." No one stopped me from leaving. That was a good sign, right?

Once I had fully exited stage left, I saw that the community officer was waiting for me in the hallway. "All done? I'll walk you out."

But instead of following her, I snapped my fingers. "Shit." I'd forgotten once again to tell anyone about a potentially important detail. It felt clunky, structurally, but I had to go back in.

I threw the door open and returned to the interrogation room where Sanchez was now facing away from the door, shouting at his three subordinates, "So I'm meant to believe—" but then he jerked his thick neck toward me. Not even bothering to smile, barely looking like the same person I'd just left, he barked through his mustache, "What!"

"Sorry," I started, ignoring his change in demeanor the best I could, "but goddamn, I keep forgetting to tell someone. There was a delivery person in a red motorcycle helmet who I saw enter the building when I was watching the desk for Alina, around the time Ernest was killed. And I never saw him exit."

"You're just remembering this person now?" Sanchez snapped.

"No. No. I-I keep forgetting to tell someone."

"And this person could have exited out of *two* other exits?" Sanchez asked.

"Well, delivery people most likely—"

"And how attentive would you say you were while sitting at the front desk?"

Ah. So it was going to be like that. He was going to use my own inattentiveness against me. "There was a large pile of Amazon boxes partially obscuring my view."

Sanchez pressed on. "And one final question, Mr. . . . ." He searched for my last name in his file but couldn't find it. "*Paul.* You're an actor by profession?"

"Why, yes. Yes, I am."

A brief silence.

"That is all for now," Sanchez said.

I knew he was using my vocation as proof that I could easily dissemble, but for some reason, I left the station feeling . . . flattered.

———

As I hurried down the street, my heel now not hurting at all (mysterious), I understood that perhaps I hadn't handled my revised statement as smoothly as I would have liked. But the opportunities this new day seemed to present were putting me in high spirits, and I wasn't willing to sacrifice my optimism to the gods of rethinking and regret. I jogged to a row of blue Citi Bikes docked outside a bright-yellow warehouse. I fumbled with the app and pulled a bike out of its rectangular wheel holder. I mounted and pedaled the ungainly thing, the hazy river to my right. Wow, it was suddenly hot and humid out. No breeze at all from the water. Stifling!

Fifteen minutes later, I huffed and sweated as I jammed the bike into the dock outside the strip of low-rise industrial buildings just north of Dumbo, where wartime ships were once assembled. I lumbered toward security, signed in, and wiped as much sweat from my face as I could while I rode the shiny metallic elevator to the third floor.

I looked a frightening, liquid mess as I checked in at the table outside the rehearsal studio. I sat next to a few other middle-aged men in the air-conditioned waiting area. No one was as sweaty as me, but this was a horror movie, so maybe perspiring heavily would be a good thing.

After a short wait, it was my turn to be led into the audition room. I looked at the impossibly skinny trio of young people behind the folding table in the large mirrored studio. As the comically stooped young man, Zack, introduced himself as the director, I was positive that the water still pouring from my face was going to help me get this part. The three of them looked at me as if they were seeing someone real. And it startled them. The director continued to explain that they were college students and this was a student film. That was fine by me. I was just happy to be out of the house.

They were so young, in fact, that they spoke a language I barely understood. For example, when I was acting out the audition scene, flinging my body in every direction, fighting off multiple imaginary Pineys, the director squeaked, "I loved how you were spinning around," and then his assistant director, a soprano, it turned out, sang, *"Helicopter, helicopter."*

"What is that you're singing?" I stopped acting and asked.

As the other two laughed, the assistant director said apologetically, "Oh, it's music that's under a lot of memes." And then they all sang in unison, *"Helicopter, helicopter."* As I did the scene again for them, their production assistant brought in sliced avocados, and they all sang in unison, "Avocados from Mexico!"

"Another meme?" I ventured.

"Yes!" they cried. And when they all reached in to grab slices, the director said, "What the dog doin'?" and they cracked up.

"Did you guys ever see Charlie Bit My Finger?" I asked when they offered me a slice of avocado.

They all shook their heads.

"Really? That's like the original viral video." And then I continued in a British accent, "Charlie bit my finger!"

They looked it up on an iPad and cackled. They'd truly never seen the father of all viral content. *Oh my God,* I thought. *We're two generations into meme culture. I've lived too long.* (Interestingly enough, the words "Charlie bit my finger" are never spoken in the video, just like Humphrey Bogart never says, "Play it again, Sam" in Casablanca. *Just* like that.)

I waved goodbye to these young people, who seemed so removed from the strangeness of my last few days. Then Zack the director called, "Hey, wait a second." I turned back. He was looking at my résumé. He said, "You live in that building where that guy was strangled." Oh, what a relief to be just a guy who happened to live in that building.

Next, I took an Uber into Manhattan, specifically to the eternal cesspool that is Eighth Avenue between Thirty-Fourth and Forty-Second Streets. The rest of the city can shift and change and grow, but apparently this stretch of gridlocked traffic, wall-to-wall with homeless people, bridge and tunnel commuters, and old-timey textile workers, is impervious to the march of time.

Still hyped up from my audition, I grew impatient with the crowd of people waiting in the lobby for the elevator, so I shot up four flights of steps, right past the agency's receptionist and into my overweight agent's office, where he was eating nuts directly off his desk and peering into his sleek pink monitor.

He looked over at me and cocked his head to the side. "Paul?"

I tossed the black plastic bag on his desk with more force than I'd intended—nuts flying everywhere—while I told him that Alina was the voice of her generation and that the agency would be foolish not to represent her. I then took a picture of him with the black plastic bag in the frame so that I could prove to Alina I'd delivered the manuscript, like Snow White's supposed heart in the hunter's bag, proof the deed was done.

Vaulting out the door, down the stairs, and back into the humid afternoon, I decided to not overthink my erratic behavior, for I would not deny myself the natural high that comes with getting shit done. I would ride that high like I was now riding this Citi Bike, careening recklessly down Broadway through the Flatiron, the Village, and SoHo. Of course, once I got to the Williamsburg Bridge, I had to dismount the bike and walk it up the incline.

I mean, Jesus Christ, I'm not a professional athlete. And while bikes are on my mind, can I just pause the narrative for a moment to express my disdain for *electric* bikes? What a bunch of fucking babies these people are who zoom around on electric bikes. Just pedal! Like a man! Electricity doesn't need to enter the equation here, folks. Or what about these fucking electric scooters, where there's no pedaling at all? Or worse, assholes who ride their motorbikes in the bike lane! Can't we all just ride normal bicycles? You have gears and wheels and pedals—what else do you need? At this point, just ride an electric couch, why don't you, you lazy dunderheads.

As I docked the rental bike and hobbled toward my apartment building, for I was hobbling—this was the most exercise I'd had in an age—it occurred to me that I hadn't thought to look for Laura today. Shit. But we've established that she hadn't seen a horrible murder; she had simply left me. And given that she simply left me, what was my responsibility anyway? And look, I don't want to give off the idea that Laura and I were wrong for each other from the start. In fact, we were crazy about each other. Lit each other up. God, we were all over each other. It was embarrassing, all consuming. I was so thin! But it was hard to remember the good times, harder still to feel them. And anyway, what was left now? Getting annoyed with each other? Taking bicycle rides together? (Although I had just ridden a bike, but for transport, not for pleasure, but it had been pleasurable.) Maybe this relationship just didn't have legs. How did other people sustain relationships? Maybe no relationship has legs. Maybe people are just too lazy to move on! Or maybe something was lacking in me, a stick-to-itive-ness? Maybe I lacked imagination of what could be? I guess we could travel? Ah Jesus. What was I going to do with the rest of my life? Did I really want a family, or was that just what I didn't have? Wanting something and simply being aware that you don't have it are two different things, after all.

So when she gets back, Laura and I will talk, I thought as I entered the lobby, nodding at the two police officers and showing them my ID. The front desk person wasn't anyone I recognized. Walking to the elevator, I suddenly realized I didn't have the black plastic bag with me anymore. Of course I didn't, and that realization made me inexplicably lonely, and I could sense my thoughts darkening. I could almost feel my eyelids start to droop, foreshadowing a depression.

It's okay, I told myself in the elevator. I am okay. I will stumble through this period of transition, just as I have stumbled through everything in my life, with only a vague idea of where I am going, mostly sure that everything will work out one way or another. Sure, I'd been unfair to Laura. Sure, I'd made assumptions. None of these things are awesome. But in the end, I am who I am. I am this guy. I am . . . an asshole?

Plodding down the hallway, I realized I was about to spend a lot of time alone. I didn't want to have to deal with myself in a shitty mood. I'm a real challenge to be around when I've lost my sense of self.

So I started to give myself a mental pep talk with such force that I was actually muttering out loud. "Maybe I'm too hard on myself. Can you really be an asshole for being incompatible with another person? Maybe I'm not an asshole at all. Maybe I'm a nice guy who took someone's shit for too long? Was that possible? (That would be awesome.) I mean, she wasn't very nice, Laura. And I think I am nice. Haven't I always prided myself on being nice even when I feel crappy? Oh, so, see, I'm not an asshole. I'm nice."

I took out my key.

"And I had an audition today. Maybe I can keep using my passable looks and large white body as a money machine. It's easy enough. And I can cry on command—I should advertise that more. Maybe I'll even challenge myself to take bigger roles. What about a return to the theater?"

I opened the door and immediately sensed there was another

person in the apartment. It was as if a certain amount of ambient noise was being absorbed by additional matter.

The gray afternoon had darkened the walls. The bedroom door was closed. And the dog hadn't greeted me. Something was wrong.

I turned the knob on the bedroom door. I put my shoulder into opening it—summer makes the doors swell. And there was Laura, lying on her back in our bed over the white comforter, her feet in white ankle socks. And I felt happy to see her toes, which confused me. Was the reality of having her here going to change all of the feelings and thoughts I'd been having in her absence? Was real Laura actually better than imaginary Laura? Had I just been focusing on all the negative aspects of her, and now that I saw her, I'd remember all the good things? I do have a habit of focusing on the negative. In fact, I may have entirely misremembered my childhood because I so tend to dwell only on the bad times.

Dim light strained through the large translucent shade. And I thought, *Huh, looks like the shade's chain is broken again.*

And that's when I saw a few metal bits of the chain scattered on the floor. And then I looked over at Laura's head.

And, reader, I'm feeling guilty because I should have prepared you better for what's about to happen. But then, on the other hand, it felt truer to put you into my own mindset. How I experienced that day. So you could feel the shock that I felt.

I saw shiny blood on Laura's mouth and chin.

I saw the line of bruising on her neck, dark, seemingly on the edge of bleeding.

Then I focused on her too convex eyes and the rivers of red running through them.

I heard myself wailing before I realized I was wailing. It was a wailing that defied gravity. A wailing that augured some other reality, a *realer* reality.

Somehow her blood was on me. Had I gone to her without realizing it?

And then I was on the floor by the balcony door, hearing scratching behind me. I turned. Theo was on the other side of the glass door, his little head on his front paws, crouched low, outside somehow, looking in.

I realized my breathing was shallow, though it didn't feel like it was happening in my body.

I must have called 911, though I don't remember doing it. I do remember that I had to use the bathroom, and I remember clinging to that pressure in my bladder to take my mind some-where else, to keep part of me separate from the shock that I could feel myself falling into. I had been around dying family members a couple of times in my life, but those deaths had been slow moving, sterilized. And of course there had been Ernest Whitaker, but that felt like looking at a surreal painting. This was like being trapped inside.

The police came.

The lab technicians wore protective white plastic.

Someone escorted me out of our apartment.

The entire building had been turned inside out. Everyone was standing outside of their doors. Whereas Ernest's death was a blip, this was a pattern.

And the lobby was a dam ready to burst. Reporters flooding in, police trying to keep them out. Police trying to get tenants to clear the lobby, tenants demanding answers. And the staff huddled around the front desk. I saw Alina among them, and as I tried to go to her to tell her I don't know what, I realized how tightly the officer escorting me was gripping my arm. Looking back at Alina's wide, frightened eyes, I thought of her novel's cool, crisp third-person prose. I wanted to rise out of myself, out of this moment, and become a detached, omniscient narrator. But I was more deeply entrenched in my own first-person narrative than ever, and it didn't look like rescue was coming anytime soon.

The police pushed me into the squad car and explained I wasn't under arrest, but I wasn't sure I believed them. And then, as we pulled away, I saw something that I didn't quite register with my full mind. There, through the passenger-side window, across the boulevard, alone in the gas station parking lot, astride a black motorcycle, stood the leather-clad figure with the cherry-red helmet.

CHAPTER 7
DEATH AS DEFINED BY MERRIAM-WEBSTER

Before I describe the forthcoming police interrogation, I want to delve into something that may seem confusing on its surface. There may have been an expectation that I'd feel nothing at Laura's passing. And that this *nothing* would haunt me. Certainly, there were moments when she was alive when I would imagine her death and ponder the possibility that her hypothetical passing could leave me cold. But now that her life had come to an end in reality, Laura existed in my mind as a totality. And that totality included the love I had felt for her. It also included the violent way she died. There was no more anxiety about what the future might hold for us; instead, there was only the ever-present burden of the multifaceted past.

In general, in the coming days, which we will soon get into, I was bereft. I'd start crying and wouldn't be able to stop. Some of my grief was because I unexpectedly missed her, but most of it was due to the horror of it all. And my guilt was overwhelming. I'd been so careless, so thoughtless. Even though I couldn't explain why this had happened, I was certain that it was my fault she'd met such an unimaginable end.

In the coming days, time would go by without me realizing it.

My sleep would be fitful and full of the visceral horror of her bloodshot eyes. Sometimes I'd become confused about where I was and how I'd gotten there.

When I'd find myself alone, I would force myself to masturbate by watching pornography, just to hold on to some other part of myself. I would masturbate joylessly, with great difficulty, until it was painful, until it was useless. But eventually, I would learn to give in to grief. I'd learn that I *was* grief. Even if my grief was selfish, unfair, unearned, it didn't matter. It wasn't something I could control or judge.

———

In the hours after I'd discovered Laura's body, I sat in the police station's pale green interrogation room, like at the bottom of a swimming pool. Someone made me take off my bloodstained shirt and gave me fresh clothes from my apartment. But even after I dressed, I was cold, shivering hard until someone else brought me a police blanket, little pieces of it coming off on my shirt and pants. Picking at these tiny bits of cloth, I let myself realize that, beyond the fact that my wife was dead (Jesus Christ), I was in real trouble here. I had, after all, found two bodies in three days. I had an inkling, even then, that I would have to figure out who had done this. That I couldn't leave that job to anyone else. But hadn't Kurlansky insisted he knew who killed Ernest Whitaker? Why hadn't he arrested anyone sooner? I felt anger. But the feeling was like a faulty firework, shot up only to fizzle in the night sky.

Suddenly, I heard Kurlansky shouting in the hallway, "How could you not have told us? That was your whole reason for being there!"

And then a voice I didn't recognize. "She came in through the other building."

This was followed by muffled sounds of arguing and shoes scuffling down the hall.

And then at some point, it must have been evening by then, I looked up, and Investigative Chief Sanchez and Detective Kurlansky were sitting across the metal table from me. We had switched positions since the last time we'd met in this room that morning. Now I was facing the door, not that it mattered.

To the best of my recollection, Sanchez asked me to go through what time I'd left home in the morning, when I'd returned, and what I'd seen when I entered the apartment.

"Look," Sanchez said, "you're obviously upset."

From the way Kurlansky glanced skeptically at him, I knew he was starting to lay some sort of cop line on me.

"This isn't the sort of thing you ever saw yourself getting tangled up in," Sanchez continued. "We're still waiting for DNA testing from Whitaker's apartment to come back." Of course, Kurlansky had told me any DNA in that apartment was most likely useless. "But look, we know your DNA is in Whitaker's apartment because you entered it, by your own admission, twice, if not more than that."

"Yeah, I did," I said.

"Twice or more than that?" Sanchez asked.

"Twice," I said.

"Okay." Sanchez nodded. "You say twice." He folded his fat hands on the table. "You have to see this from my point of view. First you claim you heard a noise in Ernest Whitaker's apartment and that's why you went in. Then you claim your wife was having an affair with him. Then you claim your wife wasn't having an affair with him. Then there is this mysterious delivery person."

"I don't understand," I said.

"Maybe you think you're smart. That by throwing confusion all over everything, you're helping yourself."

"Helping myself with what?" But I already knew what he was getting at.

"Why did you kill her?" Sanchez asked. "I think you could've gotten away with the first murder. Maybe you just got angry all over again? She said that he was a better fuck than you? You used the chain again. You said, 'This is how I killed him.'"

I looked over at Kurlansky. But he was staring down at his knees.

"I still don't understand how that killed her, the chain," I said. "She was strong. Why didn't she fight more?"

"Why *didn't* she fight more?" Sanchez asked. "Why don't you tell us?" And then he sneered, "What are you going to do now? You gonna act some more?"

"You think I'm acting?"

"You are an actor, aren't you?"

"But not a very good one." I could feel myself spiraling into an unhelpful monologue. "I only even became an actor because I didn't want to take math in college. Or a foreign language. And then people always just needed a big guy in their play or movie. And most big guys were more successful than me, so they wouldn't dream of spending their time saying a few lines, or maybe I was just more sensitive than other big guys—"

"Enough! Jesus fucking Christ! Enough!" Sanchez stamped his shoe against the concrete floor.

And he was right. It *was* enough.

Then there was a long silence. And then I couldn't stop crying. It was as if that silence made a hole through which all my sorrow poured.

"It's okay," Sanchez said. "Just admit you killed her. You'll feel better."

And I swear to God, I was feeling so awful, I almost pleaded guilty to a crime I didn't commit.

But then I remembered again, Kurlansky had said he knew the identity of the murderer. Why wasn't he speaking up? I turned to him. "You know who did this. Tell me. Please. Tell me who did it."

But before Kurlansky could open his mouth, Sanchez shouted, "You did it, Paul! You did!"

———

And yet, sometime later, I was walking back home through the heavy evening. Obviously, everything they had on me was circumstantial. That's like when it's just circumstances that are against you, right? Maybe they were hoping I'd disclose incriminating evidence during the interrogation? Or maybe they were hoping I'd break down and confess. And honestly, I'd come pretty close, and I was innocent. Jesus. A couple of nights alone with my thoughts, and who knows what I might confess to? I might confess to any unsolved case they put in front of me. I mean, I've always been highly suggestible. After I saw *28 Days Later*, part of me thought that human flesh did indeed look kind of tasty.

And there was also this. As Sanchez had held the door of the interrogation room open for me to exit, he delivered a parting shot. "If we find proof that your wife and Ernest had a relationship of any kind, you won't be walking out of here so easily. I don't care how many exits are in your goddamn building." I'd just shrugged at the time, but as I walked home, I could see where proof of Laura and Ernest fucking might further implicate me through . . . even more circumstances. How many circumstances need to pile up until the evidence is no longer circumstantial? That feels like some sort of Zen riddle or an excised verse of Bob Dylan's "Blowing in the Wind."

I checked in with a uniformed cop in the lobby of the Jax, who in turn radioed an officer in my apartment. As I waited for the okay to proceed, I nodded to Leonard at the front desk, pleasantly chubby, wearing a black suit, and in his fifties. Leonard gave me a sympathetic shrug that didn't feel appropriate, given the gravity of the situation. But what would have been appropriate? An arched eyebrow to let me know he believed I was guilty? A man hug to let me know he believed I was innocent? Actually, the more I thought about it, a noncommittal shrug was probably a smart move on his part.

One of the cops escorted me upstairs, and when we got to my door, an officer was standing in the entryway holding my old backpack full of clothes and toiletries. In his other hand, he held the dog leash. Theo sagged next to him, looking uncharacteristically bowed.

I knew I wouldn't be allowed back in my apartment, so I'd asked the local dog day care if Theo could spend the night. I hated to do that to him, but the truth was he liked it there, and the overnight guy was sweet. Looking down at the dog, I felt my legs start to give out from under me. The officer who'd escorted me up here noticed and offered to take Theo to his overnight. Overwhelmed by his kindness, I took a few deep breaths and tried to hold it together. Theo looked back at me, hesitantly letting this stranger lead him to the stairwell.

For myself, I'd made arrangements to stay with my old college buddy Bob Shapiro in Manhattan. Bob's a great guy, really fun stuff, goofy and unselfconscious. Before I left the station, I told the coordinating officer that I'd be staying with Bob, and I gave her his address. But now, in the Jax, in the hallway outside of my apartment, I was suddenly, unexpectedly alone, completely on my own. I could theoretically, though maybe not ethically or possibly not legally, go anywhere. As I approached the elevator, I allowed myself to consider once again that the cops really did suspect me of double homicide, so it would probably behoove me to present them with another suspect. And since Kurlansky was convinced someone in the building had murdered Ernest (and thus Laura), it made sense for me to stay *here*. To talk to other tenants and generate an alternate theory, though I had no idea what that theory might be. So instead of hitting the down button, I hit the up button and went to apartment 705. Maybe I could stay with Robin Nash. She had shown me real sympathy up by the pool yesterday. That wasn't a lot to hang on to, but it was something.

Unfortunately, Ms. Nash could barely steady herself as she opened her door, drunk. Improbably, she was wearing a bikini, even though it was nine at night. Her large green eyes were trying to focus on me.

"It's Paul," I said. "From 329."

"Oh fuck." Her eyes filled with tears. "What do *you* want?" She pulled a vape pen from the side of her bikini bottom and took a hit.

"Well, actually, I know we don't know each other that well, but you were so nice to me at the pool yesterday, and I don't have many friends here, and I can't bear the idea of staying with the plant people, and my apartment is a crime scene."

"I'm so sorry, I'm so sorry. *I'm sorry.*" Her condolences were erratic and a bit aggressive.

"No, listen, it's okay, but if you're willing, I really need a place in the building to spend the night . . ."

But Robin was too overwhelmed by her own emotions to listen to me. "They were even going to close the pool down today," she needed me to understand. "In *her* honor." Then a bit bitterly, "They hadn't suggested that for Ernest."

"So did they close the pool?"

Outraged. "No! A couple of tenants, *assholes*, got angry and refused to leave. Not *me!*" Then rambling. "Though I didn't leave, truth be known. I mean, we do pay a lot of money for that pool." And finally, self-flagellating. "We should have shut the pool down today. I know that!" She stood as straight as she could manage, ready to take responsibility for the building's failure to memorialize my wife's death with a day off from swimming. Mind you, she still hadn't invited me in.

And that's when I saw, over her shoulder, three twelve packs of Corona beer bottles stacked on top of each other on her kitchen counter. They were all leaning like that tower in Pisa, some on the top level nearly cantilevering over the bottles below. Then I noticed that a couple of bottles on the bottom were actually broken and the whole mess was indeed precariously close to toppling. And, oh, the bottom cardboard container was beer-soaked and deteriorating. *And* there was already some broken glass on the kitchen floor and Robin was barefoot.

"Robin, stay where you are," I said and moved forward. Startled by my tone, she stepped aside, inadvertently letting me in.

But seeing me going toward the beer, she shouted, "Leave that alone!"

"Stay where you are. You're not wearing shoes and there's broken glass."

"Don't!" She was genuinely upset. "You're embarrassing me! Leave it alone." But I couldn't leave it alone. The beer tower looked seconds from collapsing.

I pulled her garbage bin out from under the counter.

"Really, I'm fine. I've *got* it," she insisted, bare feet inches away from glass.

"You're going to get hurt." I delicately pulled a cracked beer bottle off the top tier. Oh, there was all sorts of broken glass in this mess.

Robin, meanwhile, prattled on angrily. "I told my friends not to bring glass. I said glass is not allowed at the pool. They didn't listen. No one listens!"

I extracted a second broken beer bottle off the top layer, but unfortunately, that one was somehow integral to the whole structure, and its removal triggered a chain reaction of beer and glass cascading waterfall-like down the counter.

"Look what you did!" Robin screamed, anger exploding from her chapped mouth.

"I'm sorry I'm sorry I'm sorry!" I scrambled to get paper towels.

"I told you to leave it alone!" she bellowed.

"I was trying—" I turned to her.

"I know!"

And then she hit me. She smacked me full across the face. It was hard and it hurt. My mind went in opposite directions. One voice in my head said, *Holy shit, I can't believe she fucking did that.*

And then another voice in my head said, *Thank God someone hit me today.*

I was stunned, but do you know who didn't look stunned? Robin. "I told you to leave it alone," she pouted.

"I made it worse, so now I have to clean it up." Why was I being stubborn about this? Well, I had made it worse. And even though she hit me and it fucking hurt, it was hard to be angry with her, nearly naked and drunk out of her mind.

"Fine. That's fine. It's fine." Robin tried to calm herself down. "Just next time I ask you to leave something alone, leave it alone." And with that indisputably wise advice, Robin strode into her bedroom and slammed the door shut. It was only then that I noticed Sparky, her French bulldog, sitting on the long gray couch the whole time, his ears peaked up, on high alert. God, the things these dogs have to see.

I went about picking up pieces of glass, disposing of broken bottles, and mopping up an endless flood of yellow liquid. I noticed some minor cuts on one of my hands and applied pressure with a paper towel to stop the bleeding.

Blood.

Then sometime later, I sat on Robin's kitchen floor and called Laura's friend Alex. He didn't pick up, which was no great surprise. And then I called Laura's parents. The police had informed me that they'd spoken to them. But I needed to reach out. I knew that. So I talked to Laura's distraught mother and father. I'll spare you those moments; I wish I'd been spared myself. They cried. I cried. They said they'd come down from New Hampshire the next day. As I hung up, I gave Ernest Whitaker's parents a thought as well.

I wiped down the counters and floors for what felt like the hundredth time, double-bagged the broken bottles and then disposed of all the detritus down the garbage chute. I sat on Robin's low couch and leaned my head back on the wall. I noticed framed photos of fashion models and piles of fashion magazines.

Sparky put his head on my lap. My last thought before I fell asleep was that I'd never actually asked Robin if I could stay here.

My body and mind had mercy on me and let me sleep, dreamless. That was the only night I wouldn't be haunted by what I'd seen for a long time to come.

———

In the morning, I made a pot of coffee. The dog was still passed out on the couch. Something smelled like excrement, but I couldn't locate the source.

I texted Alina. Are you at the Jax?

Alina texted back, Where are you?

I texted, Robin in 705 needs your help. Was it ridiculous to text in code? Probably. And what sort of code was that anyway? But I didn't know where Alina's head was at. We hadn't spoken at all yesterday, so I was feeling cautious. It's not like I was hiding from the police, but, on the other hand, I wasn't staying where I'd told them.

In a few moments, Alina gently rapped on the door. I opened it a crack and she crept in. As she passed me, her eyes darted down to my right hand, which was streaked with blood from the broken glass last night.

"Why is there blood all over you?"

"It's not all over me," I tried to assure her. "Robin broke some bottles."

"And why is the kitchen so clean?" Alina asked. "I've been in this apartment many times, and the kitchen is always a mess."

"I stayed here and cleaned up."

"The apartment is still . . . fetid, though." She crinkled her nose.

Alina focused on my face. I guess I was catching the natural sunlight from the window because she said, "What happened? Why is your cheek bruised?"

Oh right, that's why my face hurt. "She, Robin, hit me."

"Did you kill her?"

"Robin? Of course not!"

Alina stumbled away from me, her eyes having returned to my large bloody right hand, which had, annoyingly, begun to bleed again.

"Stop looking at my hand. Do I really seem like a killer?"

"You do right now." She backed up into a wall.

I staggered toward her. "Don't scream."

"Why would you say that?"

"Because you look like you're going to scream."

"Because you're looming over me with your giant bloody hand!"

Alina suddenly ran past me and flung open Robin's bedroom door.

"What are you doing?" I asked.

"Checking to see if Robin's alive."

I looked over Alina's shoulder, and there was Robin, alive, swaying up to a sitting position. Thank goodness she was wearing a nightgown and not her bikini—her own hygiene was at stake.

Robin, groggy, turned to us. "What are you doing here? What are you *both* doing here?"

Making sure to use my non-bloody hand, I tugged Alina into the living room.

"I need your help," I said to her.

"Don't touch me."

"Are you two just going to hang out in my apartment?" Robin called from the bedroom.

"I need to figure out who killed Laura," I said to Alina.

"The police think you did!"

"Is that what you think?"

"I don't know what to think except that you keep finding dead bodies!" And then she circled the living room, rubbing her hands on her black work pants.

"Sometimes you lack a bit of empathy," I muttered.

"Oh, do I?"

In the short silence that followed, Robin strolled from the bedroom to the kitchen, tying her plush green robe. "I don't know what either of you is doing here."

"You don't remember me knocking on your door last night?"

"I certainly don't. But thank you for making coffee." Robin pulled out a pan, and as if the idea of cooking were an absurdity, she asked, "Would anyone like eggs?" But before either of us could answer, Robin gestured to a dried dog turd and some urine on a disposable changing pad in the darkened half bath. "Paul, would you mind disposing of that? The trash chute outside will do." For a moment, I could have sworn Laura was in the room.

———

A few minutes later, the three of us were sitting awkwardly around Robin's white plastic kitchen table, eating scrambled eggs and toast and drinking coffee like we were all at a Holiday Inn on a work trip together.

To make conversation, Robin asked me, "When are the funeral arrangements for Laura?"

"It's complicated," I said, "because we don't know when the police will release the body."

"Right. Same with Ernest."

Awkward silence.

I turned to Alina. "I need someone to help me figure out what happened before the police build a case against me."

"I could help," offered Robin, dangling a bit of dry egg from her fork.

"Of course," I said to her as kindly as I could manage. Then to Alina, "My mind is so scattered, I need to talk this out."

"People find me easy to talk to," Robin said to her egg, still trying to be nonchalant.

"But Alina has an inside track with Kurlansky," I explained, making an obvious excuse.

"How is that?" Robin asked.

"He likes her. I can tell."

"Maybe you should date him," Robin said to Alina with a mischievous smile. "It would be a romantic how-we-first-met story."

We both looked at Robin in disbelief. But she just shrugged and put her fork in her mouth.

Alina and I made eye contact. I don't know what Alina saw in me at that moment. But here I was, at breakfast with two women I barely knew in an apartment I'd never been in before. Did I look lost? How could I not? Whatever Alina gleaned from my expression, it made her cry.

She looked away, but she only cried harder. "I am really sorry about your wife," she said, dabbing under her glasses with a napkin. And then I cried. Sobbed. Gasped for air. And Robin watched us while she crunched down loudly on her toast. This was easily the weirdest breakfast ever.

"Okay. Well, look, I'm no expert," Robin said. "But if you're going to figure out who killed these people, you're going to have to stop sitting here crying, and you're going to have to start asking questions."

"Right, right," I said, wiping the water off my face with the back of my hand. "Questions. Well . . ." I thought for a moment and then asked, "Why does anyone even murder anyone at all? Greed? Maybe someone would murder someone who had sex with their underage daughter? People commit murder because of gang affiliations. Do people murder for contested wills? Or is that just on TV?"

"You're spinning," Alina said.

"This is why I need your help."

Robin cleared the plates and tossed them into the sink. "How about asking *me* questions? I knew Ernest. Intimately." Alina and I looked over at her, standing there in her green robe, her arms now spread out like a cactus.

I did have a question for Robin, it turned out. I asked it before I even realized I had it. "I know you slept with Ernest, but did you love him?"

"*Yes.*"

And now all three of us were crying.

I wanted to ask Robin some sort of follow-up, but I couldn't think of one. And evidently neither could Alina.

Her emotions suddenly a thing of the past, Robin declared, "I have to go to work," and she strode through her bedroom and into the bathroom.

"What sort of work do you do?" I called after her. I'd finally thought of another question, albeit an irrelevant one.

"I'm a creative director at American Express," Robin called through the closed bathroom door. "Don't be impressed. Everyone is a creative director. I handle in-house promotion." She reopened the door, toothbrush in hand. "But listen. Meet me in the building's basement tonight, after ten. And I'll show you something that might shed some light on Ernest's death."

"Does it have to be that late?" I asked. "I'm an early-to-bed, early-to-rise kind of guy."

"Ten." She turned back into her bathroom and grumbled, "Now where the hell is the toothpaste . . ."

"It's in here." Alina pointed to the tube in repose on the bookcase.

"Oh." Robin stalked in and snatched it. "I swear my things move around." And dental hygiene implements in hand, she turned to us. "You can't *stay* here." Then she peered at me. "I've been meaning to ask you, Paul. What happened to your face?"

"Nothing," I said. "Just bruised."

"Hmm," Robin said. "Now *that's* suspicious."

A few minutes later, exiled into the barren hallway, Alina and I stood next to each other in emotionally drained silence.

"I need to go back down to the desk," Alina finally said. "And when Leonard relieves me at noon, I have to go to Manhattan."

"Why?"

"Management training."

"Oh, right."

"Turns out they fired Bonnie, who was the community manager. So now I'll be community manager for this building and two others." She walked over to the elevator.

"Do you know why they fired Bonnie?" I asked, remembering the buxom blond woman we saw as we were leaving to look for Laura on Sunday.

"No," Alina said. "But I guess maybe it was because of what's been happening here. I'll find out." She hit the down button.

"Hey," I said, wanting to get this next thought out before Alina left me. "When we were texting the other night?"

"Yeah?"

"I thought to myself, you know, I think Alina and I . . . I think we're friends."

"I don't have many friends," she said plainly.

"I know," I said. "It's a theme that runs through your book. You're comfortable at your job because the relationships are transactional."

Alina looked at me quizzically. Happy to be seen? Offended? It was hard to tell. In any event, the elevator doors opened and shut, but Alina didn't move.

"Oh shit." I pulled my phone out of my pocket. "I didn't even tell you. I gave your book to my agent." I showed her the picture I took of my agent with that black plastic bag in the foreground.

She laughed. "He looks thrilled. But thanks. Thank you. That's amazing."

"It's scary to think how happy I was yesterday," I pondered, feeling darkness encroach upon me once more.

"Where are you going to stay now?" Alina asked.

"I have an idea about that. But I need your help."

My idea was simple and stolen directly from Alina's novel. There was an advertisement hanging from the knob on the door across from Robin's apartment. I fingered it, and yep, it was good and grimy with dust, so there was a very high probability that this tenant was on a long vacation. I wanted to squat in that apartment. That way I would be able to stay in the building and figure out what had happened to Laura. All I needed Alina to do was retrieve the access key from behind the front desk.

Probably flattered that her novel had inspired me, she agreed and went downstairs while I waited in the hallway. A few moments later, she returned, and we were standing inside an apartment that was densely packed with books and heavy, old-fashioned furniture. The walls were painted dark red (good luck getting your security deposit back), and the shelves were cluttered with odds and ends from international trips.

"This is Martin Stowell's apartment," Alina told me. "He does something with corporate events. I think he said he was going to Dubai. Don't lose this key."

"Thank you," I said.

"I'll come by tonight," Alina said, "to be with you when Robin shows you whatever it is she has in mind."

"You don't have to."

"I want to."

And with that, I was alone in a stranger's apartment. In the living room, Chinese masks glowered and glared, so I sought refuge in the kitchen. I sat at the table and looked at busy wall hangings depicting the Buddha on his journey to enlightenment, their meanings impenetrable. So I turned and looked out the window, hoping for relief in the blank blue sky.

I sat alone most of that day. Alex overcame his dislike of phones and called me. He wanted to know if I needed anything. I spoke again with Laura's parents. They were driving down to the city. We talked about when we thought her body would be released. And they told me the police had asked them all sorts of awful questions about whether I'd ever acted violently toward Laura or anyone else. Or whether Laura and I were unhappy. I tried to assure her parents that all of that was standard procedure. They always suspect the spouse, just like on TV.

At some point, I spotted a maroon clothbound book on one of Martin's shelves. I don't know why it called to me, but it did. I pulled it down and opened it up. It was a blank journal. I found a lone pen in Martin's solid oak rolltop desk, and I started writing down thoughts for an eventual eulogy. How Laura and I kept meeting through friends. How one time when we saw each other at yet another party, we went right up to each other and wordlessly grabbed hands and made love at my nearby apartment. How we didn't leave the bed for a week. How we were sore with how much we wanted each other. I wrote about how we genuinely enjoyed each other's company, but then during Covid, we didn't know how to be around each other anymore. Stripped of our city as playground, we found each other lacking, uninspiring. I started to want a family. She didn't. And then I wrote about how after we moved to Brooklyn, I made all sorts of assumptions about what she was doing with her time. How I thought the worst of her.

Of course, none of that could be used in an actual eulogy. So I started again. "Death as defined by Merriam-Webster." I made myself laugh. But it was a feeble laugh. A damp match, momentarily flickering but ultimately failing to produce light or warmth or anything of worth.

CHAPTER 8
THE ORIGIN OF ORGIES

At eight that evening, I went up to the roof. I couldn't stay in that apartment any longer. I couldn't be by myself any longer. (I wanted to be with my dog. Was it possible to ask Alina to pick up Theo so that I could keep him with me in Martin Stowell's apartment?) Going for a walk in the neighborhood wasn't an option. I didn't want police officers to see me passing through the lobby and ask why I wasn't staying with Bob Shapiro in Manhattan.

As the afternoon had worn on, I watched planes descend upon LaGuardia Airport and wrote eulogies for people other than Laura, people who were still alive, just to distract myself. "I'm honored today to speak at the funeral of Robin from apartment 705. Sure, she slapped me across the face, but I refuse to let that single act of violence define her. We all know Robin struggled with depression, but she was also a caring neighbor, and when she set those large green eyes on you, you felt like the most important person in the world."

The day now dimming, I took the stairs up to the roof, barefoot, my right heel in agony. Bare feet are bad for this heel issue of mine. Huh. Another mystery solved, people. I signed in with the lifeguard using Martin Stowell's name and apartment number. I don't know, it felt prudent.

Dusk wasn't a time I normally went up to the pool area. It tends to be chilly once the sun starts to go down, but tonight the cool air felt refreshing. The pool itself and surrounding deck were empty, but the hot tub was filled with three . . . senior citizens? I'd always joked that Laura and I were the oldest people in this building, but as I stepped into the warm bubbly water, I couldn't deny that the three folks opposite me were at least in their seventies. The skeletal bald one was wallpapered in tattoos, mostly of rock and roll logos and naked women. He was pontificating to a busty woman in a black one-piece about something I couldn't make out over the rumble of the bubbles. The third geriatric, downing a can of beer, was an overweight man with a shockingly full head and chest of white hair.

I texted Alina: Did you know old people live in this building?

My ears having calibrated to the gentle roar, I heard Tattoo invite Busty and White Hair to his DJ set that night at a club in Bushwick. White Hair told them he'd had an art show in that neighborhood last week, and Busty exclaimed with a laugh that of course she would be there, and she would be bringing clients (whatever that meant).

Alina texted back: Oh yes. We call them the vampires because they only come out at night.

There was something desperate about these three, gabbing on and on about the big night they had planned. And I was pretty sure Busty and White Hair had done some coke by the way they were grinding their teeth. One of these altacockers could certainly commit murder. I mean, what did they have to lose?

Alina texted me again to say she was almost at the Jax, and I asked her to meet me on the roof.

That's when I heard Busty say, "Awful, right? Did you know either of them?"

White Hair laughed. "The guy, Ernest? He, um, politely asked me to no longer attend his parties."

"Ageism!" croaked Tattoo.

"Well, kind of, sure, yeah, okay, but look, look, when we were young, it was a different scene," White Hair said. He pressed his lips together and cracked open another beer. "I told him I'd stay out of the way, that I just wanted to go to his parties to watch. But I guess that was the wrong answer too."

I wondered what parties they were talking about.

"I think," Busty chimed in, "there's a serial killer loose in the building."

"Ooh," they both responded.

"Statistically, a serial killer is most likely!" She smacked the water for emphasis.

"Makes me nervous," said Tattoo in a high, distant voice.

"Don't be," said Busty. "So far it's just young people. No one even notices us."

White Hair laughed long and hard, but Tattoo didn't seem amused. "Jesus. With the bone cancer, I'm looking down the barrel every day as it is," he said. The other two nodded solemnly and then asked how he was planning to get his DJ equipment to the club.

I focused on the couple of thin red clouds that were losing their vibrancy over Manhattan's setting sun. My mind was muddy, but the words *serial killer* stuck with me. Was that really a possibility? My hot tub friends didn't know there was a connection between Ernest and Laura, so of course that seemed likely to them. But wait. Was there actually a connection between Ernest and Laura? Probably not. Or at least it seemed that the only connection was . . . me. But before my mind could start to make sense of that thought, I saw Alina standing over me, the indigo sky radiating around her.

She pulled off her blue frilly work shirt and wriggled out of her pants, revealing a black one-piece identical to Busty's, though

I was too sunken to pay much attention to bathing suits or female skin.

Alina slid down the three steps into the hot tub and addressed our companions by name. "Sid, Claudia, Ridley."

They all nodded at her appreciatively and then went back to aggressively yammering about Sid's (Tattoo's) set list for the night.

"Hope you don't mind that I'm joining you in here," Alina said to me as she submerged her shoulders down into the water. "Management training was stressful."

"Tell me how it went, please." I was grateful to hear her voice.

"Merit Management is located in a glass-walled office on the top floor of a Lower Manhattan high-rise," Alina began with the precision of her prose. "I spent most of the day reading company policies in their conference room. There's this enormous puzzle of the New York City skyline in the center of the large table, and executives come in during the day to fill in pieces, mostly blue pieces. I'll work from the conference room when I'm not rotating between the three buildings where I'll be community managing. My duties will include fielding complaints from tenants, sched-uling and hiring on-site employees, and conducting performance evaluations."

"At least you're out from behind the front desk," I offered.

"It all sounds perfectly awful to me."

"You'll be a published writer soon," I reminded her.

She let out a throaty laugh. "From your lips." Alina scooted in front of a jet and spent the next couple of moments willing her body to relax. Then she faced me and lowered her voice. "I did discover why they fired Bonnie Besser, the community manager before me. And it's interesting."

"Okay."

"Well," Alina continued, "part of the community manager's job is to handle disputes between tenants. And Bonnie had ignored a dispute between Ernest Whitaker and one of his neighbors. So Merit decided to get ahead of things and let her go, for that . . . negligence."

"Do you know who the other tenant was?" I asked.

"The woman who was training me didn't know," Alina said, "but I'll find out. In any event, I bet Kurlansky knows. It sounded to me like this dispute was intense and ongoing."

"It's good to know the police maybe have like one other actual suspect."

"And there's another thing," Alina said hesitantly, as if she were wondering if this was even worth going into. "Rental renewal notices went out on Friday and Saturday to a bunch of tenants whose leases are set to expire. And some of the rent increases are as high as thirty-six percent."

"Whoa."

"I don't know who received them, but I was warned that some tenants are very unhappy."

"Can they really raise the rent that high?"

"There's no regulation on buildings like this." Alina shrugged.

"Did everyone's rent get raised thirty-six percent?"

"No. The community manager and the manager of residential properties get together and come up with the rent increases. Apparently the size of the increase is based on a mixture of market value and the desirability of the tenant. In other words, if you break rules and cause trouble, they raise your rent more."

We sat for a moment and let our bodies drift in the warm water.

"Let's say this was some sort of tenant dispute between Ernest and another resident," I said, returning to that seemingly more relevant topic. "What does that have to do with Laura?"

"Maybe the dispute involved Laura."

I briefly explained to Alina why I was no longer convinced that Laura and Ernest knew each other, let alone were lovers. "I mean, do you ever remember seeing Laura leave by the back door on Saturday mornings?"

A thoughtful pause and then she said, "Actually, I think so. With her gym bag."

"And so if she wasn't having an affair with Ernest, if she was actually going to Orangetheory, the only link between them is me." Another round of emotions heaved up inside me, and I had to make some horrible squeaking noises to keep them down.

It was then I realized the bubbles had ceased, and our three geriatric neighbors were blatantly, but sympathetically, listening to us. "So sorry for your loss," Claudia (Busty) said to me.

"Thank you."

And as the trio pulled themselves out of the hot tub, Sid (Tattoo) turned to me and said, "I'm DJing a set tonight at the Mellow Yellow. If you need to get out."

"Thanks," I said. "Thanks."

"Want us to turn the bubbles back on?" Ridley (White Hair) asked.

"No, that's okay," Alina said. "The quiet's nice."

Alina and I sat for a moment. A cool breeze skimmed its fingertips across my face.

"Hey. I've been meaning to say something," I said slowly. "I'm assuming your book is mostly autobiographical."

"It is," Alina said.

"In that case, I'm sorry that your dad passed when you were still in college. It sounds like that was a hard loss for you."

Alina teared up and smiled. "I'll tell you something strange," she said. "My dad loved pools and hot tubs. He liked to sink down, so his mouth was just beneath the surface, and lightly blow bubbles. And now when I do that, I can feel him inside me. It's like for a brief moment, I *am* him." She submerged her mouth and slowly exhaled into the water. Watching her do that, it was a lovely moment.

———

A little bit later, down in Martin Stowell's apartment, Alina showered while I sat on the velvety living room couch with a towel under my damp bathing suit and wrote fake eulogies of living people to pass the time. Here's my eulogy for Tattoo Sid: "While we all knew how much he loved vintage tattoos, how many of us actually attended his DJ sets? Couldn't we have done more for this man who never once complained about the bone cancer that was slowly killing him from within? I'll never forget the night he learned of my wife's passing and showed me such tenderness. 'I'm sorry for your loss,' he said. And I believed that he was." *Goddamn, I'm good,* I thought. I could write a fake eulogy for any son of a bitch I barely knew.

At 10:00 p.m., Alina and I padded down the long corridor in the Jax's basement. Florescent lights blinked insufficiently, casting our pale green shadows onto drywall. Gaping openings in the walls revealed dark, cavernous spaces, looming deep on either side of us. Alina was back in dark business attire, and I was still in a bathing suit and sleeveless T-shirt but with borrowed socks on under my flip-flops to cushion my heel.

"Robin texted me that she's already down here," I said as we continued forward.

"Why the hell does she want us to meet here anyway?"

"No idea." I peered into the dark side rooms. "I've always meant to ask, why are there these large empty areas?"

"They're unused storage for the vacant retail stores above."

"They're creepy."

Just then, Robin's torso appeared, comically horizontal, from a doorway at the far end of the hallway. She motioned for us to come to her before disappearing again.

"Oh, she's in the tenant storage room," I said.

We walked at a clip to that end of the hallway and turned into a long room full of a dozen metal lattice lockers that stretched from floor to ceiling. Robin was facing away from us, wearing pink sweats and white sneakers. No locker was quite as stuffed full of broken furniture, clothes, linens, and indeterminate objects than the locker before which Robin stood.

"Okay," she said, not turning to us. "I need your help disposing of all this evidence." There was no irony in her voice. She wasn't pleading. It was a simple statement.

"I'm sorry. I thought . . ." I trailed off.

Robin craned her neck toward me, encouraging me to finish my sentence.

I glanced over at Alina for help, but she was speechless.

So I tried again. "I thought you were going to help us with information about Ernest's death."

"Once you help me dump these blankets and sex toys into Newtown Creek, then I'll give you what you want." She took a pull from her vape. "My car's in the garage."

"You understand," Alina said, "that Paul is already a suspect in this case. This could get him in serious trouble."

"Fine. Paul will duck down in the back seat when we pull out of the garage. Good?" When we didn't respond, Robin continued. "Listen, this is a lot of shit that needs to be disappeared. And I need a strong *man* to help me. *Okay?*"

"What exactly is this evidence of?" I asked.

"Evidence that Ernest and I were lovers. Evidence that Ernest and I used to host . . . parties in the basement—"

"Orgies?" I asked.

"Parties have a life of their own," Robin said, taking another pull of the vape pen. "Now come on, chop-chop. I don't want the police asking me questions about my sex life. Plus, if the building's management finds out that I helped host orgies down here, they'll raise my rent by thirty-six percent. Rumors are that's what management does to tenants who . . . misbehave. I can't afford that, and I'll be goddamned if I'm moving to Queens."

I was about to tell Robin that Alina was now part of the building's management, but Alina read my mind and shook her head no. I looked down at Robin's chewed-up nails, her fingers opening the padlock: 06 . . . 18 . . . 31 . . .

"I'll get a recycling cart from the hallway," I said.

Moments later, we were pulling items out of Robin's locker, like it was a giant game of Jenga, and tossing them into the wheeled blue bin. I was trying to work quickly because there was no guarantee that a policeman or tenant wouldn't find a reason to pass through. I wished I'd worn gloves because maybe it was my imagination but a couple of the blankets felt sticky.

"Is this a lava lamp?" Alina asked as she put two distinct parts of it into the cart.

"So we liked to be a little kitsch," Robin said while she sorted through a medium-size plastic container, tossing glow-in-the-dark bracelets into the recycling cart.

"Why don't you just put the whole box in?" I asked.

"You wanted clues to Ernest's death, right? Well, the clue I had in mind, it's somewhere in this box. Ah!" Robin pulled out what looked like a 5 x 7 photo album, its cover bejeweled. She went to hand it to me but thought better of it and placed it in the pouch of her pink hoodie. "Later."

Once we'd emptied Robin's locker of everything but a cardboard box of paperback books (vampire romance) and some sort of disassembled exercise machine, I clarified, "You guys were having parties down here in the basement and this is the . . . stuff you were using for them? These are the parties that the old guy with the white hair—"

"Ridley," Alina filled in.

"Right, Ridley, the parties that Ridley was disinvited to."

Robin let out a guffaw. "That old pervert just wanted to sit and watch. He needed to go play with people his own age, IMHO."

"How old are *you*, Robin?" I asked, feeling the need to get in some sort of jab. I pegged her pretty close to forty.

"Fuck off," she answered dryly. "I'm not in AARP. Not yet."

Robin spritzed the walls of the storage locker with cleaner and used a paper towel to spread it around with all the enthusiasm of someone suffering from Epstein-Barr. Then she instructed, "Move this cart out to the garage. Come on, Paul."

I pushed the cart down the hallway, conscious of the noisy wheels over the rough concrete floor, while Alina asked Robin, "Didn't the garbage smell down here bother you?"

Robin didn't deign to answer, but she did hold the door open to the underground level of the parking garage. Alina helped me surmount the bump in the doorway, and from there pushing the cart was nice and quiet on the smooth parking lot tarmac.

"My car's this way," Robin said as she half gestured to a silver BMW sedan. "Don't be too impressed," she continued without looking at us. "It's a 2017. It won't even hook up to Apple CarPlay properly. I wonder if I could afford a Tesla." She popped the trunk with a button on her fob. "I like the idea that in the Tesla, everything is black but a single touch screen." I lifted the trunk the rest of the way up. "Do you know in California even the Uber drivers have Teslas? That's how far behind we are on the East Coast." Robin's ability to divorce herself from the sordidness of our situation impressed me.

"And you're right," she admitted as she watched us load up the trunk with her disused orgy furnishings like we were her house elves. "The smell was not ideal. I think we enjoyed the fantasy that we were slumming it."

"Why not just get together in someone's apartment?" I asked, smushing a futon mattress into the trunk.

"Oh, you know the snobs who live here." Robin sighed as she leaned against the car. "They complain about everything. There are too many people in the hallway. Someone smoked a spliff and now my baby's got a contact high. On and on."

I opened the door and tossed in underwear, sheets, and one very large, creepy full-body tiger costume.

"Why were you the one to hang on to this stuff?" Alina asked as she opened the passenger door.

"You'll always be invited to the orgy if you're the one with access to the lube."

Robin backed the car out of its spot, and I slid down farther into the back seat, face-to-face with the tiger costume's head. Robin jerked the car forward, accelerated up the ramp, and skidded to a stop in front of the metal grate. She hit the button on her remote and the grate rose, screeching like a thousand dying children.

Robin jolted us through industrial northern Brooklyn, braking quickly and often, turning sharply and suddenly. I have a theory that people drive the way they make love. Robin's style was arhythmic and brittle.

"You have to understand," Robin said at a red light, inching up needlessly to the car in front of her. "Covid had us all sequestered. I mean, summer of 2020? Even the pool was closed. So 2021? Pool season was *intense*. And yes, the pool could get a little X-rated, but when we were told by management to keep our clothes on and our hands to ourselves, we listened. More or less. But once pool season was over, we were sent back to our rooms. For people like me, that was brutal. So Ernest had the idea that maybe some of us could get together in the basement. And he had all of our contact information because he'd helped so many of us train our Covid pets. And so he picked who he invited, and we would find little rooms down in the basement and set up shop on a Saturday night. Like a pop-up shop!"

Robin backed her car down an alley to Newtown Creek, the oily streak of water that separates Brooklyn from Queens. Shipping containers shielded us from the cross streets. Battered, illegal houseboats dotted the opposite side of the dark waterway.

Robin got out of the car first. Surveyed the area. Looked back at us. "All right. Into the creek it all goes," she said as if we were caterers preparing for an event. "And I want that stuff out to sea. I don't want it just sitting in the mud. So get out there."

I stepped over the metal guardrail and looked down the dirt embankment into the murky water.

Alina stood behind me and whispered, "Are we really going to do this?"

"If she has insight into Ernest's death, I think we need to. So. You shlep, I'll swim." And with that, I skidded down the narrow muddy strip and waded out into the creek. The underwater decline was alarmingly precipitous, and suddenly I was waist-deep, the thick liquid somehow warm and cold at the same time.

"I can tell by the way you dress, Paul, that you don't under-stand people like me," Robin pontificated as she sat cross-legged on the hood of her car. "I can tell by how little you care about your outward appearance that *you* are okay with being alone." Alina, meanwhile, stepped into the muck and handed the rolled-up mattress to my half-submerged torso. "But people like me? We sculpt and shave and primp and pluck so other people will look at us long enough that we won't ever be alone. Ernest Whitaker was like me. Would he really have taken the time to sculpt that pompadour in the center of his head if he didn't need the atten-tion and company of others?"

Robin shifted her attention to Alina, who was trekking back to the car. "You, Alina," Robin said. "You are pretty, but you do what you can to hide it behind those illogical glasses. I think you would like less attention than you receive."

"I'd like to receive the *right* type of attention. The type of atten-tion that sees me for who I actually am."

"You're cute enough to get that one day," Robin said without irony.

I trudged out of the water and did the next two trips, hauling bedding, with Alina, who now looked exhausted. When all of the stuff was in the water, Robin called, "I think you need to get it farther out there." She pointed to the sheets drifting back to shore.

Chest deep in the oily muck, pushing bedding away from me, I watched the glow-in-the-dark bracelets drift on a black current toward the distant neon outline of Manhattan at night.

Then I slipped and sloshed my way back to the shore.

Drenched and dripping with a liquid heavier than water, I went to open the back door of Robin's Beamer.

"Oh, you can't get back into my car like that," she said flatly.

"What am I going to do?" I asked, now shivering.

"It's only a couple of miles back to the Jax," said Robin. "Don't act like that's a lot. I run seven miles every day on the treadmill."

"Fine."

"I'll walk with you." Alina peeled herself off the side of the car.

"You don't have to do that."

"I'd like to," Alina said in a tone that made it clear she'd rather crawl home on broken glass than get back into Robin's car.

Alina and I had started to hobble down the alley when Robin bellowed, "What's the matter with you two?" She ran to us, expending more energy in those fifteen seconds than she had all night. "You forgot your reward." She pulled out the photo album she'd tucked into her hoodie earlier and handed it to me, the plastic gems on the cover coming off on both of our hands.

I opened the small book. Every page was thick with Polaroids. Snapshots of young people, tenants, in their underwear. Nothing X-rated but skirting the edge. Mock sexy rather than actual sexy. In the dim streetlight, I couldn't make out much, and although some of the tenants looked familiar, I didn't know anyone's name.

"We thought it would be fun one night to take some pictures," Robin explained. "This album should at least give you an idea of who came to our parties. Maybe that will help." Her arm remained extended in front of her for no reason other than some unconscious reluctance to part with the pictures. "If the police aren't doing their jobs correctly," she said, her face looking down, lost in darkness, "please find who did this." Then she glanced up, the muted lamppost light barely grazing her sad smile. "I can still hear Ernest saying in his chipper voice, 'Come on, let's go to the basement. Let's have a *party*. Let's do the damn thing.' Or he'd say to me, 'Are you ready to party? I don't think you're ready to party.'" Robin laughed and pushed aside tears. I thanked her for the book and told her that I was squatting across the hall from her, just in case she thought of anything else that might help us.

And then Robin walked back to her car, alone.

I continued flipping through the photo book, not really sure what I was looking for, when a business card fell out and fluttered to the street. I bent down and picked it up. "Dr. Laura Olander, Veterinarian." And it had an address for her nearby Brooklyn practice and a phone number.

"Robin?" I called to her as she opened the door to her car. "Who is Dr. Laura Olander?"

Robin looked at me, squinted, and saw I was holding a card.

"Oh, that's nothing," she called back. "That's just the veterinarian Ernest worked with. I never used her, but he gave me her card a couple of times."

I rubbed my finger over the embossed lettering. Another Laura . . .

———

A few minutes later, Alina and I were shuffling past darkened body shops. We were a pair, sweaty and dirty. Her blouse ripped at the sleeves, her pants muddy at the knees, and me looking like I'd taken a swim in an environmental catastrophe, which I had.

"What do you make of the Polaroids?" Alina asked.

"I don't know," I said. "I don't think I have the stomach to look through them any more tonight."

"Me neither."

And so we walked.

"I like New York during weird hours," Alina said as we crossed Grand Street against the light.

"Sometimes when the streets are empty, I fantasize that I'm the only one left in this city," I said.

"Yeah. I do that too." She held her torso in her arms. "If it's okay with you, I'm going to stay on the couch tonight in Martin Stowell's apartment. My sister is working and, for some reason, dumping disgusting things into the river made me feel uneasy. I don't want to be alone."

"Okay."

We walked along a desolate park. The greenery seemed lit from within. And maybe because my mind was too exhausted to protect itself, a thought occurred to me, and I started to form a theory as to why both Ernest *and* Laura had been murdered.

———

When we got back to the Jax, no cops or reporters were outside, so I used my fingerprint to get us into the stairwell.

Nauseous and suddenly overtaken by a headache, I found some Advil in Martin's medicine cabinet and some saltines in a kitchen drawer. Alina and I sat at the table, eating crackers, drinking tap water, and looking down at the occasional headlights slinking along McGuinness Boulevard. We were both wearing crisp white undershirts and workout shorts we'd found in Martin's drawers. My outfit was too tight; Alina's was too loose.

"Look," I said after a while. I wanted to tell Alina what I'd been thinking as we walked home, but it was going to take me a minute to get to my point. "I'll look through this photo album. I'll even call this veterinarian, this Dr. Laura Olander, in the morning, just to get a sense of who Ernest Whitaker knew outside of the building. And it's possible that one of these items will lead us somewhere. And also, I mean, Robin herself seems to be a lead.

She is violent and reckless. So—I don't know—maybe she killed Ernest?"

"Why?" Alina asked.

"By accident? Or jealousy of some sort?"

"But," Alina said, shaking her head, "I was pulling Robin out of the pool around the time Ernest was supposed to be killed. And when I left her, she was completely passed out. So that's an alibi, right?"

"Oh yeah," I said, putting down the saltine like it was a cigarette I'd suddenly lost my taste for. "Well, there's also this thing about Ernest having an ongoing fight with someone in the building. That's a lead."

Alina said, "Yeah. But it would have to be a pretty big argument for it to end in murder."

"But my point, my larger point, is that . . ." I tried to gather my thoughts. "My larger point is that any way I cut it, it seems to me that Laura was killed *because* Ernest was killed."

Alina made herself sit up. "I don't understand."

"First of all, we agree there is no reason anymore to think Laura and Ernest were sleeping together."

"Agreed."

"Now think for a minute about the way they each died." I could tell she was trying to focus on me through smudged glasses and fatigue. "Ernest was strangled, which makes sense in a way. He liked sexual asphyxiation, he was small, and, according to Kurlansky, he was sedated. It makes sense that he would die like that. But it makes no sense that Laura was strangled. She was never into sexual asphyxiation. And she was big and strong. It couldn't have been easy to kill her like that."

"I'm listening."

"The only reason to kill Laura that way is to connect her death to Ernest's death. And the only reason to connect the two deaths is to frame me."

"You've lost me again. Why frame you?"

"So the killer could throw the police off their trail," I answered.

"But why *you*? What makes you so important?"

"Maybe it was convenience. The killer saw me go into Ernest's apartment with you. Or maybe the killer knew that I thought Laura and Ernest were having sex. What I'm saying is that someone saw an opportunity to blame Ernest's death on me, and so they killed Laura to make sure the police suspected me. Look, even if you don't buy that, it's pretty clear that Laura and Ernest didn't know each other. Not only were they not sleeping together but also Robin had never seen them together. Laura's not in this photo book. So no matter how you look at it, the only connection between the two of them is me!"

Before I could say anything else, not that I had anything else to say, Alina stood up and took a deep breath. "Actually, I think I need to get a couple of hours of sleep," and she collapsed onto the stately red velvet couch. "I hope Martin Stowell will forgive me. I used his toothbrush earlier."

"I used it too."

"Before I did?"

"I think so."

"Gross." Then after a moment: "Look, we don't know anything for sure." Alina closed her eyes. "It could be a coincidence."

"How's that?"

"It could be a coincidence that you thought the two people who were murdered were sleeping together, it could be a coincidence that you found both bodies," she said, struggling to make sentences before falling completely asleep, without a blanket, supine, and in a stranger's white T-shirt. "Maybe there's a serial killer in the building."

"I should be so lucky," I said.

Her chuckle melted into a snore, and I envied Alina her sleep.

CHAPTER 9
I CONFESS

At seven in the morning, sitting at the kitchen table, I heard Alina's iPhone make that tinny sonar sound we've all come to accept as an alarm clock, and I watched her startle awake. I'd never fallen asleep. I hadn't even moved from the chair. I'd spent the wee hours making notes in my (Martin's) cloth journal. All the while, an ache that had started in my shoulders wound its way up the tendons of my neck and now pulsated in my jaw. I looked out at the ball of yellow sun rising over the gas station across the street and felt spasms of sinewy pain in the base of my skull, in my sinuses, in my eyeballs.

I filled the kettle with water and dumped coffee in the French press as Alina blinked her way toward the bathroom. A few moments later, we were both stumbling around Martin Stowell's impressive walk-in closet, picking through possible outfits for the day. Alina took a white dress shirt and a black business suit and staggered back to the bathroom to change. Meanwhile, I pulled on a soft pink T-shirt and lightweight lime-green pants. The waistband couldn't quite traverse my belly, but I covered the fleshy gap with a woven belt I found in one of Martin's drawers. I looked at myself in the full-length mirror on the back of the bedroom door.

My hairy, flabby midriff was showing a bit below the pink shirt, and my ankles were showing a lot below the green pants. Then it occurred to me that I'd actually brought a bagful of my own clothes from my apartment, but fuck it, I'd rather look like someone else anyway. Even if that someone else bore a passing resemblance to a circus clown.

Curious about Martin's shoes (and shoes in general, due to my aching heel), I investigated the bottom of his closet and pulled out a pair of purple Nikes that miraculously fit me, and I paced back and forth, enjoying the sensation that I was walking on clouds. Plus, the two tones of purple behind the black swoosh were very aesthetically pleasing. Had I stumbled upon a perfect pair of sneakers? And of course I should mention that I'd also put on a pair of Martin's socks. Why the fuck had I been wearing flip-flops? Socks and sneakers, people. Hashtag take care of your feet. Hashtag sometimes the most obvious solution is the correct one. I wanted to carry that last thought over to Ernest's and Laura's murders, but the throbbing pain in my neck and head made following the thought any further impossible.

I paced absently in my new sneakers, trying to convince myself that moving my body would loosen my muscles and ease this now overpowering headache. But the headache was just getting worse. My vision was getting blurry. I was squinting so as to not let in more light than necessary. At some point, Alina had entered the bedroom because there she was in her Talking Heads suit with a mug in her hand, saying, "Thanks for making coffee."

"Yeah." Though honestly I couldn't remember having poured the water on top of the grounds. "I've never used a French press before."

"It is too strong," Alina admitted. "I had to use the bathroom immediately after the first sip. How long have you been pacing like that?"

"I don't know," I said. And I tried unsuccessfully to make myself stop.

Alina looked at me uneasily. She put her coffee cup down on the counter and picked up her dainty black backpack off the couch.

"Hey," I said finally, having managed to stand still. "I don't know if you stayed here because of you or me last night. But thanks."

"If I hadn't let you into Ernest Whitaker's apartment, none of this would be happening."

"This is not your fault." I went into the kitchen and, forcing my eyes to focus, poured myself a cup of coffee, dimly aware that Alina was lingering at the front door, irresolute.

"What's the matter?" I asked.

"I'm just worried about you. Did you sleep at all last night?" she asked.

I lifted up my notebook but put it back down because even subtle arm movements were now making my head and neck throb harder. "I made a list of potential suspects, and then I wrote fake eulogies for people who are alive. 'Harrison Ford, who first resisted stardom but later embraced his best-known characters, was found dead in the cockpit of his private jet under mysterious circumstances.'"

"So this was productive," she said dryly.

"No." I turned to her and forced my eyes to un-squint in an effort to ameliorate her concern. But the gravity of Alina's expression remained unchanged. She said she would find out which tenant Ernest Whitaker had been in conflict with, and I told her I'd examine the nudie pics and get in touch with Dr. Laura Olander.

After Alina opened the door and slid out, I went into Martin's medicine cabinet and swallowed four Advil, dry.

I did my due diligence and called the number on Dr. Laura Olander's card. When the person who answered the phone said she'd taken the week off, I detected exasperation in his voice. I asked if this was a planned vacation, and he sighed, replying,

"No, it was sudden." I asked him for a cell phone or a home address, but the most he would do was take a message.

Then I paged through Robin's weird little scrapbook. Each page had a Polaroid taped to it showing one or some of the tenants laughing or exposing a bit of boob or butt. I think at another time, I would have enjoyed this sneaky peek at my neighbors' areolas or pubic hair, but I had a sinking feeling that these pictures were utterly beside the point. In detective novels, there's often a detail in a snapshot that first goes unnoticed but that later solves the entire case. But in real life? Given the chaos of any one person's life? What were the chances that these photos taken on some random night last winter said anything important?

Another thing I've noticed in detective novels is that often the murdered party has been previously orphaned. This allows the writer to skip over the victim's anguished parents. Let's face it, the emotions of a dead person's mother are a complete buzzkill. But no author spared me the full brunt of Laura's parents' pain that morning. Laura's mom called me before they left the hotel where they'd spent the night. They'd decided to split the drive into two days. She told me the police were asking about Laura's will, and she'd faxed them a copy that Laura had kept in the safe in their house. She told me they expected to be in Brooklyn by midafternoon and they'd booked a hotel. But then suddenly her reasonableness turned to anger. She cried and raged and called me some terrible names for not protecting her daughter. By the time I hung up the phone, not only my head but also my back was a torture. I couldn't find any comfortable way to sit or stand. Pain was shooting from my spinal column around to the front of my torso, down to my hips. I thought about lying on my back, but I was afraid I wouldn't be able to get back up. I took three more Advil. Staying still hurt more than moving, so I decided to walk out of Martin's apartment. To hell with the fact that I was supposed to be with Bob Shapiro in Manhattan.

Cloth journal in hand, apartment key and phone in pocket, I

focused on getting down the hallway, but each step sent a spasm of pain through my body. While going down in the elevator, two young people got in on the fifth floor. Once inside, they gaped at me with something akin to horror. I glanced at myself in the floor-to-ceiling elevator mirror, hoping to find solidarity with my reflection, but instead, I too was aghast by the sight of myself. How could I have picked out this ridiculous pastel-colored, ill-fitting outfit? Not to mention my beard and hair were greasy and disheveled, and my face was glistening with sweat. When I stepped out onto the ground floor's parqueted hallway, the walls quivering a bit through my headache and nascent nausea, a few passersby didn't even bother to hide their disgust at my presence. One suited man I'd never before seen audibly gasped as he passed me. Sure, looking at me was no aesthetic daydream, but was I really worthy of such blatant contempt? Or had something else changed, something beyond my outfit and self-care?

I took refuge behind the glass-plated windows of the communal library. After I lowered myself gingerly onto the wooden bench and squirmed a bit to try to get comfortable, I noticed that Patrick Backus, in his signature checkered shirt and khakis, was sitting at the far end of the long table, typing on his laptop. Maybe some chitchat would relax or at least distract me.

"Hey, Patrick," I said, conscious that my armpits were extra swampy. "Avoiding the family?"

"Um. Yeah. I guess." Patrick attempted a smile, but his glasses couldn't hide the discomfort in his shifty eyes.

"Any dreams lately?" I asked. It was good to talk. It was good to focus on something outside of myself even if it was Patrick Backus's pinched face.

"Um, just the normal dreams," he muttered. "Where I'm saving my kids from terrible peril. Mortal danger. Etcetera." He made a failed attempt at a smile.

I peered through the plate glass and out at the lobby where a couple of uniformed cops were now looking at me, staring like hungry dogs waiting to be let off their leashes. Just because I wasn't with Bob Shapiro? A third officer, larger than the other two, meandered into my field of vision. He dead-eyed me for a moment and then talked into his radio.

"Do you think it's all right that you're sitting here?" asked Patrick, watching the police watch me.

"Why wouldn't it be?" I tried to sound unconcerned.

"Aren't you out on bail?"

"No." I laughed a little too hard. Would laughing relieve my headache? I laughed again, just to see. Nah, laughter was not the answer here. "I'm just like, um. A person of interest." Before I could glance at Patrick to see if I'd successfully eased his concern, I spotted yesterday's *Daily News* sitting in the middle of the table. On the cover, a large candid shot of Laura in a strappy black dress laughing at something off camera. The headline: "Second Slaying at Luxury Building." I opened the paper and tried to read the article, but the words were dancing around the page. I did see a picture of myself, in the upper right-hand corner, being led from the Jax into that cop car. That picture alone would explain why my stock around here had plummeted. God, I hadn't even thought to look at the news yesterday. How could that be? Was my grip on reality . . . loosening?

"I hope you won't take this the wrong way," I heard Patrick say, but I didn't look over at him. I was too busy wondering if I appeared fat in the newspaper picture because I was hunched over or because I was actually fat. "I've started a petition to have you banned from the building." Now I looked over at him. He was no longer smiling, nor was he apologizing with his body language. He was sitting ramrod straight. Nothing like being a suspected murderer to make even the most ordinary people inflate themselves with self-righteous indignation in your presence. "Tenants saw you coming in from the street last night, in the middle of the night, covered in mud, and they find your presence here disturbing. I find your presence here disturbing. I'm telling you to your face." Patrick said this as if having the bravery to say something to someone's face exonerated you from whatever heinous nonsense you were spewing. "Once you're no longer a person of interest, as you put it, you could come back here. But my wife, for instance, doesn't think it's fair that you're making the rest of us feel uncomfortable."

"What if I promise not to murder *you*?" I offered. "And of course I'll promise to not murder your family too. That's gratis. I mean, unless you want me to." This attempt at repartee came out a lot more bitter than I'd intended.

Patrick sucked on his lips and then released them, emitting a popping sound. "I have a lot of signatures on my petition." With that, Patrick swept up his laptop and trotted around the glass wall and down the hallway.

"No one wants to be uncomfortable during pool season! Right?" I shouted to his back as he disappeared into the elevator. Poor guy would have to actually help get his children ready for the day rather than hide down here. Oh, but I'd always liked Patrick. Shit. And then I realized I'd said *shit* out loud. "Shit." And actually, cursing released some pressure in my body. So I shouted, "Shit!" again. And then I shouted it again. "Shit!" On the one hand, hurling expletives at no one made my body feel measurably better, looser, and the headache was starting to wane for the first time that morning. On the other hand, everyone in the lobby was now staring at me through the glass.

I opened my notebook, trying to look like I was busy with work, but I didn't know what to write in it. So I closed the book and closed my eyes and used this slight abatement in physical pain to try to relocate a lost train of thought. Kurlansky. Kurlansky. Right. Kurlansky had insisted he knew who killed Ernest. And I was pretty sure that he didn't think it was me. I should go see him. I should go to the station and find Kurlansky and plead with him to tell me the identity of this other suspect. I put my head back, just to gather energy for the journey, and oh, that position released some tension in my shoulders, oh, that felt so good, I breathed, I felt vertebrae in my back crack, *oh* I moaned, I moaned louder, I felt certain my belly was exposed—and then I was asleep.

Sometime later, a snore (mine) startled me awake, and there across the table, as if I'd summoned him with my brain thoughts, sat Detective Kurlansky. Sleekly cross-legged, in his trademark beige suit and open collar shirt, he sat thumbing through my cloth notebook.

"What are you doing here?" I grumbled.

"I could ask you the same thing," he said without looking up from my property . . . well, Martin Stowell's property.

"I don't think you and I are friends anymore," I said. Ooh, my head hurt again. Those seven Advil were clearly wearing off. And now I was ravenously hungry. I wished I was seeing Kurlansky with a stomach full of bagels. With me, hunger and patience rarely go hand in hand.

"Why do you think we aren't friends?" asked Kurlansky, his eyes drifting up to mine.

"You know someone other than me did this. Why didn't you say that at the station?"

"You know," he started languorously. "I took a night off last night, Paul. I had a bath. I slept. I ate a very large breakfast this morning." My stomach growled, and that made Kurlansky smile. "And I thought, Investigative Chief Sanchez is a smart guy. Maybe he's right and I'm wrong."

"Just tell me your other theory, your first theory, your other suspect," I said, not even trying to keep the desperation out of my voice.

Kurlansky gently placed my cloth notebook on the table but kept his hand on top of it. "Tell me about this notebook, Paul."

"You know what I think? You don't have any theory! I think you're full of shit is what I think!"

Kurlansky merely tapped his manicured fingers on the cover.

"That's my property! Give it back to me!" I went to grab it but noticed for the first time that my cut-up hand (the broken bottles) still bore streaks of mud (Newtown Creek). I quickly retracted it.

"Why is your hand like that?" Picking up the notebook, Kurlansky pushed his chair back, stood, strode to my side of the table, and looked down at me. "Your ankles are dirty too. People saw you enter the building through the stairwell late last night. What were you up to?"

"I'd like my book back," I said.

"About this book." Kurlansky dropped down onto the bench next to me. "Why are you writing eulogies for your neighbors? Why are you writing eulogies for your neighbors who are still quite alive?"

"I was just amusing myself!" I sounded unhinged and I knew it.

"If the book is all a bunch of gags, you won't mind if I hold on to it for a day?"

"No . . . I . . . I do mind!" I sputtered. "I need it! It has a list of suspects in it!"

"Oh, is *that* what this list is?" He opened the notebook.

"Yes!"

"Then why is Ernest Whitaker's name on this list? And why is your wife's name on this list?" He was enjoying himself. "And why are both names crossed out?"

"Their names are crossed out because how can they be suspects if they're dead!" *That* logic was impeccable. But for some reason Kurlansky wasn't buying it. He leaned closer to me, his torso surprisingly long, and pointed to the next name on the list.

"And how come," he whispered, "this woman, Robin, how come her name is next?"

"Because even though she has an alibi, I have a reason to suspect her! Two reasons!" I would turn the tide here, and he'd see my reasoning. "First of all, she slapped me really hard. See this bruise on my face?" I pointed to the yellow splotch on my cheek with one of my dirty hands. "And . . . and . . . she loved Ernest!"

"And Alina is next on your list. You're telling me she's a suspect?"

"I can't let my fondness for her create a blind spot!" My exclamation had renewed the attention of the three on-duty cops in the lobby. I could see the biggest one purposefully meandering toward us.

Kurlansky continued reading down the list. "Tell me about Ridley."

I put my head in my hands. This was a waste of time. "He's an old guy who was upset because he wasn't invited to Ernest's parties. Maybe he was mad at Ernest! I'm doing your job for you!" Oh, my blood was pumping. Annoyance and personal famine were building to a fury. I had no patience for this. My wife had died, and this man, rather than helping me, was toying with me.

"This next guy doesn't even have a name! You just wrote Angry Gym Guy," Kurlansky said.

"Yeah! He's that guy in the gym who seems really angry when he runs on the treadmill! Like too angry! He could probably commit murder! So he's on my suspect list!"

"And Earbud Guy. Who is that?" Kurlansky asked, running his finger farther down the page.

"He's another suspect!"

"Why?"

"I see him around here, and he's always opening and closing his earbud case, like clicking it over and over. It's compulsive behavior!"

"The plant people?" Kurlansky asked.

"They're friends of ours—*friends of mine*—who have a lot of plants, like too many plants."

"Why do you suspect them?"

"I'm exploring all avenues!" At this I rose, but now I was trapped between the bench and the table.

"And this last guy on this list. Craig Finn? Who the hell is that?" Kurlansky demanded as I awkwardly sidestepped toward the far end of the bench.

"He's the lead singer of the Hold Steady, a very famous rock band. He lives around here. I see him at Café Grumpy sometimes!"

"Why is he a suspect?"

"I don't know!"

Kurlansky stood up and slammed the book on the table. "You know what this looks like to me, Paul? It doesn't look like a suspect list. It looks like a kill list."

"You skipped one name on it," I said petulantly from the head of the table.

"I saw it. It was *my* name!" Kurlansky shouted.

"Because sometimes in these things it turns out the detective did it!" I felt like I'd scored a point, but I wasn't even sure what game we were playing. "Anyway, how could that be a kill list?" I asked. "It's too long. Do I seem like an ambitious guy to you?" Kurlansky didn't have anything to say to that. "Tell me who your other suspect is," I pleaded, "so at least someone can investigate this!"

"I'm trying to investigate this, Paul, but goddamn it, the equation has changed since your wife died. You must see that. And then with you sneaking back here in the middle of the night, muddy? When you're supposed to be with Bob Shapiro in Manhattan? And then with you coming down here with cuts on your hands, a bruise on your face and dirt on your legs, and eulogies for your neighbors? I'd look like an idiot to *not* suspect you!"

"Who is your other suspect?"

"I can't tell you! But I can tell you this. I'm capable of changing my mind!" He pushed the bench farther behind him with his leg and faced me. Oh, he was really angry now. We were in a real argument. And the three lobby cops were encroaching upon the Library entryway.

"Before Laura died, who did you think did this?" I yelled desperately.

"You really want to know who I thought did this?" he yelled back.

"Yes!"

Then he smiled devilishly and drew really close to me and whispered so that the cops behind him couldn't hear. "I thought the building did it, Paul. I thought the building did it. Are you happy now?"

I staggered back from Kurlansky. I tripped over my own foot and fell into the bookcases behind me.

"You're fucking with me," I said as I tried to pull myself up using the shelves, knocking off books and knickknacks in the process. "That was your theory? That an inanimate object was the murderer?"

Kurlansky impassively studied me. I had nowhere to go. I was stuck between the shelves, a lamp, and a potted plant.

When Kurlansky finally spoke, he sounded casual, almost disinterested. "I nearly forgot why I came here. Sanchez asked me to tell you something. Are you calm enough to receive new information?"

"Sure." My voice shook.

"Your wife had a very generous life insurance policy, and you're the main beneficiary," Kurlansky said. "You stand to gain one million dollars from her death. Congratulations."

He stared at me blankly.

I stared at him blankly.

"Come see us at the station, Paul."

And with that, Kurlansky turned and strode past the officers into the lobby.

I don't know if it was the reemergence of the headache, the need for sustenance, the news of Laura's life insurance, or this spiraling sense that I was going to go down for these murders, but I called, "Wait."

Kurlansky turned back, now framed by the tall glass double doors, white sunlight beaming in behind him.

"Come back!" I shouted. Did I just not want to be alone? Alone with this strange news that Laura's death, for which I already felt responsible, was going to make me rich? Richer? Jesus, was I just going to keep stumbling around having undeserved money and comfort thrown at me? Oh, and her parents were coming to New York, and they knew what the will said. Oh Jesus, no wonder her mother was so angry with me.

"I mean, fuck, you guys now have two motives for me. Jealousy and greed." I realized I'd moved into the lobby. I was adrift in the middle of all that empty space. "I mean, I should just confess now and save everyone a lot of trouble."

"*Are* you confessing?" Kurlansky asked.

"Yeah, sure," I said with some sarcasm. But was it enough sarcasm? And was that sarcasm clear to the cops who were now surrounding me? *Maybe I was just telling a joke,* I said to myself. Maybe I was just playing the part, you know, for the humor. "Sure, I'm the murderer!" I continued. "I killed my wife and her supposed lover for the life insurance. Lock me up! I did it! I did it!"

Boy, did that change the tenor of the room. And I had said it in front of so many people. Kurlansky! Three cops! Leonard at the front desk. Hi, Leonard. Jesus. Leonard was confused enough on a normal day! And fuck, a random assortment of my hipster neighbors was gathering around me.

Pretty clear from the cops' expressions that they were uninterested in whether this was an actual confession or a humorous bit. Subtleties of tone or authorial intent were understandably not their forte. They were all three approaching me. Two of them had their hands hovering over their guns, and the third was unhooking handcuffs from the back of his belt.

"Paul Downing—" Kurlansky started.

"That's not my last name . . . that's my wife's last name . . . she kept her name," I stammered.

"I'm arresting you for the murder of Ernest Whitaker and Laura Downing . . ."

But those were the last words I heard because when the handcuffs clicked open, the metallic clink echoing throughout the lobby, the reality of my situation came crashing down on me. I didn't want to go to jail—what the fuck—so I turned and ran. I fucking bolted past the Library and out the back door of the building.

Thank Christ I had on my purple sneakers. The discovery of comfortable footwear had come in the nick of time.

As I sprinted across the grassy knoll, I hauled an outdoor chair with me and slammed it against the reclaimed moldy brick wall. Climbing up the chair, I heard Kurlansky say, "Don't shoot!" God bless him. One cop grabbed my foot as I tried to haul myself over the top of the wall. You know that story about the mother who was so full of adrenaline that she picked up a car with one hand to save the life of her baby? Well, I was that mother *and* that baby. With superhuman strength, I kicked the cop away (definitely a crime) and managed to vault myself over the wall and fall down on the other side. I landed on my back, mercifully in the middle of a lush garden, but still, Jesus, my whole body vibrated with pain. But no time for pain, Dr. Jones. I rolled over and scrambled to my knees and found myself, surreally, at the feet of the pretty, elderly Polish physician whose general practice sat catercorner to the Jax. She was standing in the middle of her backyard, smoking a cigarette. I looked up at her long enough to notice that her oblong boobs weren't completely covered by her tank top and then scrambled to my feet. Behind me, one of the policemen was trying to pull himself over the wall. "Police! Freeze!"

"I un-confess! I un-confess!" I yelled at his angry red face and then I darted through the physician's back door into her house. I looked back and said sorry, but the Polish doctor smiled, merely curious.

I sprinted down the long dark hallway, passing a messy bedroom and half-open closets full of medical supplies. Stuffed animals were scattered all over the floors for some reason. I pushed myself through a swinging door that led into an examination room covered with posters of the human anatomy, and then I threw open a light wooden door and found myself in an empty waiting room. I struggled with the chain lock on the front door and then tumbled onto residential Calyer Street. I pushed my legs against the cement as hard as I could, turning onto Eckford Street before I heard the cops yelling at me to stop. I bolted across the street and strained my legs and heart, veering right toward Manhattan Avenue.

My mind started making plans all on its own. Maybe it was the physical strain, but something in me became unblocked and ideas flowed freely. First idea: Get to the hardware store on Manhattan Avenue and make a copy of Martin Stowell's key. This was important because I wanted to be able to stay in the Jax so that I could keep looking for the real murderer, and once the police saw Martin's access key was missing from the building's lockbox, they'd know which apartment I was hiding out in. So I would make a copy and then get Alina to return the key she'd taken. Plus, who would look for me in a hardware store?

I pushed on past the Polish homeless coalition sitting on the corner, conscious that I was looking oddly like one of them, dirty and in bright mismatched clothing. The heavyset woman who perpetually hangs out there even said hello to me in a friendly way.

I slowed down as I turned and joined the jet stream of pedestrians on Manhattan Avenue, my body burning like the inside of a cigarette.

Two patrol cars with flashing sirens passed as I slipped into the narrow, stale-smelling hardware store. Praying adrenaline would continue to be my friend even though I was no longer running, I moseyed down the store's single aisle, passing power drills and gardening supplies. I put my elbow on the counter and ran my hand through my hair, but my hand got caught in a nasty tangle. I delicately extradited my fingers as a thin unshaven man turned to me, looking like he'd stepped unironically out of *Deadwood*.

"Can I get a copy of this key?" I managed to say, startled by the choppy sound of my own voice. I pulled the key out and placed it on the counter.

"Sure. It'll be three bucks," he said evenly.

"No problem," I said as I took out my phone to use Apple Pay.

"Cash only."

"Oh, I don't have any cash."

"Can't do it." He slid the key back to me.

"This is kind of an emergency."

"Three bucks."

Don't be deterred, I thought to myself. *Don't give up*. The old Paul would have given up. The old Paul almost turned himself into the police because he was unable to work through his pain and guilt. So fuck that guy. I'll figure this out.

This new Paul was *undeterred*.

"Be right back," I said, an idea already forming.

I slid out of the hardware store. Noticing a few police cars cruising toward me, I skittered sideways like a crab up the sidewalk, against the buildings, and then slipped into a trendy coffee place. "Undeterred," I muttered to myself. I liked that mantra. I'd stick with it. There was a time a couple of years ago when I was getting testy at auditions, snapping at the monitors and bitching to the other actors. Trying to reign in that behavior, I'd whisper to myself, "Gently." And it helped calm me down. I think I got that technique from a book by Jeff Bridges about Zen Buddhism. *Life is in the adverbs*. Gently. Well, my new adverb was undeterred. I pushed to the front of the line—fuck the customers' grumbles—

reached my hand into the tip jar, pulled out a bunch of bills, stuffed them in my pockets, and fled out the front door.

"Hey!" someone shouted as the door slammed behind me.

Undeterred.

Only after I'd fast walked back into the hardware store did I think to myself, *Shit. I just committed a crime.* And wait, hadn't I kicked that cop? Shit. I've now committed two crimes. Oh, and shit, I fled the police in the first place—*three* crimes.

I gave Wild Bill Hickock three bucks, and I still had two left. Crime pays, etcetera. He was copying the key when some bro with a display case of muscles burst through the door. "I saw what you did in the coffee shop! You can't fucking steal money!" he shouted. A fairly obvious yet demonstrably false statement.

Was I going to have to fight this guy?

The hardware store proprietor warily put both keys in one of those little brown envelopes. I snatched it from him and turned to face muscle college boy, who was still heaving with a rage that probably had more to do with the vicissitudes of his own life than my petty theft.

"People can't just go around stealing things!" he yelled. Oh, he simply wanted to live in a just world. Cute.

I didn't know what to do, but this alleged tip jar theft couldn't become a thing, so I simply yelled my face off—"Aaaaaaaaah!"— and charged, slamming him into shelving and knocking him down (but oof, that hurt the side of my body), and then I continued forward, lumbering out the door.

But before I completely emerged into sunlight, I saw three police officers walking by, so I had no choice but to duck back into the hardware store. I looked down at muscle boy, who was still on the ground. "Hey, what are you—" he grunted. He tried to get up, but his leg looked pretty fucked up, like twisted the wrong way. Shit. This was my fourth actual crime. "Please don't get up," I pleaded with him. "Because, like, my next move is to like step on your leg that already looks broken. I've seen that sort of action in the movies, and it looks painful. So let's just learn from mass entertainment and be cool. Besides, I'm a nice guy in a desperate situation." I kinda laughed so he'd know it was okay for him to laugh. But he didn't laugh.

I glanced back at the hardware store guy, and he was just watching us silently like he could have done with a bag of popcorn.

Keeping low to the ground, I peered out the store window and watched the police move on. I opened the door and made a run for it in the opposite direction.

Now the next thing I did is going to seem really insane, so brace yourself. Rather than head back toward the Jax and figure out how I was going to reenter the building, I continued instead toward the dog day care where Theo was still incarcerated—although actually he loves that place. He'd probably rather be boarded with other dogs than hanging with me. But the idea of spending hours alone in Martin's apartment seemed unbearable. I wanted my dog back.

I burst into Barking Up the Right Tree and then skidded into a counter-lean as casually as I could, dog leashes hanging on the hooks to my right. Somehow this place had the same ramshackle feeling as the hardware store. And somehow I was once again leaning on a counter.

Through an interior window in the wall, I saw the jovial young woman with blue hair who ran the place. She saw me too, scooped up Theo, a chorus of dogs barking around her jealously, and headed through the doorway to the waiting area where I stood. Theo was so happy to see me that the nice lady barely got his harness on before he flew at me, licking my face and mouthing my hands.

Theo and I jaunted down the street where he immediately took a huge dump. I think he doesn't like to go when he's in the day care. Oh did it smell bad; it had been in the oven way too long. So after unspooling the poop bag from the leash and picking up and disposing of the biggest shit I'd ever seen in my life, I put my head down and started to power walk toward the Jax. But with all of these cops looking for me, how would I sneak back in? So, after a moment's thought, I turned around and headed farther into Brooklyn, away from home, toward Bushwick. I knew where I could go until things settled down.

Theo, meanwhile, was pulling at the leash, super wound up from the stimulation of having been with all those dogs. He barked at every passing car and downright tried to maul a couple of joggers. He was overwrought. I could relate. In fact, it was one of those hot summer mornings when the whole city felt over-wrought. Small explosions everywhere—jackhammering, honk-ing, clanging construction. Everything louder than everything else, as Meatloaf once proudly sang on his underrated album *Bat Out of Hell II*. (RIP Marvin Lee Aday.)

A couple of turns later, Theo and I found a narrow street lined with distinctively tall trees that fell blissfully quiet as if it were covered by a soft, warm blanket. But after a moment, this blessing of silence was abruptly interrupted by a lone motorcycle shooting toward us. The two-wheeler passed with a rumble so deep it made my penis vibrate and made Theo scream-bark at such a high pitch, my ears rang. The dog went so berserk that he practically levitated. With a super canine burst of strength, Theo ripped away from me, the leash stripping skin from my already cut-up hand, and tore furiously after the bike.

The motorcyclist, I suppose seeing this insane yet tiny demon through their rearview mirror, skidded to a stop at the end of the block so that their bike was catercorner to the curb. I jogged over to the biker, everything hurting, especially my shins for some reason (shin splints?), and grabbed the dog's leash—not that this stopped him from futilely attacking the motorcycle's tires. Then I looked up and saw the biker's helmet—cherry red.

But just as I managed to say, "Wait, I know you," the driver turned the handlebars away from me and skidded down the street, straightening out, picking up speed, and blowing through a red light toward the Jax itself.

Yeah, the dog was still barking, but my mind isolated itself, trying to work out what, if anything, this could mean. It couldn't be a coincidence that I saw this figure the day Ernest died, the day Laura died, and just now when the police were trying to arrest me. But I couldn't follow the cyclist back to the Jax. I couldn't go back there so soon, dressed like this, looking like this, with a dog barking his face off. So I continued into the urban wilds of Bushwick, thinking about the cyclist but following the plan.

———

Thirty minutes later, I was holding my head under a steady stream of hot water, vaguely aware that dirt was coursing from my body, sloshing around the old yellow tub and swirling down the drain. Alex had given me refuge just as he'd given Laura refuge a few days ago. When he'd answered the door, I was still feeling like Harrison Ford in *The Fugitive*, expecting that train on fire to catch up to me at any second. Alex had hastily waved me in while finishing on the phone. I knew how he hated his phone, so the conversation must have been important.

As he put water out for Theo, he explained he'd been talking to Laura's mother. The police had told her I was now a suspect and that if she saw me, she should tell them. But instead of asking me to leave or calling the police, Alex quietly recommended I get in the shower.

He now knocked on the bathroom door and opened it a crack. "I'm putting clothes for you on the toilet. You're bigger than me, but I think these should work."

"Thank you," I called from behind the curtain. "Alex?" I wanted to talk to him, but water pouring down on me in an anonymous bathtub wasn't a pleasure I was ready to leave behind.

"Yeah?" he said.

"It was awful the way she died."

I could hear Alex moving the clothes and sitting on the toilet seat.

Alex: "Why do the police think you did this?"

Me: "Because I confessed. But I did it sarcastically!"

Alex: "Do cops make that sort of distinction?"

Me: "I don't think so."

Alex: "Why would you confess at all?"

I turned the water off and grabbed the towel that was slung over the curtain rod.

"Guilt." I dried off in the tub with the ratty, frayed green towel.

"Did you strangle her?" Alex asked.

"No," I said, still behind the curtain.

"Someone else made that decision?"

"Yes," I answered.

In the silence that ensued, I tied the towel around my waist and opened the curtain. Alex was still sitting on the toilet. He looked up at my bare torso. It couldn't have been a pretty sight.

"Paul," he said simply. "You did not kill Laura. Maybe you had complicated feelings, maybe you weren't the most attentive partner. At worst, maybe you cheated on her."

"I didn't."

"Regardless," he said evenly, "you did not murder her. Someone else did that. So stop being a little bitch and avenge your wife's death."

In a black T-shirt and jeans, I sat in Alex's kitchen gazing at an unfinished watercolor on an easel. The easel stood in a patch of natural sunlight coming in from the back patio window. The painting in progress, Laura.

"You get nice light in here," I said.

"For an hour or so a day," Alex responded as he opened take-out tins filled with pancakes and bacon and put them on the counter.

A snapshot of Laura was taped to a corner of the easel. She was looking at the camera, expressionless. Wearing a black dress. Oh, the photo was from the night we were at Alex's opening. The night she told me she didn't want to have children. The night that chasm opened. The night I should have made any decision other than to start ignoring her. But just as I was about to tumble down that rabbit hole again, I had a new thought. I turned to Alex. "This must be very painful for you," I said. "I'm sorry for your loss."

"Thanks," he said, his eyes glistening. He took a seat next to me at the counter and started to pick at bacon from one of the aluminum pans. "Do you know who did this to her?"

"No," I answered. "But I'm fairly certain Laura was only killed to make it look like I'd killed Ernest."

"So who would want to kill Ernest?"

"It seems like he had a lot of friends in the building." I reluctantly tore a piece of bacon off. Now that food was in front of me, I wasn't sure if I wanted it. "I looked Ernest up a bit last night on my phone. He's from Pennsylvania. He was in the military for a few years where he trained dogs. He had a prosperous dog training business that he ran from his apartment."

"Dog training?"

"Yeah," I said.

"Huh."

"What?" I asked. Our hands both grabbing for more bacon at the same time.

"I don't know. There's something familiar about the dog training thing. But I can't bring it back. Continue with what you were . . ." Alex trailed off as he chewed.

"Well, there was another side to Ernest. He was in conflict with the building's porters because his apartment always needed repairs. I mean, there were dogs going in and out all the time. And apparently he had a lot of female company." The bacon had whetted my appetite, so I delicately used my fingertips to pull a rubbery pancake onto my plate. "Oh. Ernest was also known to enjoy asphyxiation."

"Which is how he died, right?"

"Exactly."

"So maybe it was a lover?" Alex asked as he stood and poured me a cup from a burned coffee pot.

"Maybe, but the only one I know, she doesn't really have a motive—"

"Jealousy of other women?"

"Maybe? But she knew he was involved with other women. And she has an alibi."

"How about pissed-off neighbors?"

"I thought about that," I said. "You'd think with the sex and the dogs, he would be loud. But those apartments? They're like super insulated. However, he was having an issue with another tenant, but I don't know what that issue was. My friend Alina is helping me there."

"Any other leads?"

"There is one other person I'm trying to get in touch with." I pulled out Dr. Laura Olander's card from my phone case and held it up to Alex.

Alex took the card from me and examined it.

"This is the veterinarian Ernest worked with," I explained.

"Another Laura."

"I called her practice just because I wanted to get a sense of who Ernest knew outside of the building. But when I called, the person at the desk said she'd suddenly taken this week off."

"Huh." Alex considered. "You looked her up online?"

"I haven't and now I'm too afraid to turn on my phone in case the police are tracking it."

Alex reached down the counter, pulled his computer over, and started typing. He turned the laptop toward me. An image search for Dr. Laura Olander had revealed a dozen or so marketing photos of the vet in a long white lab coat crouching down, very seriously examining various dogs. There was no denying that this woman looked similar to my Laura, our Laura, Laura Downing. Not a twin but a wiry sibling or cousin.

I glanced up at Alex. "They look . . ."

". . . alike."

I scrolled down the page of images. At the bottom, one picture was very different from the others. It was a candid shot unmistakably of Dr. Olander. But in this one, the beach and the sun were behind her. She was standing by the side of the road, next to a motorcycle, red helmet in the crook of her arm . . .

So my mysterious delivery person wasn't a delivery person at all.

"I could message her on Facebook," Alex offered.

"That's okay," I said after a moment's thought. "It might be better if she's unaware that anyone's looking for her." And then after another moment's thought: "I might have an idea about how to get in touch."

Alex nodded. One of that man's best characteristics is that he doesn't fill the air with unnecessary questions.

Finally, I asked, "Did you hear about Laura's life insurance?"

"Her mom told me." He stood up, opened the back patio, and lit a cigarette. Theo emerged from wherever he'd been sleeping and trotted outside.

"I keep thinking of this Bob Dylan lyric," I said. "This Dylan lyric that was later co-opted by Hootie and the Blowfish. 'She inherited a million bucks and when she died, it came to me, I can't help it if I'm lucky.' You know Bob Dylan considered suing Hootie over using that line in their song "I Only Want to Be With You," but he decided against it. I respect him for letting that go. Too many artists are suing other artists over quote, unquote stolen music. All music is stolen, after all. You know that."

"Because I'm Black?" Alex asked.

"Well, yes. And because you're an artist."

Alex took a final drag from his cigarette and snapped his fingers. "Ah! Yes! Yes! Now I know why the dog trainer thing was bugging me!" Alex tossed his stub into a can and came back inside, pungent with cigarette smoke. "When Laura was here the other day, someone called her. It was late afternoon." He sat back down next to me. "She was sitting out here. I came out to smoke a cigarette, and I heard her say into the phone something like 'There go our doggie downers.'"

"Huh," I said.

"Yeah. It was like . . . it was like someone gave her some gossip, and her response was 'Oh well, there go our doggie downers.'"

"You think that person told her Ernest Whitaker had died?"

"That's what I think." Alex got up again and paced. "I think someone called her and told her Ernest had died and she said, 'There goes our supply of doggie downers,' or something like that. This feels significant, right?"

I watched Theo settle himself down into the weedy grass outside. "Was she doping Theo to keep him calm? No. I mostly fed the dog. I would have known. Besides, there was never any marked change in Theo's behavior."

Alex shrugged. "Maybe Ernest was supplying them to people, the doggie downers."

"To Laura?" I asked.

"I don't know," Alex said.

The idea of Laura taking some sort of exotic tranquilizer didn't seem impossible.

I looked at the snapshot of her taped to that easel. And she looked right back at me.

———

The afternoon passed without me feeling it. I sat in the shade of the backyard, much as Laura had done when she'd visited Alex. Then I napped intermittently in the downstairs bedroom with the dog at my side. It occurred to me at some point that I'd left my notebook in the Jax's library. Oh well, Kurlansky could have it. He'd already read the best bits anyhow.

As evening set in, Alex walked me to the front door. He nicely suggested that I leave the dog with him, and I couldn't argue. I squatted and pet my buddy, his tail waving energetically. I picked some of the matted bits out of the fur on his big ole schnoz. I looked up and asked Alex, "Do you think something is wrong with me that I relate to this dog more than I relate to most humans?"

"Therapy," Alex responded. "When this is over, Paul, go get some therapy."

Hands in pockets and borrowed blue cap pulled down over my bowed head, I made my way back toward the Jax. I had to be inside that building if I was going to get to the bottom of this. So, feeling more hard-boiled than I'd ever felt in my entire eggs-over-easy life, I stalked home.

As much as that last sentence feels like a fitting end to this chapter, one thing happened during the walk back that would influence my thinking in the days to come. I was heading down Bushwick Avenue, trying to remain anonymous among people coming home from work or crowding around portable speakers. At some point I took a left, just to vary my course, onto a street with large low-income apartment complexes on both sides. Twenty yards ahead of me, the driver of a small black sedan was trying to parallel park. And he was doing a pretty bad job of it. The spot wasn't small, but the driver just kept cutting the wheel too tight. Behind him, a large SUV was trying to get by, but there wasn't enough space to pass. As I got closer, the SUV started to honk. But the sedan kept trying to park, in and out, in and out, in and out, never leaving the SUV enough room to get by. Then the

SUV started really laying on the horn. A wall of blaring honking that continued as I walked by them. Almost at the corner, I heard a car door open, and I turned back on instinct. A young man was bounding out of the sedan, brandishing a handgun, yelling, "Honk again, motherfucker! Honk again!" And as I fled, I was left with this thought: *That's* why people commit murder. They get pushed and pushed until, in a moment of stress, they snap.

CHAPTER 10
I GOT THE PART!

squatted behind a car in the parking lot adjacent to the gas station across the street from the Jax. Squatting is not my favorite position, but personal comfort wasn't much of a consideration. Though, in the interest of full disclosure, I had just taken the risk of buying a bucket of chicken from the KFC down the street with cash that Alex had loaned me. You pay all this money for hipster fried chicken and it's not nearly as delicious as a $3.99 bucket of Kentucky Fried. Am I right? And it's not like hipster fried chicken is healthier. Fried chicken is fried chicken—there's only one way to make it, and that's to fry the chicken. Anyway, I was squatting behind a parked car, watching the Jax from across the four-lane boulevard. Uniformed officers at the main entrance, of course. A man whom I figured to be a plain-clothes cop between the stairwell entrance and the parking garage gate. But if I managed to walk really low on the far side of a car as it pulled into the garage, I might make it in undetected.

So when I saw a car slow before the rising, screeching gate, I jaunted across all four lanes and squat-walked on the far side of the vehicle as it rolled down into the underground part of the garage. Smooth. I was smooth. Maybe I'd always been smooth but couldn't give myself credit? Once inside, I darted to the door that led to the basement hallway. It was fortunately ajar (would my fingerprint still work on the trackpads?), so I scooted right in and then hopped into the elevator, hat over my face as far down as it would go.

I got off at floor seven, pleased with my good luck. But as soon as I let myself feel a bit of relief, I saw Robin sitting outside Martin Stowell's door, weeping.

"Oh, Paul, thank God you came back," she called, wiping her eyes and standing.

"Robin, shhh! What the fuck," I whispered, unlocking and opening Martin's door.

"Are you going to invite me in?"

I hastily ushered her inside by her arm.

"I just needed someone to talk to," she said, pulling away and then recovering her balance. She looked around Martin's heavily furnished apartment. "*Masterpiece Theater* called. It wants its stuff back."

I'll say this, Robin looked good in her shiny black suit that hugged her slender hips and gave her gender-neutral sex appeal. Her dark hair was slicked back with gel, a bit rock and roll.

"I'm sure Martin has something to drink here," I said, looking through the cabinets.

"No, thank you." She wiped more tears from her face with the back of her hand. "I'm sober for the time being." Restless, she prowled into the bedroom. "I'm just going to smoke on the balcony."

"I'd rather not draw a lot of attention to the fact that someone is in here," I said, following her outside. I peered over her shoulder to the street below, but I couldn't pretend anyone looked interested in us.

Fading into a charcoal sky, she lit a cigarette.

"What happened to your vape?"

"It's not cutting it." She luxuriated in the first inhale and . . .

exhale. "There was a memorial for Ernest today in his parents' Upper East Side pied-à-terre." She gestured toward what maybe she thought was Manhattan but was actually a cluster of skyscrapers in Queens. "They normally . . . the family normally lives on their farm in Pennsylvania, but they had this gathering in the hope that Ernest's friends would come. Hardly anyone showed."

"It's a workday," I offered.

"His parents, his siblings, and one suspiciously short army buddy," she continued. "No one came from the building but me." Her eyes were full of hurt. "I just can't understand how someone who was adored by so many is missed by so few." She threw her cigarette down to the street. But then realizing she actually wasn't done smoking it, she said, "Shit" and struggled to light another. "Ernest did so much for people and. And. They loved him. They. They did. They loved how he treated their pets, and they loved the parties he threw. And he was funny. Do you know what he wanted to call his dog training business? Sex, Dogs, and Rock and Roll. Isn't that *funny*? But now that he's gone, it's a shrug. Why is it a shrug?"

"I don't know." I leaned on the balcony's doorjamb. "I mean, maybe in the end, it's really just family that misses us."

"Well, then I'm fucked!" She laughed. "I don't talk to my parents. I don't have siblings." She pulled so hard on her cigarette, I worried she'd swallow it. "I don't have a husband. I don't have kids. You're telling me my friends won't miss me when I'm gone?" Robin stalked past me and continued smoking her cigarette in the middle of Martin's bedroom. "I don't accept that my friends won't miss me!" she shouted. Then, realizing she had to ash, she went into the dark bathroom and flicked embers into the sink. "I just thought you'd relate to this wave of despair because of your wife."

"Actually, now that I think of it, maybe I'm wrong. My wife has one close friend who seems quite upset by her passing."

Robin tossed her half-finished cigarette into the toilet and flushed. "Who am I kidding? I don't even have any friends." And before I knew it, she was in front of me, kissing me. She clung to my lips with her teeth in a way that I frankly found attractive. I was strongly considering going with the flow here, but then I heard . . .

. . . the sound of a dog barking.

The sound was coming from the apartment below.

I pulled away from Robin and shut the balcony door so as to not be distracted by the street noise. I stood in the center of the bedroom. Robin went to say something, but I held up a finger to silence her.

I heard the sound of the dog barking again.

"What?"

"Shh." I stepped silently across the doorway into the living room. I put all of my attention on my ears; they felt warm, a little waxy. Then, after a moment, I heard the dog bark again. And then I heard, "Hamlet, quiet!"

"What are you doing?" Robin demanded.

"That dog barking," I said.

"What about it? Dogs bark!"

I stood there in the silence. And then I heard footsteps above me. "Huh." I walked past Robin, back into the bedroom, and pressed my head against the far wall. "I hear a TV."

"Naming things you hear is a very strange way to avoid having sex with me."

"In my apartment, I never hear any noise from my neighbors," I explained, "so I just assumed no one in this building heard noise from their neighbors."

"Are you kidding me?" She slogged into the living room and dropped onto the couch.

"I always figured it was the luxury insulation."

Robin growled a laugh. "There's no luxury insulation. I hear every fart and murmur from next door. Your unit is just at the end of the building! And that skinny bitch who lives above you? She must weigh ninety pounds!"

"So you hear everything your neighbors do?"

"We all do!" she shouted. "New York real estate. You know! Even when it's nice, it's still crappy."

Robin picked up the scrapbook of nearly naked pictures from the coffee table and paged through it, first disconsolately but then lovingly. "Maybe if I have a party here in the building for Ernest, then people will come to pay their respects. We'll do something in the basement. Like we used to." Her eyes implored me to agree with her. But dear lord, a basement party in honor of Ernest just sounded like a good way to get crabs. And fuck if I was going to haul another set of bedding out to Newtown Creek. "Well, I'm doing it with or without you," Robin said, resolved. And then I had the thought that no one had invited me to these parties when Ernest was *alive*, why the hell would I go to one now that he's—

But then I heard the dog below (Hamlet) bark again. And it jarred my thoughts back to this new truth—everyone in the building could hear everything their neighbors were up to. So what had *Ernest's* neighbors heard the morning he died? What had my neighbors heard on any given night? And something else along that line was bothering me, but I couldn't quite get at it. Surely someone else had told me that they never heard their neighbors. Who was that? I went to grab my cloth journal just to remind myself to follow up on that question later, but then I remembered my journal was missing. Shit. I rolled open the desk and pulled out some kitchen drawers looking for a pen and paper or even a sticky note. Just so I could focus my thoughts into some sort of linear . . . something. I didn't want to turn on my phone, so typing notes on that was out of the question, and I hadn't thought to bring my laptop with me. I opened hutches and scanned shelves. No pens. No pencils. Why was writing a note for myself suddenly impossible? I looked over to Robin. Maybe I could dictate to her and she could type on her phone? But her eyes were once again glued to that photo album.

"Do you have anything I can write with or on?" I asked Robin with too much impatience.

"Why do you need to *write*?" she asked as if I'd said I was taking up ice sculpting.

"Because something is tickling my brain, and if I start to write things on paper, my thoughts make more sense."

But under my explanation, we both heard a knock at the door. And then in our attentive silence, the knock repeated itself.

I peered through the peephole, and there stood Alina in her too-large suit, anxiously cracking her knuckles. I yanked the door slightly open, and she slid through the crack.

"I'm just dropping by quickly. I wanted to check on you," Alina said, sounding surprisingly emotional, but then she saw Robin on the couch, and her voice lost all expression. "Oh. Robin."

Robin, eyes still on the photos, lifted her hand in a motion that might one day grow up to be a wave.

"What does a guy have to do to get a drink around here?" Alina asked me as she headed to the kitchen.

"I'm taking the night off from alcohol," Robin said, as if anyone had asked.

Alina pulled a bottle of Chivas Regal out of the cabinet above the sink and poured two fingers into a water glass. "Boy, this place is a mess," she said, surveying the open drawers and dirty dishes.

"Do you have a pen and paper?" I asked with more vigor than those words usually warrant.

"Nice to see you too." Alina fell into a chair at the kitchen table. "What did you two do today? *I* worked."

"I confessed to a crime I didn't commit," I said as I sat across from her. "Then I fled the cops. Then I took a shower."

"I went to Ernest Whitaker's dispiriting memorial." Having

looked through that picture book a dozen times or more, Robin tossed it onto the armchair, slid her shoes off, and curled her feet up on the couch.

"Well," Alina said, forcing down a bit more Chivas, "I'm having lunch tomorrow with Bonnie, the previous community manager. Hopefully she can tell me who Ernest was having a conflict with."

"Thank you," I said.

"And I did find out that Ernest was one of those tenants who got a renewal notice in the mail the day before his death," Alina continued.

"And how much was his rent raised?" I asked.

"Only five percent," Alina said. "I'm surprised too. It's curious that his increase was so small when apparently others had their rents raised multiples of that."

"Well, for my part," I said, "I called the number on Dr. Olander's card."

"I'm the one who gave you that card," Robin said unnecessarily from her recumbent position of privilege.

"I haven't gotten through to her," I continued, "but I'm pretty sure I know how to find her."

"The police think I'm just in the building to pick up some things for work, so I need to go." Alina stood and took as big a sip of the Scotch as she could tolerate. "This drink is disgusting."

"When this is over, I'll buy you all the Midori Sours you want."

"Kurlansky called me today," Alina said, ignoring my impressive memory for other people's drink orders. "He warned me not to help you. He says you're not helping yourself."

"That's an understatement," I said.

"We have to come up with another suspect, quickly," Alina said.

"What does that mean?" Robin asked. "*Come up* with another

suspect?" And then, as if this were our job, "Shouldn't you find who *actually* did it?"

"Dr. Olander feels like a lead," I said.

Alina didn't look convinced. She could barely make herself shrug.

"Are you okay?" I asked her.

"I have to go home and figure out next week's front desk schedule for all three buildings. Maybe work disagrees with me." She grabbed the glass off the table and forced herself to finish the Chivas. "Can I ask you an annoying question?"

"Sure," I said.

"I know we have bigger fish to fry," Alina said, "but do you think your agent has looked at my book yet?" Her face flushed. "Sorry, sorry. I shouldn't have asked."

"No, I'm glad you asked." And before she could apologize again, I got up and said, "I don't think I should turn on my phone, but when you get home, check my email, see if he emailed me— my agent." I gave her my login information.

As I walked Alina to the door, I explained to her that I'd made a copy of Martin's key and asked her to return the original to its proper place. Then Robin appeared next to us with the inhuman speed of a vampire. "It's time for me to leave too."

As I closed the door behind them, I heard Robin tell Alina that she was going to throw a party downstairs for Ernest. And then I heard Alina say, "That's batshit insane." At least she was standing up for herself.

Still without pen or paper, I forced myself to sit and think. It felt weird.

All right, brain. Who was it who had agreed with me that they couldn't hear anything from other apartments? I went through a mental list of every person I'd come in contact with over the last couple of days. Ah—there it was! It was Patrick Backus. When I was riding down the elevator with that officer the day Ernest died, Patrick Backus had told me that he too couldn't hear his neighbors. Well, given his upstairs neighbor was Ernest, that was obviously bullshit. So why would Patrick Backus lie? Why wouldn't he have said, "What the fuck are you talking about, Paul? I hear every yap and footstep and female moan."

I didn't want to go over to Patrick's apartment until after 9:00 p.m. when the tenants would likely be settled in for the night, so I sat down on the couch and, every once in a while, muttered to myself, "Visit Patrick Backus" to make sure I didn't forget.

About an hour later, I crept down the hallway and knocked on number 725. I stood to one side so that Patrick or his wife wouldn't be able to see that it was me through the peephole.

Someone opened the door a bit, and immediately I put my foot in the crack. "Don't freak out," I whispered to Patrick as our eyes met.

"What the hell?"

I gently pushed the door open, and Patrick backed up as I entered. He was wearing flannel pajama bottoms and a plain red T-shirt that hung from his clavicles. "Please don't hurt me."

"Why would I hurt you?" I heard the door shut behind me.

It's really interesting to see how different tenants personalize these expensive white boxes we live in. Ernest Whitaker had turned his into a circus for dogs. Robin Nash had used hers as a repository for fashion magazines and dog shit. Martin Stowell had painted his red and stuffed it with dark furniture and international memorabilia. And the Backuses had covered theirs with their children's artwork. The drawings and paintings were hung haphazardly at odd intervals. A couple of pieces of poster board were even taped so low that they were near foot level. Honestly, most of the art was . . . meh.

Noticing my critical eye, Patrick said, "A lot of the drawings are a couple of years old. The kids are better now."

"You're really pushing these kids into the visual arts," I said, noticing some poorly thrown pottery lined up on the spotless kitchen counter.

"Not pushing," said Patrick. "You follow a child's natural inclinations. There's so much art on the walls because when we first moved here, the kids really missed their old apartment, and this book we read said to cover the new apartment with their work." Boy, people love to talk about their kids.

"A frame or two might help," I suggested. "Or maybe some curation?"

Patrick managed to blink himself back to the situation at hand. "Listen, I think I should call the police."

"Why?"

"Didn't you confess to murder?" Patrick asked.

"I unconfessed immediately." But Patrick didn't appear persuaded, so I said, "If you call the police, I'll scream."

"You'll scream? That doesn't even make sense." Patrick calmly took his phone from the all-purpose table that also held his laptop and stacks of what I assumed were work binders.

"If I know one thing about parents," I said as I pulled out a chair and sat, "they hate it when their kids are woken up. Am I right? Do you really want to go through the bedtime routine again? Do you, Patrick?"

Patrick put his phone back on the table. "As a matter of fact, I don't."

"I have a couple of questions, and then it'll be like I was never here."

Patrick scratched the skin on his thin, pale arms, leaving behind long white contrails. "Fine. Just be quick because my wife is due home, and she will be extremely unhappy to find you here."

He walked backward to the fridge, I guess not wanting to take his eyes off me, and poured himself a drink out of a clear cylindrical bottle, spilling a little. This dude was nervous. Nervous because I was asking questions or nervous because his wife might find me here?

"What's that you're drinking?" I asked.

"It's seltzer. I have a seltzer stream." Why be defensive about a seltzer stream, Patrick?

"Are you happy with that purchase?" I asked. It was off topic, but I was interested.

"It's fine."

"I've long since considered getting one, but the CO2 cartridges aren't cheap."

"Well, as long as you confine yourself to the lowest carbonation setting, the cartridges will last," Patrick said. "Obviously, if you're undisciplined and use the highest setting, yes, you'll use cartridges too quickly."

"How are the flavors?"

"I like it plain." He took a sip, put the glass down, and placed both of his sinewy, scratched-up, hairless arms on the island counter. "What do you want to ask me?"

From my chair, I ran one hand along the beige partition that cut the living room in half. The temporary wall wasn't unlike what you would find separating cubicles in an office. Presumably, Patrick and his wife slept on the other side of the partition and their children slept in the sole bedroom. I heard people laugh from the apartment next door, as if they were reminding me why I was here. *I'll get to it, laughing next-door neighbors. Relax.*

"How's your petition to have me removed from the building going?"

"Honestly, it doesn't seem necessary now that you've confessed to the crime." He laughed a weird high-pitched strangled laugh. Why had I never noticed just how tightly wound this man was? He looked to me now like the kind of man who easily becomes motion sick during long car rides.

Patrick's phone pinged. "My wife is almost home."

I stood up and drifted toward him in the kitchen. "A few days ago when Ernest Whitaker died, I saw you in the elevator, and I said something like 'I bet you didn't hear anything because the walls are so insulated.'"

"This was when a police officer was escorting you out of the building?"

"Yes, but my point is, you agreed. You said I was right, you never hear anything." I leaned on the counter, across from him.

"So what?" Patrick asked, his hand reaching for his glass of bubbly. Goddamn, that seltzer looked refreshing. I bet it would be even better if it was flavored like blueberry or strawberry . . .

"You can hear everything that happens in the other apartments! I can hear people laughing next door right now! The insulation is shit! Why lie?"

"Why lie?" Patrick's pale skin was tingeing pink. "You said something stupid, and I agreed so you would stop talking!"

"Keep your voice down," I said, like we were a couple having a marital spat. "The children."

"What exactly are you getting at?" he asked.

"You must have heard a lot from upstairs that morning, so why say otherwise?"

"No, I didn't hear anything. I was down in the Library because Shaina was getting the kids ready. You really have to leave." Patrick came around the island to me, but I stood my ground.

"Well then, you must have heard things other mornings! Other evenings! Other midnights!" I could see Patrick calculating if he should deny this. "Are you really going to tell me that Ernest Whitaker wasn't an annoying upstairs neighbor?" I demanded. "With the parade of women and the circus of dogs? It defies rationality!" This was going quite well.

"Is the point of you coming here to ask why I didn't tell you that Ernest was an annoying neighbor while a police officer stood behind you on the day of Ernest's death?"

"The noise must have really bothered you," I said with mock

sympathy. "You were even having nightmares about sounds in the walls."

"*I* will not be harassed by *you*," Patrick hissed imperiously and lifted his now empty glass as if he might smash my face with it. And I swear to God, looking into his squinty, rage-filled eyes, for an instant I was certain this man could easily be provoked to murder. But lucky for both of us, his wife came in the front door at that moment. He put the glass down with all the gentleness he could muster and seethed at me. "Do you know what I do all day? I work on cybersecurity for city hall. I protect this city."

"Like Batman?" I asked.

"Exactly like Batman," he said through clenched teeth.

I glanced over at his wife, in a long thin black coat, looking exhausted, standing in the doorway, warily assessing the situation.

"And do you know what my wife, Shaina, does all day?" Patrick asked rhetorically. "She's a social worker at Riker's Island. Also like Batman." The analogy seemed stretched thin, but I let it go. "What do you do?" Patrick asked. "Except play make pretend detective?" *Also like Batman,* I thought, but I kept that to myself. "What do any of these idiots do?" he said, jaw pulsating, arms gesticulating sharply to invisible neighbors on all sides.

Shaina pulled out her phone. "I'm calling the police," she said simply. I was momentarily distracted by her pretty, makeup-less face. I felt like I'd seen her recently, more recently than the other day in the elevator, like I'd seen her in a dream.

Just to show that I could read social cues, I took a couple of long steps toward the front door. "I'll go." Shaina in turn backed up into the living room, phone to her ear. "But answer me this first," I said to Patrick. "Were you and Ernest Whitaker in some sort of long-standing feud?"

"Yes!" Patrick whisper-shouted as he approached me, his wiry figure suddenly looking razor-sharp. "So what?"

Shaina put her hand on the phone and said, "Patrick, shut up."

And then into the phone, "Police, there's an intruder in my apartment."

"Ernest Whitaker was loud! I'd put my children to sleep while listening to him fuck women up there!" Patrick spat, his eyes suddenly unfocused. "And he was running a business out of his apartment, which is against the rules!" I will reiterate that Patrick had a laptop and binders on his table, clearly he worked from home, so you know, pot, kettle. "And the worst, the worst, the very worst dispute Ernest Whitaker and I had—"

"Patrick, stop!" Shaina yelled. I mean, she flat-out yelled. And then she told the police exactly who had invaded their apartment.

"What was the worst dispute?" I asked.

Patrick said, "Get out," as Shaina said, "The police are on their way up," so I spun around on my good heel and sprinted down the hallway toward the stairwell, dogs seemingly barking from every door I passed.

"One more question!" I yelled back to Patrick whose scarecrow body was craning out of his doorway. "Have you seen a red cloth notebook? I just—it's impossible to replace my own notes, you know?"

That seemed to be too much for Patrick to take. "Fuck you! And fuck your fucking notebook!"

As I skidded into the stairwell, from the Backuses' apartment, I heard a startled child cry, "Daddy?" Boy, getting those kids back to sleep was going to be a bitch.

I hid out in the stairwell for thirty seconds and then darted across the hallway into my temporary residence, the door shutting just as I heard officers emerge from the elevator.

———

A few moments later, I stood in the darkness of Martin Stowell's kitchen, staring out the window, down at the gas station across the street. It was brightly lit in contrast to the great black sky above and beyond.

On our side of the street, a couple of squad cars carelessly pulled up to the Jax, blocking a lane of traffic. A few cops ran into the building, the predictable result of Shaina's phone call. But I was curious to see if someone less predictable would show up now that the police had been called. While I watched and waited, I contemplated how keeping my phone off had allowed my mind to form sequential thoughts that deepened in complexity the longer I teased them out. I still hankered for a pen and paper, but even without these implements, my brain was forming connections that surprised even me, its humble passenger.

I thought about what I'd learned during my brief time with Patrick Backus. Patrick had been right about one thing, of course. Sometimes the most natural response when someone says something is to agree. The fact that he'd nodded along with my erroneous statement about the walls being effectively insulated didn't mean much. However, there were other reasons to suspect him. He was certainly a guy who seemed quick to upset. It was easy to imagine him becoming apoplectic about an inconsiderate upstairs neighbor. But was that really motive enough to kill? Regardless, his conflict with Ernest was clearly ongoing, so it was more than likely that he was the other party in the feud that Merit Management had neglected to address. And tantalizingly, Patrick hadn't told me about their worst dispute. His wife had stopped him before he spat it out.

And something else pointed to Patrick. My theory was that Ernest's murderer killed Laura to throw the police off his scent and onto mine. So that meant the murderer most likely knew that the police were already interested in me. And of course the day of Ernest's murder, Patrick saw me in the elevator with a cop. I could feel anger tingle in my nerve endings. Did that narrow man really end Laura's life? I almost laughed, it felt ridiculous. But Jesus, also? He didn't have an alibi, at least not for Ernest's murder. He claimed to be down in the Library, but I was at the front desk, and I didn't see him.

Ah! There! Not in the gas station parking lot this time, but in the supermarket parking lot, across McGuinness Boulevard and on the other side of Calyer Street. My less predictable person showed up after all. Illuminated by a single streetlight, there was the motorcyclist with the red helmet. He or she (but let's face it, probably she) showed up the last two times the police were called, so I'd hoped she would show up tonight. My motorcyclist must somehow be monitoring police activity.

Then, holy shit, the helmet came off, and she looked up at the building as she shook out her long brown hair. Goddamn, even from up here, Dr. Laura Olander bore a resemblance to my Laura, to Laura Downing. Getting out to the street to talk to her tonight was an impossibility, but now I knew how to beckon her. Raise hell and make sure someone calls the cops.

From my darkened corner of the kitchen, I could hear police officers knocking on doors and dogs barking in return. The knocks were getting closer and closer. I didn't think they'd come into apartments where the tenants weren't home or the doors weren't answered. Not tonight. I had to believe that. There was nowhere else for me to go. Finally, an officer knocked on Martin's door. "Police." I didn't answer. After a moment, the cop's footsteps moved on, and my sphincter released.

I actually found the repetitive knocking peaceful as it trailed down the hallway. My eyes started to get heavy, and I sat down at the table, resting my head on my arms. *The first hour or so of sleep will be restful,* I thought. But after that I'll find myself half-conscious, going down the long hallways of my mind, passing open doorways of horrific visions and mournful remembrances.

At some point during the night, I wandered about, finished the Chivas, took a few more Advil, and studied my face in the bathroom mirror. One eye was bigger than the other, distorted from crying and stress. What was I going to do with myself to pass the time? I couldn't sleep. There was no TV or computer in this apartment, though on some level that hirsute penance pleased me. I sat on the lid of the toilet. I could feel myself roiling at the unfairness and senselessness of Laura's death. And I could feel my fury building toward Patrick Backus, but I had to remind myself that his guilt was just a theory. Yet part of me wanted to get up off the toilet and knock on his apartment door again, for no reason other than to see his face and for him to see mine. It was almost like . . . like I had a perverse crush on him.

Then—a metallic clink, a key entering the lock of Martin's front door. My ears instantly alert, I sat as still as I could and listened to the front door squeak open. Shuffling sounds. Fabric on fabric. Scraping. Maybe Martin Stowell was home? But it didn't sound like a homecoming. It felt like a break-in. I stood up and slowly crept out of the bathroom in my (Martin's) boxer briefs and undershirt.

The noise I made getting up must have startled the intruder because by the time I entered the dark living room, his bulky form was quickly tottering back toward the entryway. When he pulled the front door open, I saw his oversize figure silhouetted by the hallway light. Then he pushed the door closed behind him.

I threw the door open and watched Stovan shuffle-run diagonally across the hallway and into the stairwell, holding his pants up with one hand, never even looking back. What the fuck?

———

At six in the morning, there was a gentle knock at the door. I'd drifted into an unconscious state at about four, and whatever sleep cycle I'd just been woken from, it wasn't so bad. I looked out the peephole, and there was Alina, dressed like her normal self in a frilly white button-down and straight black pants. She wasn't cracking her knuckles this time. She was smiling right up into the peephole, her face large and happy.

I opened the door. "Hey, what's up?"

"Can I come in?" she asked, one exhale away from a giggle.

"Yeah, of course."

She slipped inside and looked down at my hairy legs. "Stop looking at my hairy legs."

"Maybe you want to put on some pants?" she asked, crinkling her nose. Was she trying a bit too hard to be cute, or was I just irritated by her unexpected perkiness? In any event, I grabbed orange sweatpants from the floor.

"That's not really your color." Alina smirked.

I grunted and rubbed my face.

"Hey, don't be grumpy," she said. "Better to deal with the fashion police than the actual police." Boy, she was chipper. "But," she continued, looking at the clothes that were strewn about, "you should clean this place up."

"I was in a fugue state last night," I told her. "At some point I became obsessed with finding clothes that were comfortable. As if finding a combination of the right texture and temperature would allow me to sleep. Let me make some coffee."

I loped into the kitchen with Alina at my heels. "Please put less coffee in the French press this time."

I scraped yesterday's grounds out of the glass beaker and into the trash. Then I realized there was no bag. Shit. All that mushy black sludge was in the plastic bin. I knew myself; there was no way I was cleaning that out.

"Okay, so here's the amazing news." Alina was pacing in front of the kitchen windows, the sky brightening behind her. "I checked your email last night," she said. "There was a message in there from that agent of yours. He passed my manuscript on to the literary department, and the agent there, *she likes my book*. He was asking you for my contact information," she said, trying to keep her excitement from bubbling out the top of her head. "I've already emailed him back, and I'm going to meet with the literary person tomorrow." She shook her head in disbelief. "Every time I cross the street, I'm certain I'll be hit by a car." Was her happiness irritating me? Does other people's happiness in general irritate me? Maybe I prefer my people to be disgruntled? Maybe I don't like recognizing a more joyful existence is possible?

"That's great news."

"But wait." As I filled the kettle with water, Alina vied for my attention. "Paul! There's more. There was an email from some movie guy for you. Something about Pineys and New Jersey? You got the part!"

I turned the burner on under the kettle and looked at her. It took me a minute to contextualize what she was saying. Then I remembered. Oh, right. That audition. So some of this good news was for me? It was like a previously unseen lamp suddenly flooded the apartment with the golden light of possibility. "They were getting worried because they hadn't heard from you," Alina continued, "so I took the liberty of responding that of course you're interested, but you're just dealing with important personal business." I scooped some coffee out of the tin. How the hell much coffee goes into a French press? I almost asked Alina, but I was still trying to digest this news about my career (career?). I put three scoops of coffee in. That didn't look like enough, but I let it be.

"I am very happy for you," I said. And this time I believed it a little more.

"For both of us," she insisted. "Look, I don't want to minimize all of *this*. But doesn't it help to know that there might be something good on the other side?" I wondered if she really thought there was truly any getting to the other side for me.

"I don't have a pencil or paper and I don't want to turn on my phone, so can I just kind of talk through where we are with all of *this*?" I asked.

"Yes, of course. Yes," Alina said. She sat ramrod straight at the table and looked up at me. "Oh! Take my laptop today." She pulled a chunky Hewlett-Packard out of her backpack.

"That's not necessary," I said.

"No, it is," she insisted. "So we can be in touch by email. And you can keep track of things!" She placed the laptop on the table and smiled at me primly.

"Okay, thank you." I poured the nearly boiling water onto the coffee grounds and put the plunger on top.

"Three minutes," she said.

"What?"

"You have to wait three minutes before pushing the stem."

"Oh, thanks."

She opened her computer. "Okay, you talk, I'll type up notes. Then we're going to have a cup of coffee, and I'll go to the corporate office." She looked at me expectantly.

"I went to Patrick Backus's apartment and had a talk with him last night," I said as I pulled down mugs.

"Patrick Backus?"

"Yeah."

"Oh good," Alina said.

"Why good?" I asked.

"Well. He lives below Ernest, and he always seemed like a jerk."

"I think he might be the tenant who Ernest was in an ongoing conflict with."

"You know, Patrick as a suspect, that tracks," Alina said. "When he first took my statement, Kurlansky asked me if I'd seen Patrick Backus in the Library that morning."

"And did you?"

"No," Alina said.

Alina typed while I tried to figure out if three minutes had passed. I literally had no idea if one or ten minutes had gone by, so I pushed the plunger down and hoped for the best.

"Was there anything unusual in Patrick's apartment?" Alina asked. "Because it seems to me that we'd need some evidence before we went to Kurlansky."

I brought over two black coffees.

"Well," I joked as I sat down, "his kids' art was *unusually* crappy. Their work looked like the Crayola ravings of a lunatic."

"Oh, that," Alina said. "That . . . um . . . why do I already know that? Oh! Stovan told me! This was a while ago. He said he was in there fixing something and that papers are hung in strange places, right?" And then, "This coffee is much better."

"Yeah, the drawings are hung at weird heights and . . . What did Stovan make of it?"

"He thinks that Patrick sometimes punches and kicks the walls. Like in anger? And uses the kids' drawings to cover the holes."

"If that's true, it could illustrate that Patrick has violent tendencies."

But then Alina saw something on her computer that changed her demeanor. She started rubbing her palms on her thighs. "I just got an email," she finally said. "From Merit Management. 'Today law enforcement officers will be patrolling the halls in increased numbers and requesting access to each unit multiple times. Merit is encouraging all tenants to allow the police entry and will be contacting those by phone who are not home to obtain permission.'"

"Then I better find somewhere else to stay," I said.

"Yeah, in case Martin Stowell gives them permission by phone. Where will you go?"

"There's always Bob Shapiro in Manhattan."

Alina kept typing for another few minutes, quickly and intently.

"What are you typing now?" I asked.

"Just answering emails," she said after what seemed like a very long moment. When she looked at me again, her face had darkened.

"What?" I asked.

"I don't know. Maybe my endorphins are drying up. I-I'm

worried about you." She stood and took the photo album off the couch. She started to leaf through it, absently, nervously, tugging at the pictures for a few moments before she thought to ask, "This thing do any good?"

I shook my head but promised, "I'll look through it more today."

She tossed it back down. Looking at her newly hunched posture, I realized now that Alina was worried. I felt better. Maybe I really did prefer my people disgruntled. Huh. In any event, she reminded me that she was having lunch with the former community manager, and I told her that I was going to try to talk to Ernest Whitaker's neighbors. And that I really wanted to have one more conversation with Patrick Backus before I left the Jax.

Once Alina was gone, I found scissors and a straight razor in Martin Stowell's bathroom and went to work at losing my beard, facial hair soon covering the sink and floor. Ten minutes later, I looked in the mirror at my newly hairless face. Where the hell had my chin gone? Thank God *I* didn't have to look at this face all day. That was a problem for the rest of the world. I put on a non-insane outfit from my own clothes—T-shirt, jeans. I stuffed the photo album and Alina's laptop into my backpack. From the front door, I surveyed the apartment once more. The floor was covered in books and clothing. The kitchen was a mess of dirty dishes. And it all smelled vaguely of Robin's cigarettes and my masturbation. With no time to clean up, I laced up my (Martin's) purple sneakers and headed out, knowing I would never be back.

CHAPTER 11
(OR IS IT 12? WHO CAN KEEP TRACK?) DETECTIVE SHIT

t was still early, so the hallways weren't yet teeming with police. I ducked from Martin's place into the stairwell, narrowly dodging an encounter with a tenant leaving her apartment. I jaunted up one flight of steps and paused before I entered the eighth-floor hallway. I noticed I wasn't out of breath. *If I make it through this*, I thought, *I should publish a book: How to Lose Weight Like a Fugitive.*

The coast was clear, so I walked with purpose to the apartment next to Ernest Whitaker's and knocked. If this went wrong, I could always run. In my mind I was now a very fast runner. And skinny.

The tenant in 823 opened up right away. I got the feeling he hadn't even looked through the peephole. It was Icon Hat guy. You know, that South Asian guy who's always wearing a black baseball cap that says Icon in large white letters? Maybe I haven't mentioned him. Well, that's who it was, standing there, holding the door open with his knee, slurping from a cereal bowl. He was a tall son of a bitch, comically so. "Yeah?"

"Can I come in for a moment?" I asked, cowed by his height and self-proclaimed icon status.

Icon shrugged and moved to the side. I guess being tall and wearing a ridiculous hat means you don't fear much from the outside world.

"I'm sorry to bother you."

"What do ya need?"

"Do you know who I am?" I asked.

He shook his head and put his lips fully around the head of the spoon.

I took a moment to glance around Icon's apartment. I can't stress enough how interesting it is to see inside your neighbors' domiciles. Why don't we have like open door night in apartment buildings? Why all the mystery? But at the same time, it's a drag to have to describe them, especially as I'm trying to build some momentum here, and I know, as a reader myself, I mostly skip descriptions. So it's like why even take all this time to form these sentences when most people are going to skim, at best? Well, I guess for the audiobook. You can't skim past this shit in an audiobook.

Suffice to say, Icon's apartment was full of comfortable furniture covered by an abundance of blankets. This place seemed designed for naps. Tasteful, abstract line drawings hung framed on the walls.

"My mom made those," he said. "She's a great artist."

Surrounded by his mother's art? This guy truly feared nothing.

"I wanted to ask a couple of questions about Ernest Whitaker, your deceased next-door neighbor."

"And who are you?" Not that he really seemed to care.

"I'm Paul. My wife was also . . . . killed." Boy, that was a fucking weird thing to say. I remembered how strange it was to call Laura my wife when we were first married. My eyes felt hot with tears, but Icon didn't notice. Was he . . . laughing?

"Oh shit!" he said. "You're that guy? The cops! Man! They've been knocking on our doors! The building is emailing us to get into our apartments! They're looking for you." My fugitive status clearly raised me in Icon's estimation. "You're that guy!"

"I know," I said, smiling, because it's nice to be considered special. "But I didn't. I didn't do anything. I'm hoping you can answer a couple of questions about your deceased neighbor?"

Icon was off to the races, suddenly talking a mile a minute, only pausing to slurp milk, now directly from the bowl. "Shit. I mean, I can't ask you to sit down, but I'll tell you what I told the cops. He was a noisy fucker, always with drama and people and dogs. Jesus, the dogs! He would train those fuckers in there. Not that I cared about any of it. I mean, I can sleep through anything! Even that morning, before he died, at like nine, he had a huge fucking poodle in there. I'll tell something funny!" Boy, this guy had serotonin to burn. "I'll tell you *two* things that are funny! First, he was always inviting me to parties, which was kinda gross cause he was so old."

"Wait, I'm sorry," I interrupted. "Wasn't Ernest Whitaker like thirty?"

"Yeah! But I'm twenty-three, bruh!"

"Oh."

"He smelled old!" Icon tossed his bowl in the sink and then tossed his head back and laughed. "I'm not going to some old guy's party!" And why should he? This guy could have fun all by himself. "The second thing. I saw all this stuff in the news. About your wife. And at first I was like, oh shit, she was over at Ernest's all the time. But then I was like, no. It was just a woman who looked like your wife."

"Dr. Laura Olander."

"I don't know, was that her name? I was like, that's some *Double Indemnity* shit."

"I think you mean *Vertigo*."

"What?"

"*Double Indemnity* is the one with insurance fraud. *Vertigo* is the one with the woman who looks like another woman."

"Aw shit, my man knows his Hitchcock!" Icon slapped me on the shoulder.

We were suddenly friends. It's nice to have friends. Still, I couldn't help but mutter, "*Double Indemnity* was Billy Wilder."

"But anyway, then I was like, nah. I saw your wife over there too. Not at the same time, but I know I did. I saw *both* of them."

"Wait, what? Are you sure?"

"Pretty sure, 'cause I was like, hey it's that hot-ass older woman again, but then I was like, nah, she just looks *remarkably* like that other hot-ass older woman. Oh, no offense."

I wasn't sure which part I should be taking offense to, so I asked, "Do you know what my wife was doing there?"

"I saw her in the hallway. He gave her a couple of pills. Loose. He did that sometimes. Like for the dogs."

"Oh. Did she have our dog with her?"

"Nah," said Icon. "Look, you should go. I've got a Teams meeting in two."

"One more question. Any opinion about Patrick Backus?"

"Who's that?"

"Guy who lives below Ernest, has a family."

"Oh, that uptight prick? Yeah, he came up here and yelled at Ernest like twice a week. Poor fucking guy, Ernest. Who needs that, right? Live and let live." Icon showed me his perfect white teeth and then showed me the door. I never even learned his name.

I skipped past Ernest's door, which was still covered with police tape, and went to his other next-door neighbor. As I was about to knock, I heard the elevator open and saw Robin step out in a business suit.

"What are you doing here?" I called sotto voce.

"Inviting people to Ernest's memorial slash party tomorrow night. What are you doing?"

"Detective shit. Don't bother knocking on that door. Icon doesn't want to go to your party."

"Why not?"

"He thinks you're old."

"Fuck you."

"*I* don't think you're old. I think you're young. *He* thinks you're old."

"Still fuck you," Robin said.

Again, I went to knock on apartment 827, but the door opened first, and an overweight man with an asymmetrical face lumbered out.

"The fuck are you?" he grunted.

"Sorry." Backing up, I noticed his MTA uniform. "I'm just asking some questions about Ernest's death."

"Get a fucking load a this!" MTA called back into his apartment where moving boxes were scattered about. A woman with unkempt hair in a long Minnie Mouse T-shirt that stretched at her large breasts appeared from the bedroom.

"Whaaaaaat?" she asked, making a whiny full-course meal out of the word.

"That guy da police are looking for? He showed up at our door!" MTA was clearly astounded. And maybe flattered?

"Oh my Gaad. Harry! Call the cops!"

"What da ya want?" Harry asked as he leaned toward me conspiratorially.

"I just want to know if you had any trouble with Ernest, you know, before he died."

"I'll tell you something!" Mrs. MTA stormed to the door. "This whole fucking apartment building is awful!"

"She don't like it here. I win the lottery for the lower-income apartments, you know, each of these buildings has to offer a couple to normal folks at prices we can afford. Anyway, I move her to this nice place. She hates it."

"It's loud, and everyone is ruuude." She yelled at Harry, "I was happier in Jersey!"

"I tried to do something nice for us!" Harry yelled back.

"Nice?" she shouted. "Nice is Manhattan! I don't know *what* this is!"

"It's away from your fucking mother, *that's* what it is!"

Under all of the arguing, I could hear Robin trying to convince Icon to go to her party. "I'll think about it. I have a meeting. I gotta go," he was telling her. That's when I saw two cops enter the floor from the stairwell farther down the hallway. I darted into Mr. and Mrs. MTA's apartment.

"Hey, where are you going?" Mrs. MTA shouted.

I implored her, "Please, shh. I'm just trying to get to the bottom of what happened to my wife."

I darted around their cardboard boxes, unlocked the glass door to their balcony. and flung it open. Before I shut it behind me, I heard Mr. MTA say to Mrs. MTA, "I didn't see nothin' and we're not sayin' nothing.'" God bless old-school New York.

I crouched on the floor of their empty balcony. Looking up, I couldn't help but realize it was a gorgeous morning. What a clear blue sky, a sky that didn't need the sun, a sky that seemed to produce light of its own accord. Muffled voices told me the police had entered this apartment. I had to get off this balcony. I looked to the left. Could I leap to the next one? And then I realized that was Ernest Whitaker's balcony. God, I'd stood there just a few days ago when there was only one dead body. Simpler times. In any event, no way could I jump the ten feet to the next balcony. I looked up. Could I climb to the roof? What would I use as handholds? It was a brick facade, but to get my thick fingers into the grouting around the bricks? No way. So that left down. I could hear the cops' voices getting closer to the glass door. "The living room is clear," one said. "Check the balcony." Down it would have to be.

I flung one leg and then the other over the metal railing. I held on to the top rail and crouched like Spider-Man, clinging to the outside of the balcony, suspended eight stories above the parking lot. I slid my hands one at a time to the bottom of the posts, and just as I heard the door open, I blindly swung my feet down and toward the building. Letting go with my hands, I fell, my butt hitting the top rail of the balcony below, and I tumbled forward and down into a menagerie of potted plants. I rolled onto the cement floor, taking a few ferns and palms with me, and laid in a fetal position, covered in plant dirt, listening to the cops above. "Clear. No one's out here."

Huh, I thought to myself, *Patrick Backus definitely could have swung down from Ernest's balcony to his own*. And with his slim, athletic frame, his descent would have been a lot more graceful than my desperate tumble. I felt my shoulder ache, my butt ache, and then I thought about the backpack I was still wearing. Staying low to the floor, I slid it off and pulled out the laptop. The computer didn't look cracked or broken. That was good news. More good news, the wicker furniture on the balcony was giving me some cover from whomever might be inside this apartment. Boy, I wished I'd landed on that settee. *Fuck you, settee.*

Figuring it best to just lie low for a minute, I thought about what, if anything, I'd found out so far that morning. Icon had confirmed the extent to which Patrick was in conflict with Ernest. But he also thought he'd seen my wife outside Ernest's apartment. I wished I'd asked more questions about that, but I really didn't know what I should have asked. I couldn't make that piece fit, so I pushed it aside and stayed focused on Patrick. I wanted one more discussion with him before I left this building today. What was his worst dispute with Ernest about? The more I thought about it, the more it seemed obvious that this uptight, tightly wound, by all accounts volatile man was the murderer. But why was I so sure? Was I just hell-bent on getting revenge for my wife and latched on to the first possible suspect? Or maybe playing out this detective/suspect fantasy was keeping me from mourning the true horror of what had happened? Wait. Fantasy? Why had I thought the word *fantasy*? No. No, no, no. After all, my suspicion of Patrick was based in facts. Fact: Patrick was annoyed with his upstairs neighbor. Fact: Patrick has a short fuse. Fact: Patrick's alibi is bullshit. Fact: Patrick knew the police already suspected me, so I was the best person to frame. He killed Ernest in a rage brought on by women and dogs and then killed my wife to frame me.

I had to look Patrick in the eye again. I was certain if I looked him in the eye one more time, I'd know if he'd done it. Maybe I could even get a confession out of him. But how would I record it? I couldn't turn my phone on. Shit. I didn't even know where my phone *was* anymore. I didn't know where my phone was. I didn't know where my notebook was. I had always attributed the fact that I lose so many *things* to my alignment with Buddhist philosophy and a lack of attachment to possessions. Anyway.

I slid the laptop back into my backpack beside the photo album when I saw that a picture had slipped out of the album and lay loose at the bottom of the bag. I pulled it out. It was . . . holy shit, the picture was of Patrick Backus's wife, Shaina. Goddamn. Shaina Backus had been to Ernest's parties. That's why she'd seemed weirdly familiar to me last night; I'd glanced at this picture. In the photo, her pretty, almost defiantly plain face was staring boldly at the camera. She was wearing a black blazer and underpants. And nothing else. Had Patrick known his wife was going to his mortal enemy's parties? Ooh, the betrayal. Juicy. Maybe this was the worst dispute! If nothing else, I could use this photo to prove that Patrick was prone to uncontrollable rage.

I was so close to Patrick's apartment—just next door!—but before I could show him a pic of his wife in her skivvies, I had to get over there. I stood and looked through the glass door of this apartment. Maybe someone would let me in. To my surprise, I knew this place. The plant people lived here! I was peering into their verdant private paradise. The living room looked like a forest at dusk with a couch in the middle, like a fawn might pass by at any moment. I couldn't see anyone, but diffuse light was coming from the bedroom. Surely, my good old dull friends the plant people would give me a hand.

Right as I was about to tap on the glass, I heard, "Paul?" I snapped my head to the right, and there was Patrick Backus, in the flesh, standing on his balcony, dressed in his standard uniform. He leaned over toward me, his knuckles (bruised?) clenching the side railing, inhaling and exhaling slowly, rhythmically. Was he internally counting his breaths to calm himself? I do that sometimes. Finally, he asked, "What are you doing? Are you hiding from the police?"

"Well . . ." I wanted to keep Patrick talking to me, so I made my voice as high and sweet as I could manage. "Hey, I owe you an apology for last night. I asked a lot of stupid questions." Hopefully this gentle tone would engender some trust.

Patrick looked me up and down, and then with much effort, he said in a tightly controlled tone, "Look, we're both upset by what's going on. And obviously what's been happening with you is . . . unimaginable. Why don't you come over and we'll talk for a minute. I have to monitor a few things on my laptop, but at least I can offer you a cup of coffee."

"Thanks," I said. "Hey, do you use a French press?" When he looked at me quizzically, I said, "Never mind. I'm just curious about how many scoops of coffee are appropriate."

All he said in response was, "You shaved your beard. It looks okay."

How about me and Patrick. Two angry white guys trying to control our tempers.

"All right. Give me a minute," I said, dusting off my pants. "I know these people. Hopefully they'll let me in without freaking out or calling the police, and then I'll be right over."

"The plant people live there," said Patrick disdainfully. Then, with an aggravated shake of his head, he retreated into his apartment. Boy, even plants got under this guy's skin. But honestly, vegetation annoys me too. It tickles my nose. Acts like it's better than everything else because it relies on soil for its nutrients.

Through the glass door, I could now see Randy and Lisa (their human names) wandering aimlessly around their dark, interior wilderness, both in sleeveless undershirts and gym shorts. They each had earbuds in, captive to their individual, aural worlds.

I tapped on the door. Nothing. I tapped a little more loudly. Nothing. I went full fist pound.

Randy and Lisa looked over like startled deer.

Randy, earbuds still in, meandered over and opened the door. "Paul, what are you doing out there?" he asked mildly, as if people sometimes appeared on his balcony.

"It's a long story?"

"We were very sorry to hear about Laura," he said, his words disappearing before they were fully formed.

Lisa nodded behind him.

"Then you know the trouble I'm in?" I asked, coming inside.

"Well, since she died, I would imagine you're very sad," he whispered.

"Has anything else happened?" Lisa said with so little inflection I wasn't sure if it was a question.

"We've been working from home. Getting groceries delivered. Trying to stay away from it all," Randy explained.

"It's too upsetting to fully let in," Lisa said, opening her eyes wider, as if to show me how easily sorrow permeates her soul.

"Yeah, sure," I said. And we looked at one another. They smiled kindly. We looked at one another some more. "What are you two listening to?" I asked.

"Oh, I'm listening to commentary on *Better Call Saul*," Randy said. "The TV show? It's enlightening."

"I'm listening to a deconstruction of Taylor Swift's best songs," Lisa said.

"We have interests other than plants," Randy added with the defensiveness of one who knows his reputation. Lisa said nothing more, but by the bobbing of her head, I had a feeling she'd reengaged with Taylor Swift's *Reputation*.

"Okay, well, I'm going to go. Oh, wait. One more thing. What do you think about Patrick, your next-door neighbor?"

"We mind our own business." Randy shrugged. "It's better for the plants."

"Right." And with that, I exited the biosphere.

"Look, obviously, *if* you didn't murder your wife, this is awful for you," Patrick said a few minutes later, placing a ceramic mug of coffee on the table in front of me. "I mean, I guess it would be awful for you even if you did kill her. Sorry, am I being rude?"

I shrugged and took a sip. "I'm used to people thinking I might have killed Laura. I don't take it personally anymore." God, my ass hurt from the tumble I'd taken onto the plant people's balcony.

"Baxter, get off the couch," Patrick said to a sleeping pit bull. Baxter barely looked up at him.

"I didn't realize you had a dog," I said.

"No?" Patrick said. "I guess he was already asleep on our bed last night. He doesn't react to much. He doesn't have to go out much anymore. He's an old boy. When they're young, you want them to calm down. When they're old, you wish they'd do something." He looked at Baxter sympathetically.

"How old is he?" I asked.

"Thirteen years and two months." Patrick went back into the

kitchen, wrapped a pill in a bit of cheese, and brought it over to the dog, who licked it up with one lazy motion of his large pink tongue. "He has melanoma. It started in his mouth. His vet has really helped us manage the pain." He knelt before the dog and pet him. Then he looked at me and made a face like he just had a thought. "You know. His vet looks strikingly like your wife. Sorry."

"Dr. Olander?"

"Yeah. You know her?"

"Not yet," I said.

"They share a first name too. Laura." Patrick slid down and sat on the floor, leaning back against the couch. "Strange, don't you think? But then again, patterns occur in nature, and they're usually quite random."

Boy, Patrick was being very nice to me this morning. Was he trying to convince me that he's a swell guy? And what was all of this talk about his vet? It just felt a little . . . stage managed.

"Again, sorry if I was uptight last night," Patrick continued. "Sometimes at the end of the day, I'm just done. You know, when we moved here, we chose luxury over space. Maybe that was a mistake. It can get to be a pressure cooker in here." He forced out an unnaturally high laugh. "Yet, honestly, we still want to live here. My mistake was thinking this apartment could be semi-permanent."

"Why can't it be? I mean, now that Ernest is gone."

Patrick went to answer but stopped himself. He pressed his lips together so that only a *hmm* escaped. Then he got up without using his hands (I'm always impressed by this). "Now that the dog has had his medicine, I think I'm going to take mine." He went into the bathroom. "I never thought I'd be the type of person to take Xanax, but you know what, Paul?"

I waited in suspense until he came out of the bathroom and swallowed the pill dry. "I want people to enjoy me at home. And at work. I really do."

"Do people not enjoy you at home?" I asked.

"I have a temper." He shrugged. "And yeah, it's annoying to hear noise upstairs every single night. I mean, we run white noise machines in here so loudly it's like sleeping on an airplane." He leaned over the table and typed a few things on his laptop while he said, "I hardly need to say this out loud, but that's no reason to kill somebody."

"Not on its own." I sipped my coffee and thought about the photo album in my backpack. *Not yet.* I was enjoying this more relaxed Patrick, so I decided to ask him some questions about his life, which was, in many ways, a life I envied.

"What's it like, having kids?" I asked.

"Why do you want to know?" He eased into the chair behind his laptop, across the table from me.

"Before Laura died"—those strange words—"that was our major point of contention, whether to have children."

"You wanted them, or she did?" Patrick asked, glancing at his computer.

"I did," I said. "She didn't."

Patrick pursed his lips. "For Shaina and me, we both wanted children. We both wanted the same things *for* our children. That helps. I think in some ways we wanted children more than we wanted each other."

I thought about that. I guess in the beginning, Laura and I wanted each other more than anything. Where that passion went was an open question, yes, but I didn't think Patrick was the person to help me solve that particular mystery. He was more likely to help me solve the mystery of do I really want kids. (And of course the mystery of who murdered Ernest and Laura.)

"But," Patrick pontificated, "you asked what it's like to have kids." A smile blossomed on his face. "If you're really going to raise them and not push the actual rearing off on a partner or hired help, it is the most boring, the most anxiety-making, *the most joyful* experience in the world. *If* you're going to put in the time.

Sure, this place is small," he said, "but we are all always together. We can't hide from one another. These kids know me for who I am, faults and all." Patrick stood up and laughed. "Whatever flaws you have, the sleeplessness and the stress of having kids will make those flaws more apparent." He shook his head, sympathizing with himself.

I stood up too and went to a piece of construction paper on the wall. I gently lifted the scotch tape at one corner. Yep, there, underneath, was a hole in the plaster, the size of a fist. I looked back at Patrick. His wry smile betrayed nothing but amusement.

"They don't *all* cover holes," Patrick said through his grin. "Hey, better to hit the wall than a person."

"Hard to argue with that," I said. "Must be hell on your knuckles."

Patrick took my empty cup to the sink, daring me to look at said knuckles. "I feel like you're putting together a story of me that's really not true."

"If it's not true," I ventured, "tell me about the biggest dispute you had with Ernest Whitaker."

"You think if I tell you about this dispute, it will prove my guilt?" Patrick asked with a laugh.

"Maybe." I laughed too. Just for the hell of it.

Then Patrick leaned back against the counter, a glassy patina covering his eyes. It looked like the Xanax was starting to work its magic. "I'm not telling you shit."

"Why not?"

"It will indeed reinforce what you already believe to be true."

"That you killed Ernest Whitaker and then killed my wife to frame me?"

"That's the one." I could see the tension drain from his body and face. I really would rather have had this discussion before he took the Xanax. I felt like he was hiding behind a wall of pharmaceuticals.

"What if I told you I already knew what this dispute was about," I said.

"I wouldn't be surprised to learn that's true." Patrick shrugged.

"What if I told you I had a picture of it?"

Now that seemed to perplex him. "A picture of what?"

"Of your wife."

"What about my wife?" Now he indeed looked a little angry. *"What about my wife?"*

"You mean your biggest dispute wasn't about Shaina?" I asked.

"It certainly wasn't," Patrick said. He continued leaning back against the counter, but I thought I could see his body compressing.

God, I really should wait to show him this picture, I thought. I should show it to him when he isn't medicated so that he doesn't have so much self-control. But then again, I'd always had a hard time keeping a secret.

"I want to know about this picture. I want to know about my wife," Patrick hissed.

"Absolutely," I said, all joviality. "No problem!" I grabbed my bag. "I just need to use the bathroom first!"

When I emerged from the bathroom a minute or two later, I unzipped my bag and produced the picture of Shaina in that blazer and those black undies.

He looked down at the photo, Shaina frozen in time, leaning defiantly toward the camera. He backed up a step or two.

"When was this picture taken?" he asked.

"It's a photo from one of Ernest's parties."

"Ernest had parties?" he asked, the color draining from his face.

"In the basement," I said.

"And my wife attended them?" Patrick looked like he was having trouble keeping me in focus.

"You didn't know?"

"I didn't."

Patrick looked pained, like he'd just learned something new. But maybe he was pretending. I wondered if I could pretend to look pained like that. Wait, I'm an actor. Of course I could.

I decided to go out on a limb. "I think you're lying to me, Patrick. I think you knew about the parties. I think you knew your wife attended them. I think what's making you go all pale is the fact that I have a picture of it."

"You should leave," Patrick said. So we were back to that.

"I think what I have here is motive," I said, brandishing the photo and backing away from him so that he didn't snatch it. "I have a stronger motive than just annoyance. I have *jealousy*. Furthermore, you're an angry guy." I motioned to the pictures on the wall. "And guess what, Patrick, your alibi is crap. Alina says you weren't in the Library the morning of Ernest's death. She'd fucking testify to that." I was on a roll, right? I mean, I might actually get to avenge my wife's murder. How many people have the opportunity to do that?

We looked at each other in silence. Did you ever have one of those moments when space and time step aside and leave you alone? This was one of those. I could just feel in my bones that I was locked eye to eye with my wife's murderer.

"You have no evidence," Patrick said in a soft voice. And with that, time resumed, like a giant spool of tape, spinning once again.

"I think I'm close to getting an eyewitness."

"You can leave now." Patrick's soul seemed to have recessed into the deepest parts of himself.

"Will you do me a favor?" I asked.

"No."

"Will you call the police on me?" I asked.

"I don't know why you want me to do that, but I won't," he said, all intonation gone from his voice.

All right, it was time for me to go, but goddamn it, I just

couldn't resist asking one more time, "Let's just say for the sake of argument that your worst dispute with Ernest Whitaker wasn't about your wife. Then what was it about?" But Patrick had completely shut himself down.

———

As I descended the stairwell to the basement, I heard the little pill bottle jangling in my pocket. When I was in his bathroom, I'd swiped Patrick Backus's Xanax. Next time we spoke, there'd be nothing to keep him from indulging in murderous rage.

CHAPTER 12
DR. LAURA OLANDER

I f the basement was any indication, intensified police patrols had begun building wide. I found myself hiding in the tenants' storage room, listening to a couple of cops pacing down the long hallway. I knew they'd search this area soon enough, so I tried to remember the padlock code to Robin's latticed unit so that I could tuck myself inside until they passed. I'd seen her open it. It was small number, medium number, large number . . . After ten or twelve wrong combinations, my fingers sweaty because I could hear the footsteps getting closer, I finally hit on three numbers that were close enough for the lock to pop open. I shimmied behind Robin's remaining plastic bin and piece of exercise equipment, right as two cops sauntered in. They turned on the lights, gave the storage room a cursory glance, and moved on.

My priority was getting Dr. Laura Olander to come by the Jax on her motorcycle just as she had the past three times there were incidents involving the police. I needed to talk to her. Since she was in the building when Ernest Whitaker was murdered, there was a serious chance that she'd witnessed something, if not everything. And of course the question still remained: Why did she keep coming back?

As I stood there in the darkness, I'll admit, I considered turning myself in and letting the police find Dr. Olander themselves. But that was no good. What if they weren't interested? What if they only wanted me? And I *had* assaulted that gym bro in the hardware store, so they could hold me on that. They could even book me on that. I could go to Rikers. And I'd seen that HBO show *The Night Of*. Even though that dude was innocent, his time in Rikers broke him. Isn't that what happened on that show? Remember John Turturro's feet? What was wrong with his feet? He was like picking dead skin off his gross, dying feet. That took up a *lot* of screen time. Was it a metaphor? Maybe for our decaying judicial system?

Back to the matter at hand. The trick would be to create enough of a ruckus to attract the police and thus, hopefully, Dr. Olander's attention. But I couldn't create so much of a ruckus that I'd be immediately caught and arrested.

I didn't hear any more footsteps in the hallway, so I crept out of Robin's locker and sprinted on tiptoes to one of the caverns off the main corridor. Alina had said that these were potential stockrooms for the vacant retail above, so I reasoned there must be a way to access the storefronts from down here. And sure enough, there was a stairway in the far corner. I headed up the shadowed steps and found myself in an empty store, sunlit by floor-to-ceiling windows. The front door had a vertical bolt lock that went into the floor. I could easily pull that open and exit the building. From there I could dart diagonally across the intersection and hide in the supermarket parking lot. That's where Dr. Olander's motorcycle had stopped last night. Now to create a ruckus . . .

There was a ladder leaning against the drywall to my right. I grabbed it, and like a medieval jouster, I rammed it as hard as I could at the back window overlooking the building's parking lot. I took three running goes at the glass. The first two hits made spiderweb cracks, but the third one shattered it completely. Holy Moses, it was raining glass! I ran to the front door, threw the bolt, and shot across the four-lane boulevard—cars honking and screeching, and one bumper hitting my thigh hard enough to knock me onto the grass strip at the far side of the street. Onlookers screamed. I crawled on my hands and knees and slid behind the gas pump. Okay, that might have been too much of a ruckus. It's really hard to create just the right amount of ruckus.

I peered around the pump across the street where police convened and pedestrians pointed toward my hiding place. I crawled behind some parked cars and darted across Calyer Street, where I hid behind a car parked in front of the KFC next to the supermarket.

I crawled flat under that car and watched police officers and patrol vehicles amass outside the Jax, praying Dr. Laura would get here soon. Had I really pinned my hopes on the theory that she constantly monitored police activity? I assumed she was doing that on some sort of . . . app?

"Hey!" shouted a grizzled, angry face leaning down to look under the car. "What the fuck are you doing? Get the fuck out of there!"

"Okay, no problem," I said, scooting out.

"What the fuck were you doing?"

Come on, Dr. Laura. Where's your motorcycle?

"Frankly," I whispered to this elderly, unshaven man, "hiding from the police."

The guy looked up across the intersection at the army of cops amassing. "He's here! The man you're looking for is here!"

"Thanks, dude."

I started to scurry away, but my leg hurt. Jesus, this was hopeless. I just didn't have the stamina to spend another day running from cops. I'd have to go to Riker's and rot, like John Turturro's feet. I turned and got a good look at the cavalcade of police organizing outside the Jax. I was ready to accept my fate. I was about to put my arms up, like Jesus on the cross, when—wait—there it was! A beautiful black motorcycle roaring down McGuinness Boulevard, a red helmet gleaming in the midmorning sun. Sweet Lord, it was Dr. Olander, like a vengeful Valkyrie from Valhalla! Her black steed bearing toward me with increasing acceleration. But—oh shit—she stopped at the red light on Calyer Street. Damn. The police cadre was now charging across the boulevard, hands hovering near their waists. Squad cars lit up their lights and squealed away from the Jax and over the median strip, pointing at me like snipers. A group of cops and dogs by the gas station was now running across Calyer Street toward me. But wait! The red light turned to green! The cycle roared over to the supermarket parking lot and stopped mere yards away, between me and the swarms of approaching police. I ran, seemingly toward the cops, who were now running toward me, guns drawn. Before Dr. Laura could figure out what she was in the middle of, I hopped on the back of the cycle. She turned her torso, about to elbow me off, but then, maybe recognizing me, hesitated.

I shouted, "Dr. Olander! Drive! Now!"

I gripped her leather midriff, and she peeled down McGuinness, all the greens in our favor, praise Allah, and we shot right across the Pulaski Bridge, goddamn the Newtown Creek below us, which I'd waded in just a few nights previous, and yeehaw, we tore down Vernon Boulevard with a dozen cop cars on our tail. Dr. Laura Olander leaned low over her handlebars and zigzagged between lanes of traffic, some of it oncoming, and then made a series of hairpin turns until we were lost in the wilds of Queens. The borough's nonsensically numbered streets jutted away from us at all angles—Forty-Fourth Avenue, Forty-Fourth Road, Forty-Fourth Lane. She continued to choose routes at random until we were just one among many, traveling casually under the elevated train on Queens Boulevard, no police cars anywhere in sight. Dr. Laura tossed her bright red helmet onto the sidewalk—smart— while keeping her bike at a steady pace, her long dark hair now blowing all around me. And before I knew it, we were crossing the George Washington Bridge, heading west into the deep greens of northern New Jersey.

———

After thirty or so minutes, we pulled into the driveway of a suburban ranch-style house with wide porches and deep eaves, draped in American flags and surrounded by rolling hills. I let go of Dr. Laura's midriff, my fingers red and stiff. Bowlegged and vibrating, I hobbled a few steps away from the bike, feeling sticky with sweat and encased in dead mosquitos. Dr. Laura dismounted and ran her fingers through her greasy black hair. She turned to me. Her cheekbones were wider and her body was slimmer, but her resemblance to Laura, to Laura Downing, was striking. It was too much to take in. I watched her familiar yet alien face pixilate, dissolve, and then re-form in front of me.

"So," Dr. Laura Olander said from across the bike. "I look like her, right? Like your dead wife."

"Yes. It's . . . it's . . ."

"Shocking?"

"Yeah."

"Like I am a demon from hell here to punish you for your sins," she said without a smile. "I joke." Strange sense of humor made stranger by her accent, which seemed part Slavic, part something I couldn't yet place. "That was risky back there," she said, still serious. "I am a veterinarian, not a stunt motorcycle driver."

She punched a code into the pad next to the garage, and the wide roll-up door rose in fits and starts. As she pushed her bike inside, she asked me without looking back, "Are you going to stand there?"

I moseyed in behind her like a man who'd dismounted a horse.

"My sister and her family are away at Disney World," she explained, her voice now echoing in the double garage, a small sedan parked to her right. "No one should look for us here. I live in Brooklyn too, but it felt wise to get farther away than McCarren Park." Before opening the door that led into the house, she looked me over and nodded with grudging respect. "You were clever to keep me coming back to that building by creating . . . disturbances. In truth, since Ernest passed away, I have been watching for police activity at the Jax. I use the Citizen app." Ha, it was an app. I knew it. "Are you familiar? The things one sees on that app, they're quite terrifying." She spoke in guttural, nasal tones that I associated with Russian villains. But she also had these Midwestern *o*'s like a character out of *Fargo*. This mash-up made her seem partly like a purveyor of harsh truths and partly like a baker of homemade pies.

I followed her into the warm, dark house, all shades drawn. It was the kind of home that feels deeply lived in, even when its inhabitants are absent. The walls were filled with children's art and family pictures. But unlike Patrick's apartment, these drawings were framed and hung at reasonable intervals. The creased wooden floorboards creaked as I followed Dr. Laura into the rustic-style kitchen. "Take whatever you want from the refrigerator," she said, turning toward me. Somehow every time Dr. Laura faced me, it felt like a confrontation. She unzipped her leather jacket and tossed it on the back of a kitchen chair, leaving her in a denim button-down, leather pants, and a few necklaces with pendants that hung low between her breasts. "I have not been in my sister's house for a while," she said, surveying the well-worn furniture and rugs that filled the adjacent living room. "It is full of happiness." This statement almost sounded positive, but then she continued with contempt, "The kind of happiness that makes you sleepy." She picked up a photo. "All my siblings are doctors. Our parents came to this country as doctors and raised us in the middle of this country to become doctors. I, however, am merely a veterinarian." She smiled wearily before she said what felt like a well-used line: "I always was the rebel." She turned away, opened the sliding door, and slipped out onto the back deck. Her body was now surrounded by the bright wilderness beyond. A rich mixture of cut grass and damp wood crept inside, the smells of childhood summers. I thought about my parents, still together, living on the beach in South Jersey. Had they tried to be in touch? I'd be sure to email them today.

I stepped out of the warm house and onto the hot porch where I allowed my body to bake in the sun. The heat on my face felt both affirming and oppressive. Dr. Laura turned to me once again. She was crying, freely, openly. There was a plea in the way she stared at me. I went to offer her comfort, but she raised an arm.

"I just need to do this," she said. "I feel so guilty." She wept. And I watched her weep.

After some moments, I said, "On the morning Ernest died, I saw you come into the Jax. And I never saw you leave. I assume you were there to visit Ernest."

"Correct," she said. "Ask me everything. Please. I want to unburden myself."

"Have you spoken to the police?" I asked.

"No," she said.

"Why not?"

Dr. Laura shook her head. "Ask me anything but that."

It was too hot to laugh, and I wasn't sure she was making a joke. So I got to the point. "Honestly, all I really want to know is if you saw who murdered Ernest that morning."

"I did not," she said. "But maybe I can be helpful in other ways. Let me get us some water. I am lightheaded."

I took a seat on a vinyl outdoor chair. I'd really hoped that Dr. Laura would tell me she'd seen a tightly wound, narrow, middle-aged man fleeing Ernest's apartment. But I took a deep breath, wiped the sweat from my face, and told myself to be patient. There were other aspects to be understood.

"Did you come to see Ernest often?" I called inside.

"Only on Saturday mornings," Laura called back as she opened the refrigerator door and pulled out the Brita filter. "He wanted me to come more. I mean, Ernest wanted me to live with him, marry him, have his little hipster babies."

"You didn't want that?"

"Not with him. He was a nice boy, but he had problems. Problems with pills." She poured the water. "Also, no career. I mean, with those dogs. But not even a doctor of dogs like me, which I admit isn't much. But he is—was—just a taker of rich people's money to teach them how to make the dog *shhh*." She chuckled. "No, I wanted—want—a man. Not a boy with pills and puppies. Believe me, I have enough puppies in my life." She came back outside, handed me a tall glass, and sat across from me. She took a small sip but grimaced, as if water were a necessary evil.

"I'd like to hear more about the pills. What sort of pills was he taking?"

"You keep getting directly into what I do not want to talk about."

"Then maybe start by walking me through what happened the morning of Ernest's death," I suggested. "You went up to his apartment."

"That's right," she said. "I knocked on his door, but he didn't answer. Which was strange because he looked forward to my visits."

"Did you text him or call him?" I asked.

"No," she said. "We didn't communicate like that."

"Why not?"

She hesitated. "Again, that is hard for me." She crossed her legs, leaned back in her chair, and found the sun with her face. "When he didn't answer the door, I thought maybe he'd left town for the weekend, so I went downstairs to the building's parking lot to see if his motorcycle was there. It was. And so I thought, well, he just went out to the deli or to check on a client, whatever.

I took the elevator up to the roof, sat there for a few minutes, and then went back down to Ernest's apartment. This time, however, the door was open." Dr. Laura abruptly stood up. "Come, there is a trail through the woods out back. This will be easier to talk about if I am in motion."

And so, soon we were pushing low-hanging branches gently out of our way, getting ourselves through the bramble behind Laura's sister's backyard and onto a manicured path that ran through the hilly neighborhood.

"Are the pills the reason you haven't talked to the police?" I asked.

Dr. Laura nodded. "That's right. I think you already understand my involvement in this." She was maintaining a brisk pace now that we were on the trail. "There's a lake up beyond the bend," Laura said.

The chirping birds filled our silence.

Yes, I did think I was beginning to understand Dr. Laura's place in this story, largely due to Laura Downing's comment, "There go our doggie downers." But also because of the pill Patrick Backus gave his pit bull this morning, the pill that came from Dr. Laura . . .

"So when I left the roof and went back to Ernest's apartment," Dr. Laura said, looking down at the path, "this time, his door was open a crack. That wasn't all that unusual. He had clients in and out, you know, with their dogs."

"Why didn't Ernest have a dog of his own?" I asked, just trying to keep her talking.

"He'd sometimes have rescues in his apartment that he'd train until they were ready to go live with someone else. So he couldn't have his own dog. But his family, in Pennsylvania, *they* have a beautiful farm, and there are lots of dogs there, dogs that he considered his own."

The trail continued downhill, away from the suburban development. The trees on either side loomed larger and closer.

"So you went inside Ernest's apartment," I prompted.

"I went inside and he was dead. Sprawled out in bed."

We approached a lake hidden from the outside world by concentric circles of pines.

Laura considered the modest body of water. It was bright white, a mirror reflecting the sun. "I like nature. But I never know what to do with it," she said.

"What happened after you saw Patrick lying there?"

Laura shrugged.

"Were you there when Alina and I came into the apartment?" I asked.

"I was in the closet. I heard you say that you were scared of the dead body but that you were also interested in the layout of his apartment. I almost laughed."

"I used to be funny," I said.

Laura nodded solemnly. "And then when you left, I went out to the balcony and stood on Ernest's outdoor table, grabbed onto some exterior holds, and climbed up to the roof." She shrugged. "I do some rock climbing. Convenient, yes. Difficult, no."

"Did you see anyone else coming into or going out of Ernest's apartment?"

"I saw no one," Dr. Laura answered.

"Did you know Patrick Backus?"

Laura laughed. "The asshole from downstairs?"

"Yeah."

Laura considered. "His dog is a patient. So yes. And yes, they were always fighting, Patrick and Ernest, over noise, over every-thing." She shrugged. "We saw the lake. It's a lake. Let's go."

During the walk back, I sifted through what Dr. Laura had told me. She didn't seem to mind the silence, and honestly, I was luxu-riating in it. Even the birds were quiet now. You never realize how much noise you're surrounded by in the city until you escape.

As we approached the house, I said, "It seems to me that I saw you come into the building around nine forty-five. And then I went to Ernest's apartment after ten thirty, and you said you were still there. Even if you went down to the garage and up to the roof, that seems like a long time."

"Right," she said.

"So how long were you in the apartment with Ernest, after he'd died and before Alina and I came in?"

"A long while. I didn't know what to do." Laura looked up at her sister's house. "Come, let's go back inside this house that isn't ours."

"Wait." I grabbed her arm. "I'm going to tell you what I think. I think you were cleaning up."

"No," Laura said. "Someone had already cleaned up the bedroom, which was very strange. Usually it was a huge mess."

"Then you were looking for something," I persisted.

"That's right," Laura said.

"And what you were looking for, that's why you couldn't go to the police."

"Just say it so I don't have to."

"You were looking for any evidence that you had ever been in Ernest's apartment. I think you were especially concerned that there might be prescription drugs lying around and so you hunted for bottles or pills."

"That's right." Dr. Laura sighed. "And I guess you've figured out why *I* specifically would be concerned about drugs being found in Ernest's apartment?"

"I think you'd been illegally supplying him with doggie downers. And they weren't just being used by the dogs. Ernest was taking them. And he was giving them to others."

Laura nodded. "Have the police figured this out?"

"I don't know," I said. "Last I heard they found a bunch of Xanax in his system."

"Xanax and acepromazine, what you are calling doggie downers, have similar chemical compositions. But acepromazine is dangerous to humans."

"But the high is . . . ?"

"Different. Better. It relaxes you and slows your breathing. Like a touch of death," Dr. Laura whispered. "Ernest liked to take them and some other people in the building did too . . ."

We let that hang in the glaring midday sun.

"How did you figure out people were taking the pills?" Dr. Laura asked.

"Yesterday one of my wife's friends told me that someone telephoned her after Ernest died. And apparently my wife's response was, 'Well, there goes our supply of doggie downers.' And our dog wasn't taking any pills. So I thought maybe they were circulating for human use."

"You are correct."

"It also explains why Ernest died so easily. Those beaded chains, they aren't strong, and they break all the time. So something was suppressing his breath already," I said. And the same went, of course, for my Laura, but I wasn't able to speak those words.

Dr. Laura steeled her face, refusing to let herself break down again. "I cannot cry all the time," she said. "It's exhausting. Let's go inside, please. I'm hungry."

Once back inside, Dr. Laura announced there was nothing to eat. She'd have to go to the market. When I suggested she was using food as avoidance, she said, "We have to eat."

———

After I heard the sedan back out of the garage and found the Wi-Fi information on the fridge, I opened the laptop Alina had loaned me, which was really very nice of her, wasn't it? The manuscript for her book opened up automatically, so I minimized it and wrote down some of my thoughts in the Notes app on her computer.

I couldn't entirely discount Dr. Laura Olander as a murder suspect. It was possible that she had accidentally killed Ernest in the midst of an asphyxiation sex act. Or maybe she even had some other reason for murdering him. But I had a hard time imagining her ending Laura Downing's life. After all, there was no reason to throw the police off her trail if they didn't suspect her. They hadn't even interviewed her.

There were still questions I wanted Dr. Laura to answer. Did she know my wife? Did she know Patrick's wife? But I had one important question that I didn't think Dr. Laura could answer. Who called Laura Downing the day of Ernest's death? With whom did she discuss the doggie downers? Surely by now Kurlansky would know who'd called my wife that day. Right? But I didn't dare get in touch directly with him. I mean, not only had I attacked a guy in a hardware store but also I'd now destroyed private property and led the police on a high-speed chase. Yikes. How the hell was I ever coming back from all of *that*? I shrugged off the reality of that situation and logged on to the Wi-Fi. First, I emailed Alina and put the question to her: "Do you think you could find out if the police know who called Laura the day Ernest Whitaker died?"

I got up and paced around the living room. Ernest Whitaker's memorial/death party was scheduled for the next night. How could I take advantage of that event? How could I use it to prove Patrick Backus's guilt if he was indeed guilty? I had his Xanax, so provoking him into a rage was a possibility. I also wanted to get back into his apartment. Maybe there was some sort of physical evidence. And then I thought it would be really great to have someone filming this basement memorial so that if anything incriminating happens, there will be a record. That's when I thought of my Pine Barrens job offer.

I went back to the laptop and emailed Zack, the director, and said I'd gladly take on the role he was offering me in his student film. In the meantime, would it be possible, *in lieu of any monetary renumeration,* for Zack to meet me at the Jax tomorrow evening? "As you know, things have been pretty dramatic there, and I think you'll be interested in some of the . . . theatrics. Just bring your phone to record." When Zack had last emailed me, I wasn't yet a wanted man. I wondered if that would make him more or less excited to work with me.

Glancing down through my dozen or so unread emails, I spotted one from Alex. He'd written to tell me that Laura's parents would be staying with him for the next couple of nights. He just wanted me to know.

Feeling warm, I got up again and fiddled with the AC controller on the wall. And then I sat down again. I maximized the draft of Alina's book so that everything would be the way I'd found it. As the document expanded back onto the screen, a name toward the bottom of the page caught my attention: Brent Dixon. "Brent Dixon strolled up to the front desk, plaid shirt tucked tightly into his khakis." Oh, no doubt that was based on my buddy Patrick Backus. I read on. In this passage, Brent Dixon was looking for a package that had gone missing. "He insisted on going behind the desk and into the back room. Even as Trina explained to him that there were rules against this, *he* explained to Trina that he had every right to locate his missing property. Brent didn't push Trina out of the way, but the anger emanating from him acted as a physical force moving her aside." Alina went on to write how Brent threw packages around the back room with increasing ferocity. And that she considered calling management but thought it better to let the situation burn itself out. As Brent stormed out of the mail room and into the lobby, he turned back to Trina. "Trina had the feeling that Brent wanted to apologize but just couldn't get himself in the proper place to say anything evenly. His pent-up rage was quite literally distorting his features. If that anger were ever fully unleashed, Trina certainly wouldn't want to be on the other side of it. This was a man capable of violence."

This passage hadn't made any sort of impression on me the

first time through. I honestly didn't even remember it. *But goddamn,* I thought, *it just seems more and more likely—*

At that moment, I heard Dr. Laura enter through the garage. I turned to see her striding toward the kitchen, swinging a couple of plastic grocery bags at her sides.

"I bought some white fish. I'll broil some vegetables."

"Is it even, like, a mealtime?" I asked as I closed the computer.

"Does it matter?" Dr. Laura tossed the bags onto the counter. She pulled out a cutting board and started efficiently chopping garlic and an onion. Keeping her back to me, she poured some olive oil into a frying pan and spoke. "I first met Ernest Whitaker a few years ago. He was recently back from a stint working with animals in the army, and he was starting his own business training dogs in the neighborhood. One day he brought in a dog he'd found on the street for me to evaluate, and, very quickly, I became the vet he recommended and he became the trainer I recommended. Then the pandemic. And business for him boomed. People, for the first time ever, were home all day with their dogs. And the people were anxious. And so the dogs were anxious. Behavior issues of course. Barking, chewing, urinating. Ernest would go into these apartments, mask on, and try to help. But sometimes, when training wasn't doing the trick, he would ask me for acepromazine."

"Doggie downers."

"To calm the dogs down. He asked more and more." Dr. Laura slid the onion and garlic off the cutting board and into the frying pan. Sizzle. "As we entered the later months of 2020 and into 2021, people were purchasing more and more puppies. Out of boredom? Whatever. My number one priority is that dogs aren't abandoned at shelters. So if Ernest was asking for more and more and more samples of acepromazine and if this was ensuring that puppies stayed in their new homes? Well, terrific." She took hold of the fish fillets with her fingers and placed them in the frying pan one at a time. "But still, it was a lot of pills! And I hadn't seen

Ernest in person for a couple of years. So I said, 'Ernest, I would like to come by your apartment, see how you are working with these dogs.' We sat in his apartment. We had a few drinks. He invited me up to the pool. And that night, after a swim, he confessed in that boyish way of his that he took the occasional acepromazine himself." And for the first time since she'd gotten back from the market, Dr. Laura looked at me. "I should have told him to fuck off. But the truth?" Dr. Laura smiled. Her smile made her so vulnerable that I understood why she deployed it so rarely. "Every once in a while? I took one too. And I told him that. I guess knowing he did the same lifted some of my shame." In her eyes, fondness shimmered, then sadness, then regret.

We ate at the large dining room table. The varnished tabletop was marred with ink and paint spots. Kids, I guessed. It was midafternoon. The sky had clouded over. I looked out the back window. I thought I could see a haze of mosquitoes.

"How many people in the building are taking—were taking—acepromazine?" I asked.

"I don't know," she said, putting a forkful of fish dutifully into her mouth. "I never went to the parties. I never got to know any of the tenants socially. I wouldn't even let Ernest call my cell phone or text me unless it was an animal emergency. I was worried about the amount of acepromazine he was taking. I was taking. I knew if we were found out, I'd be in trouble. See, while were indulging in sex and recreational drug use, another animal tranquilizer, a drug very similar to this one, was making its way onto the streets. It was being mixed with fentanyl. And it was killing people, especially, for some reason, in Philadelphia. So veterinarians were under some scrutiny by law enforcement, and that was making me paranoid."

"It sounds dangerous," I said.

"I think we were both depressed in those days." As we drank more white wine, Laura's accent slid farther from Minnesota and closer to Mother Russia. "But as life came back to New York City, as restrictions eased, I had more to do, more to see. Family. Friends. Career. Future. I don't know. Concerts? Whatever. But Ernest? This is the paradox of that boy. For all of his fun? He liked to be alone or just with me. Funny boy. So I told him I would only come to see him once a week now. He wanted more. I did not. Too depressing. Too much of a confused little rich boy. Started to turn me off." She shrugged. "Sometimes you're just done with a person. Is that cruel?"

"I don't know," I said.

She poured herself more wine. "I am worried if the police find any trace of me in Ernest's life, I will lose my license. I will go to jail."

I couldn't think of any reasonable way to rebut that statement.

After a moment, Laura continued. "I am not a very good person. And because I am, at root, not a very good person, I am prone to making mistakes when I am not careful." She emptied her third glass of wine in two long swallows. She wasn't far from drunk. "I think I am better off alone. Maybe I'll go to Mexico."

The sounds of chewing. The clinking of silverware.

"You said you'd met Patrick Backus," I said.

"When he would come up knocking on the door, telling us to be quiet. Our lovemaking was keeping him awake. That man had sharp hearing. Most of the time we were gasping for breath."

"Did you ever see Patrick get violent?" I asked.

Dr. Laura shook her head no. "But you never can tell what a person will do."

"And their pit bull goes to your practice?"

"But his wife takes the dog to me," Laura said. "Melanoma. The dog. Sad."

She poured me more white wine even though my glass wasn't even halfway empty. Then she poured the last little bit in her own glass and swallowed it.

"This is getting boring." She stood up, swayed into the kitchen, and grabbed the corkscrew. "I am clearly only interested in Ernest's death as it relates to my feelings of guilt." She pried open a second bottle, all the while bitterly laughing at herself.

"I'm almost done with my questions." I drank the rest of my wine as quickly as I could, mostly to appear companionable. I brought my empty glass into the kitchen, and she refilled it. "Did my wife take the dog medicine?"

"I don't know. I only know one thing about your wife."

"Tell me, please." We both stood at the counter and drank our wine quickly, as if it were a race.

"After I told Ernest that I didn't love him and that I would only come once a week to have sex with him and sexually strangle him as a kindness . . ." Dr. Laura laughed. "I am getting drunk and I don't care! Where do we have to go today?"

"Nowhere." I drank more too.

"After I told Ernest I was on my way out of his life, he started following your wife around. He pointed her out to me one day. 'Doesn't she look just like you?' he asked. He told me he would strike up conversations with her when she was alone and pretend he was talking to me. I mean, how ridiculous! What a stupid little boy!"

"You're saying Ernest propositioned my wife?" I asked. I was feeling suddenly uneasy, a premonition that reality was about to shift again.

"Yes! Because she looked like me!" She poured us both more wine, most of it splattering down on the floor tiles at our feet.

"Do you know what my wife said? When he tried to flirt with her or proposition her, what did she say?" I was intaking wine as quickly as possible in anticipation of the blow I somehow knew Dr. Laura was about to unwittingly strike.

"You'll be happy to know that she turned him down flat." Laura shook her head. "Poor bastard. He told me exactly what she said to him. She said, 'You seem like a nice boy, but I detest it when married people flirt. But not as much as I detest it when they cheat. All of that behavior, it's weak.' That's what she said to him. Face it, Paul, you had a loyal wife."

It had suddenly gotten very dark outside. I focused on the light reflecting from the spilled wine at my feet.

"Does it bother you so much, that your wife did not want to cheat on you?" I heard Dr. Laura's voice say somewhere in the distance.

I was struggling with an overwhelming sense of vertigo. I felt myself toppling into a sea of guilt . . .

"Those pills?" I asked, my voice very far away.

"The acepromazine?"

"Do you have them?" I asked.

"You'd like to try?"

"I would."

A silence that felt like an eternity.

"This is the last time," Dr. Laura said.

I followed her to the garage. She opened the back hatch of her bike, took out a black leather bag, and gently laid it on the workbench. She unzipped it, opened both sides flat. It was full of bottles, vials, and needles. She pulled out a plastic bottle and shook loose two circular white pills. I held my hand out, and she dropped one into my palm. It was chalky, crushable, fragile. "It also comes in an injectable form. But I don't recommend it."

I followed her into the kitchen. She downed a pill with a gulp of wine. I took her glass and did the same. I had no idea what I'd done with my drink. I followed her into the bedroom. She had no problem taking her clothes off and lying naked amid the embroidered pillows on her sister's king-size bed.

"Are we having sex?" I asked.

"Unless you want to watch TV." She stretched out, pushing the pillows onto the floor in the process. I've always found other people's nakedness overwhelming. There's just so much skin. Despite the similarity of their faces, Dr. Laura's body looked nothing like my Laura's. Dr. Laura was tight and narrow whereas

Laura Downing had been generous and curvy. I thought for sure that if *this* was what Ernest Whitaker was looking for, my Laura would have let him down.

I started to take my clothes off. Should I bend down to pull my pants off my feet or lift one foot up at a time? Is there a non-awkward way to take off pants? Side snaps, I guess? I hadn't been naked in front of a woman other than my wife in a very long time, and I remembered how self-conscious I used to be, when I was single, about the size of my penis in comparison to the bulk of my torso. I always thought my penis would have looked better on a smaller man. Maybe after I die, I'll donate it for penal replacements, "best used on slim frames." But I didn't share any of this with Laura as I got into bed with her. It didn't seem like we were in that kind of play. And besides, forcing enough breath out of my lungs to create words was beginning to feel daunting.

As soon as I lay down, lightheadedness rushed over me. I felt like someone was sitting on my chest, but no, that's not quite right. I felt like everything inside of me had shrunk. As if I had little-boy organs that were no longer powerful enough to operate my man-size flesh. I tried to enjoy this feeling, but I couldn't settle into it. And then the dizziness overtook me, and I started to gasp, so I grabbed Dr. Laura's shoulders and blindly got on top of her. I just needed to hold on to something—something to keep me in this world. She looked up at me and smiled a smile that had nothing to do with me as an individual. She put me inside of her with only a touch of logistical difficulty—I'm sure I wasn't help-ing. I eased down and buried myself in her neck. She squirmed under me to create friction. Driven by something instinctual, I started to slowly partake in the act, moving my heft forward and backward. Soon this movement became one with my constant struggle for breath.

Then suddenly, out of nowhere, I wheezed a laugh.

"Why are you laughing? You're not supposed to be laughing."

"I think I'm laughing because I don't want to die. This is ridiculous; this is indulgent."

Dr. Laura rolled me over, got on top of me, and put me inside her again. Her face was suddenly angry. "You want to live, do you? Then we're not doing this right." She put her hands on my throat. "This is meant to be an act of defiance. An act of death." She pressed her hands harder on my Adam's apple until I was certain I was bruising. But then I realized I was also coming. The orgasm was weak, but it hit strange high notes inside of me, high notes that vibrated in my body for what felt like a very long time. And just as I was starting to feel guilty that she certainly hadn't come, I blacked out.

When my eyes opened, the bedroom was dark. It felt luxurious to breathe, in and out, in and out. How much time had passed? I rolled over, and there was a woman lying on her side, facing away from me, with long dark hair. Her naked form an incandescent blue.

"Why didn't you just tell me you weren't cheating on me?" I asked whichever Laura was lying next to me.

She answered, "How could you think that I was?"

And I closed my eyes and went back to that night Laura had told me she didn't want to have children. It was one of those nights with many parts. A night that rolls from event to event, from phase to phase, one of those nights you inexplicably have energy and space to spare. One of those nights when the city is happy to infect you with some of its giddiness. We'd been to Alex's group show, and we'd been to the after party, but now I was remembering being in bed with her that night, facing her. I hadn't really digested the fact that our ideas of the future had so significantly diverged. I was running my hand over her hair, my hand getting heavier with each stroke as I dipped in and out of sleep like a ship lifted and lulled by rolling swells, and Laura said to me . . . (had she said this to me, yes she had). She said to me . . .

"Paul. If you need to leave me, leave me. But please know I love you."

I murmured, feeling safe and warm, "Love you too . . ."

"Did you see what Alex was up to tonight?" Laura asked.

"Mmmm."

"He was with some guy I'd never seen before. I understand that his boyfriend was out of town. I understand that this was a big night for him. But . . . Paul?"

"Yeah?"

"I don't think he should have been kissing that other guy. I just think that cheating is cowardly. Do you understand?"

"I agree."

"Misery in a way is noble. Leaving is brave. But flirting and cheating are appalling. Appalling in their weakness. I will never cheat."

And I drifted off to sleep.

When my eyes opened again, Laura was on her back, facing the ceiling now. Her profile in charcoal gray.

Without looking at me, I heard her say, "Why didn't you listen to me?"

"We say so many things to each other. How can we know what's important?"

"You didn't have the guts to leave me and so you made up all sorts of stories to turn me into the bad guy. Only to justify your own wandering eye."

I didn't have an answer to that. So I just laid there and listened.

"But it doesn't matter," Laura said. "You have made too many mistakes. You have made too many assumptions. And now I'm dead. And you're going to die too."

CHAPTER 13
LET'S WRAP UP SOME LOOSE ENDS

There are few things more pleasant in middle age than waking up late in an unfamiliar bedroom. Here is a place that is entirely new. A place that has no associations with the burdensome past. Here is a place uncontaminated by . . . you. That is, until you see your dead wife's doppelgänger sauntering out of the shower in a towel, her face pale and creased. Oh, and then you swallow and it hurts, and you're reminded that your dead wife's doppelgänger choked the shit out of you last night. Yeah, those things tend to bring you back down to the life that is uniquely, inescapably . . . yours.

I took my turn in the floral-patterned bathroom and examined my bristled, puffy face. The yellow bruise on my cheek where Robin slapped me. The darker bruise on my neck where Dr. Laura choked me. Not to mention the ache in my thigh where that car hit me. And man, my rear still hurt from falling onto that balcony railing. I put on yesterday's clothes over my swollen, discolored body as Bob Dylan whispered in my ear, "It's not dark yet, but it's gettin' there . . ."

Out in the kitchen, Dr. Laura was pouring a cup of coffee, her hair tied messily back, a New Jersey Strong T-shirt hanging from her shoulders and athletic shorts showing off her shiny legs.

She handed me a cup of coffee and perched on the counter. "So what do you do now?"

"I go to a party. And hope that something is revealed."

"Not a great plan."

"Nope."

"You really think this downstairs neighbor did it?"

"Either him or you."

Dr. Laura smiled. "Why would I have killed a man I liked?"

"It would have been an accident. You went up to asphyxiate him for leisure and you did it a little too hard."

"And how does that explain your wife?" she asked.

"The only way I can ever explain it. To frame me."

Dr. Laura thought for a moment. "I don't know. I think if I'd killed Ernest, I would have just run away."

"And yet," I said, "you keep returning."

"Exactly." She buttered some toast. Handed me a piece.

I took a bite, but swallowing felt like sharp fingernails dragging down the inside of my throat. I dipped the next piece in the coffee to soften it. "I could have this whole thing wrong," I admitted to Dr. Laura. "Could be I'm missing a piece."

"Sometimes I think we're all missing a piece."

Dr. Laura disappeared into the bedroom, and I sat down at Alina's laptop.

A new email from Alina: "Hey. I'll be at Merit's Manhattan office for the first half of the day. Then I have a meeting with your agency at three. Then I plan to go to the memorial/party tonight. I hope you're okay, wherever you are." New paragraph. "I had lunch with Bonnie Besser yesterday, the former community manager. She confirmed that Patrick Backus was indeed the tenant who Ernest Whitaker was in conflict with. And she claims that her bosses told her not to intervene. She also told me that both Patrick and Ernest received lease renewal notices in their mailboxes on

Friday. Ernest's rent was raised only 5 percent but Patrick's rent was raised 36 percent. When I asked her to explain the discrepancy, she said that officially Patrick was paying well below what the market would bear, but she admitted that the building was looking to maintain a young, hip reputation, and Patrick and his family didn't fit that profile." *Ah,* I thought, *could this be the source of Patrick and Ernest's very worst dispute?* Could Patrick have become aware of the financial disparity in their renewal notices? They *had* received them the day before Ernest's death . . .

Suddenly I remembered what Kurlansky had said when he'd had me cornered in the Library. He'd said the building murdered Ernest Whitaker. Holy shit, had he, in a roundabout way, been right?

Alina's email continued, new paragraph. "Oh, and I did text Kurlansky about Laura's phone records. He hasn't answered."

And there was also a new email from Zack. He'd be "stoked" to meet me at the Jax and record the proceedings. "Just tell me what time."

Then Dr. Laura came up behind me and put her hand on my shoulder. I jumped a little—who can blame me? This woman might garrote me in her sister's kitchen just for fun. She was back in her leather pants and leather jacket. "Time to go. Where to?"

I considered for a moment. I was pretty certain that no matter what transpired today, I was going to end up arrested tonight. So I thought I'd do my best to tie up all loose ends. "Drop me off in the Financial District."

———

I stood, arms akimbo, looking up at 74 Broad Street. The small *Fearless Girl* statue stood in the same position a few blocks north looking up at the New York Stock Exchange. To the south, across a couple of cobblestone streets, the four-story, brick-laden Fraunces

Tavern hunkered. That's the bar where George Washington had his first beer or got his first blow job or something.

I strode through the office building's gold-trimmed doorway and beneath its lobby's tall frescoed ceilings. The faded angels above me laughed with rounded mouths, mocking my muddle-headed thinking.

Usually at this point in a mystery, the detective (I wouldn't presume to call myself a detective, of course, but if you insist) confronts a systemic force he knows he can't actually overcome. But because he holds fast to some sort of ideal, he must rail against this head of industry, even though he knows in the end he will most likely come to bodily harm. Simply put, I'd decided it was time to yell at an authority figure. Besides, I had a few hours to kill before the party. Aaaaand I had one more secret motivation . . . the aforementioned tying up of loose ends. Today was the day to settle all scores, to repay all debts. For all I knew, it might be my last day as a free man.

I marched into the nearest elevator and pressed the top-floor button, but it wouldn't stay lit. The security guard appeared in front of me, yet one more person with arms akimbo. "Honey, you can't go up there unless you've got a key card." Leading me back to the security desk, she agreed to call up to Merit Management. "Alina Serrano, you have a Paul . . . I'm sorry, what's your last name, hon?" But before I could answer, she waved her hand and said into the phone, "Oh, all right." And then to me, "She knows who you are. She'll be right down."

In less than a minute, Alina clip-clopped out of the farthest elevator, staring at me with wide eyes. Here Alina and I were, in another building at another front desk. It's disappointing, but the world contains endless variations on very few themes. She grabbed my hand, big smile to the security guard, and then pulled me to the side.

"What are you doing here?" she whispered urgently.

"I just feel like this is the part of the story where I storm a citadel of power," I said.

She released my hand and took a step back. "Well, you look less crazy than you have in a while," she considered. "Though I liked you better with the beard. Where did your chin go? And why does your neck look like you were strangled?"

"You really don't want to know."

"Explain to me the point of you being here?" Alina asked, scampering behind me as I headed to the elevator.

"To hold power to account. Plus a secret mission of my own."

"You'll get arrested," she said, swiping her card and pushing the button to the top floor.

"I don't plan to get arrested until tonight. And before then I want to set some things straight." I even went so far as to wink at her.

"I feel like I want to say something clever," Alina said. "But the exhaustion of the past few days has robbed me of my mastery of language. So I'll settle for *oh boy*."

The elevator was slow and we were still going up, both doing that thing where you shift your weight from foot to foot, so I asked her, "Are you looking forward to your meeting with the agency today?"

Alina smiled an unguarded, childlike smile, a gift to whomever beheld it. "I am." And the elevator doors opened.

Alina lingered uncertainly at the plate-glass entrance to Merit Management as I blew past the receptionist and charged straight toward a corner office. Any corner office would do, but happily I stumbled upon the director of residential properties' stronghold. I flung open the door, which revealed a trim bald man with his back to me. He was staring out a window that in turn revealed a baby-blue sky. He rotated his torso slowly. Tight body, shiny head, slack jaw. A muscled chest beneath a shiny shirt tucked so seamlessly into suit pants, it eschewed the very idea of a belt. At that moment, I hoped to live long enough to experience life as a fit man. Utterly unconcerned, he said, "Yes?"

"You run this place?" I asked.

"I'm the director of residential properties."

"What's your name?"

"Stacey Wren." A dude tough enough it didn't matter he had a woman's name. A real "Boy Named Sue" situation. He was looking me over, taking his damn time. "I know who you are," Stacey Wren said.

"Do you feel any responsibility for what happened to Ernest Whitaker and my wife?" I demanded. Oh, I was in the eye of the hurricane now, and it was as still and quiet as they say.

"Why should I?" Stacey Wren eased himself down onto the leather couch that ran perpendicular to his desk. "Aren't you the one who killed them?"

I wanted to mimic his calmness, but it was beyond me. I sputtered petulantly, "N-n-no!"

"Don't worry, Paul. I'm not calling the police." He gestured to the leather chair on his right. "Sit."

"No, thank you! Sitting tends to make me lethargic!"

"I'm curious to know why you hold *me* responsible," Stacey Wren said evenly. He leaned back into the couch, but his eyes tightened as he continued to examine me. What was he looking for? I saw him clock my bruised cheek, my discolored neck, my large hands. I in turn looked at *his* large hands. Long fingers, big knuckles. They were draped over the knee of his crossed leg. I glanced back up at his eyes, which met mine. His were dull and gray, like headlights turned off at night. Was *this* man a murderer? Not that he'd murdered anyone I knew, but there were a lot of dead people in the world. I thought, *Maybe this man is a murderer looking for another murderer. Maybe Director of Residential Properties Stacey Wren wanders through life alone, looking for someone like himself, just so he doesn't feel so alone.* But I was not this dude's psychic twin, and he clearly agreed because he said, with some disappointment, "You're not a killer."

I know it was irrational, but he scared me. Like he was talking to me from another plane of existence. I couldn't control my voice; it was shaking. "Why . . . why did you not answer residents' complaints?"

"Excuse me?"

"And then . . . and then . . . and then why raise the rent so much?"

"The rents are what the market will bear." He wasn't patronizing me; he was just answering my question. "I don't run the whole show here, but it is my primary vocation to oversee the team that keeps rents high and vacancies low. For all of our buildings."

"But . . . but . . . to not answer complaints and then raise the rents different percentages, don't you see how that's . . . combustible?" I really should have gotten my thoughts together before I came in here.

"I see what you're getting at," Stacey Wren said with a smile that communicated, *Don't worry, I'll do the thinking for both of us.* "You think I'm responsible for Ernest Whitaker's death because we didn't intervene in this ongoing feud with his downstairs neighbor? And that's who you think killed Ernest Whitaker? The police were here today, again, asking about this Patrick Backus."

"That is what I think. I think you wanted Patrick Backus out, so you didn't address his complaints."

"We're not the tenants' mommies and daddies." Stacey Wren sighed.

"But to raise his rent thirty-six percent!" I shouted.

"Is that how much we raised it?"

"You raised it that high because he didn't fit your building's ideal profile!"

Stacey laughed. "Profile?"

"He's a family man and you wanted sexy singles!"

"That's a story you made up." But clearly I'd amused Mr. Wren. "Maybe you've noticed the retail spaces at the bottom of the building are still empty? Maybe you've noticed there's a pool on your roof? The building needs money. End of story."

"Do you deny you wanted Patrick Backus out?" I asked.

Stacey smiled wide. "Or to pay more money." He was having fun. "Did you storm into my office to defend the man you think murdered your wife?"

"No. I've come in here to attack a system that pushed a man to the edge!" Honestly, between you and me, I was losing faith in my argument.

"You know, in the old days," Stacey Wren said as he luxuriously cracked his knuckles, "when I handled management for low-income buildings? If a loudmouth like you came in? Know what I would do? I'd take him out back and beat the shit out of him." This wasn't a threat; it was a fond reminiscence. Stacey Wren rose and stretched. "Wait until you see how much we're going to raise *your* rent."

"I can pay it! Now that my wife has died, apparently I'm a millionaire!"

"Oh good. Then it's a win-win." Stacey shrugged. "You get money. We get rent. I knew you and I could find commonality."

He put his hand on my shoulder. To my great shame, I let him. I like when people like me. It's a flaw.

"I can tell you didn't kill anyone," Stacey Wren said. "So let me give you some advice," he continued, like we were country club pals. "I live in Westchester. Do you know why I live in Westchester?"

"I don't."

"Because I am an adult and I make adult decisions. And I would never choose to pay the rents you and your neighbors do. Why would I? To feel young? To be near a few bars? To not have to face down the dark void of suburban living?" Stacey Wren seemed to consider all of these reasons. "So as much as I would like to charge you seven thousand dollars a month next year, my advice is that maybe it's time for you to move to the suburbs and be an adult too. Look into the void. You might like it."

"Why would you give me advice that goes against your financial interests?"

"Oh, because if you move out, someone else will pay that rent in a second. Idiots—there's no shortage of them." He was enjoying how quickly he'd made me an ally, and he was now leading me out of his office with his arm still around me, parading me down the hallway.

"Look," I persisted for the sake of persisting. "It just seems if you'd treated your tenants humanely, if you'd answered their complaints, if you hadn't jacked their rents—"

"Paul, our friends and family members must treat us humanely, not our landlords." As he said those words, over his shoulder, I spotted Alina, who was sitting nervously at her laptop in the glass-walled conference room. Meanwhile, Stacey Wren was mumbling something about *Oh, you poor privileged people who don't even realize how rich you are.* But my mind had moved on.

I turned back to Stacey, forcing my voice into a low, steely tone. "Do me one favor, Stacey Wren. See Alina Serrano in there?"

Stacey nodded.

"Fire her," I said.

"Why?"

"So she can escape this capitalistic hellhole and write her books."

"Do I have cause to fire her? I don't want a lawsuit," he said plainly.

"Well, she's the one who let me into Ernest Whitaker's apartment," I said.

"We've already decided to overlook that," he reminded me.

"*And* she just now let me into your offices, which seems to be a serious lapse in judgment."

Stacey Wren smiled. "If I do this for you? Will it make you feel like you gained something by coming here?"

"Yes, sir," I said. Fuck. Why did I call him sir?

Stacey looked from me to Alina and back to me. "It's a shame. She's cute." Stacey Wren ambled past me into the conference room. Instantly harnessing a surprising amount of fury, he shouted, "Hey, you! Serrano! How dare you let this psychopath into our offices! You put all of our safety at risk! You fucking idiot! Now get the fuck out of here and don't ever show your fucking face again!" Stacey turned, strolled toward me, winked, and, for good measure, slammed his office door behind him.

I looked back through the glass at Alina. She was crying. Stacey may have overdone it.

—————

"No, I'm appreciative, I guess?" Alina said, wiping tears from her eyes as we hustled past the statue of the bull, up Broadway, the ocean wind at our backs. "I just, you know, I'm a people pleaser, and when someone isn't pleased, I cry." She wiped more tears away. "I mean, that is what I wanted, to get fired. I didn't really want to get yelled at, but . . . thank you? I don't know."

"I'm sorry if I fucked up," I said, keeping pace at her side.

"You didn't."

"But now you can go into this meeting a new person."

She smiled at me. "Oh, that's a nice thought."

We hustled uptown, passing Trinity Church and the grave of Alexander Hamilton and other musical theater characters.

"What am I supposed to be like in this meeting with the literary agent?" Alina asked me. "Confident? Humble? Demanding? Acquiescent?"

"The great thing about art, whether it be writing or acting— the thing speaks for itself. *You* don't have to *be* anything."

"That's helpful."

"You know, when you're in your forties," I told her after some thought, "even if you're a fucking idiot, like me, you still know a few things. You can't help it."

I smiled at my friend. And she smiled back.

One World Trade Center rose to our left as we descended into the Fulton Plaza subway station. The moment we got down to the platform, the mighty A train roared into the station, perfectly timed, and we boarded without breaking our stride.

As we sat on the blessedly cold train, I thought to myself, *Stacey Wren had been right in a sense.* It's not capitalism's job to make us happy. That's the job of friendship. And love, I guess. I hadn't done a great job with love. Maybe before whatever fate awaited me this evening, I could prove to do a better job with friendship.

I looked over at my seatmate.

Me: "Can I tell you something?"

Alina: "Yes."

Me: "It's nice to see you again. I want to pat you on the head. Can I pat you on the head?"

Alina: "Sure?"

Me: "I feel fondly for you. For all of your help. And none of this is in a sexual way. I just want to tell you all of this today in case I get sent to Rikers and come back unrecognizable. Maybe with some awful foot fungus."

Alina looked at me and smiled sadly. I felt like this friendship thing was going okay. No doubt, we were in different places in our lives. She had things to look forward to. I was just trying to avert catastrophe. Some of that had to do with our specific circumstances. Most of it had to do with age.

Me: "Can I tell you something else?"

Alina: "Yes."

I rested my head on the car wall. I felt the metallic frame of the subway map on the back of my head—oh shit, was I getting a bald spot? That's all I needed on top of everything else.

Me: "I had sex last night, and it put me off sex for good. I think from here on in, I'm only going to have sex for purposes of procreation. Maybe children will give my life some . . ."

Alina: "Ballast?"

Me: "Yeah. Not that having kids seems to have helped Patrick Backus much."

Alina: "Can I tell *you* something?"

Me: "Yeah."

Alina: "I'm really hoping to feel like myself again. Like the self I always imagined I could be."

Me: "I'm hoping for that for you."

———

I stood outside the colossal Eighth Avenue building that housed our now mutual agency. Alina was inside meeting with a woman in literary. I could, hypothetically, go see my guy, talk over the contract for the Pine Barrens movie. But it felt unnecessary. I could handle any paperwork on this small independent movie, if I managed to avoid jail. And if I managed to avoid the debilitating grief that I could sense waiting for me around every corner. I had to get angrier. Angrier at the person who actually committed these murders. Patrick Backus. There was no way the police weren't going to arrest me for something next time they found me, so I had very little time to provoke Patrick into giving himself away. Maybe I could talk to his wife, Shaina. Maybe she would confess to knowing something. God, if Patrick saw me talking to his wife, or maybe even accusing her of murder, that would provoke him for sure. A plan was forming . . .

I pulled out the blue cap from my backpack and wore it low over my face. I watched the swarms of passersby. I watched them the way some people watch the ocean. There was raw truth in that constant onslaught of sweaty human existence. But I could not put into words the nature of that truth, let alone figure out how it could be of service to me.

Sometime later, Alina skittered out through the revolving door, so excited she almost went around twice. She grabbed my arm and hugged me. "When their assistant asks if you want something to drink, should you say yes or no? I said no, but I felt like everyone was disappointed, so then I said yes and asked for water because I *was* thirsty. But then I drank it too fast and coughed, and dribbled, and I didn't know what to do with the empty glass, so I just awkwardly held it while we had our conversation. Which was *great*. She loves the book and gets the book. She has a couple of things she wants me to look at, *minor*, and then she's going to send it around. Can you *believe that*?"

I hugged her properly. I hugged her in a way that gave weight to the moment. (Hugging is like sex for friends, don't you think?) And then I recommended we take the E to the G back to Greenpoint.

"Now our focus is on you," Alina said as we waited for the train in a station so hot you could pop popcorn, not that Alina noticed. Her endorphins kept her talking fast and optimistic. "So what's the plan?"

"Provocation," I said with a solemn nod.

The subway doors opened, and we held on to a disconcertingly damp pole amid a bunch of boisterous high school kids who probably just got out of school for the day. Or the week. I think it was a Friday.

"Provocation shouldn't be much of a problem," I continued. "I've already taken Patrick Backus's antianxiety medication away from him."

"A morally ambiguous act," Alina considered.

"Admittedly."

"I should be the one to provoke him," Alina said.

"Absolutely not."

"I should at least *help* provoke him," Alina insisted. "Like most middle-aged men, he resents beautiful women. And I'm at least cute."

"You're very cute," I said. "And I don't resent you at all. If I had a son, I'd want him to marry you."

"Is your son like a baby in this scenario?"

"Yes, I want you to marry my imaginary baby son."

She laughed, even though it wasn't funny. Maybe that *was* our thing. And as we got out of the E train and traversed the brightly lit corridor to the G, I realized it was now, somehow, understood that she would assist in baiting the bear.

On the G, we worked out the details as the train slid through the next couple of stations. I asked her to use my email account to get in touch with Zack and set a time to meet him at the Jax. I told her he'd agreed to document what he could on his phone so that we would have a record of anything important that transpired. A lot of our plans hinged on Robin's willingness to help. I wondered how enthusiastic she would be about assisting us, rather than us assisting her, but Alina seemed to think that as much as Robin wanted a successful memorial/rager, she also wanted to see Ernest's killer brought to justice.

When we rose from the subway into the sunshine, I gave Alina back her laptop, and we went our separate ways. Alina was going home for a couple of hours, and I was going to Alex's apartment. I was hoping that Laura's parents were still there. Loose ends. I continued down Metropolitan Avenue, and Alina hopped on a bus. I thought about telling her that I'd had a dream (premonition) last night that I would die. But that seemed like a downer.

———

To my surprise, Laura's mom opened the door to Alex's ground-floor apartment. White hair pulled tightly back. Wearing high-waisted jeans and a paisley button-down. Ever the stylish academic. She told me that Alex was downstairs painting. He'd been down there for hours. Behind her, I saw Theo waking up from a nap, his head looking squished, probably from having smooshed it against a pillow while he slept. He looked up uncertainly, stretched out his back, and padded sweetly toward the door. I anticipated how warm and comforting his body would be even before I held it.

For a moment Alice Downing and I avoided the fact that a wanted man had just walked into the apartment. She told me that Alex had been a wonderful host, giving Joshua and her the master bedroom, such as it was, while he took the spare room. She felt that being in an unfamiliar place had helped her; none of this felt connected to her normal, real life. She poured me a cup of coffee while I cradled Theo, heavy in my arms, and she walked me through what they'd learned over the last twenty-four hours. Tox results had come back. Strangulation was the cause of death, and there were a lot of antidepressants in her system with a certain anomaly that no one was able or perhaps willing to explain. Then I watched as a wave of grief overtook her and dragged her under. At that moment, Joshua padded in, unshaven in a wrinkled T-shirt and flannel pants. He hugged me, held on to me for dear life, as the undertow of grief subsumed him as well.

Joshua told me that he didn't understand how I'd gotten involved in any of this. He understood that they often had to look at the husband, but he insisted he'd never thought I would have had anything to do with it. The whole thing was obviously absurd. Alice nodded in agreement, and I wondered how I'd ever let myself get carried along in that narrative. They'd also become aware of this neighbor as a suspect. The police had asked them if they'd heard of Patrick Backus. And they wondered why the police hadn't arrested this man.

"I just don't think they have evidence," I said. "But I'm going to fix that."

I went downstairs. In an unlit corner, Alex was painting. Mercifully, it wasn't a portrait of Laura. It was one of his fuzzy, abstract watercolors, though the dim light made it hard to make out much.

"Hello, Paul."

"Thanks for taking care of Laura's parents."

"I'm glad I can do something," Alex said. "And I hope you don't mind that I'm painting while I'm talking."

"No," I said. "I understand."

"Having them here," Alex said, "witnessing their grief? It's like giving shelter to a collapsing supernova. It threatens to consume all of time and space."

"Look," I said. "I really just have one question, if you don't mind."

"Sure."

"When Laura got that phone call the day Ernest Whitaker died. The call about the doggie downers?"

"Yeah," Alex said.

"Did you get the sense that she knew the person?"

"I did," Alex said.

"And did you get a sense as to whether she was talking to a man or a woman?"

Alex held his paintbrush in midair. "I'm sure it was a woman. Just by the way they were chatting."

"Did Laura ever mention a Patrick Backus or a Shaina Backus?"

Alex shook his head.

"I'm working on a theory. I think Laura was leaving me that day. I think that I'd pissed her off with being inconsiderate. And I think whoever called Laura was luring her back to the apartment with the promise of some acepromazine—doggie downers."

"I didn't know she was taking anything," Alex said. "But I should have."

"It's the problem with being a single human being," I said. "You can never see the whole picture." We stood in the darkness.

"I'm really trying to not fill in what I don't know with assumptions."

"That's the smartest thing I've ever heard you say," said Alex, moving his brush against the shadowed canvas but to what effect it was almost impossible to tell.

I hugged Laura's parents. I kissed the dog on the mouth. And before I knew it, I was standing by the curb, alone, waiting for my ride.

Soon Robin's silver BMW screeched to a halt in front of me. She opened the driver's-side door and convinced her body to extract itself. In a trim purple blazer, she strolled to the rear of the car, looked at me, and shook her head in disappointment.

"You liked me better with the beard?" I asked.

"I have a party to host." Robin sighed.

"I thought it was a memorial."

"Can't it be both?" Never was a human being so exasperated by my presence. "I don't need whatever this is, whatever you are." She pulled open the trunk. "Get in."

I turned back to Alex's apartment. From the window, Laura's parents watched me step into the tiny trunk.

"You two idiots couldn't have picked a worse night," Robin continued as I folded myself into the fetal position. "I'm giving a eulogy. And I'm very nervous."

"Don't you want to catch Ernest's killer?"

"What does catching his killer have to do with the man he was?" Robin asked. It was only after she slammed the trunk above my head that I remembered she was a terrible driver.

CHAPTER 14
BOARD GAMES

just wasn't feeling vigilante vibes. Maybe I needed a cup of coffee? Or maybe I was starting to doubt this whole enterprise. I mean, how could I be certain Patrick Backus was the murderer? He was like my first actual suspect! Was I really that lucky? Probably not. It really did seem like he was the guilty party, though, didn't it? The feuding, the violence, the unfair raise in his rent. Not to mention the possibility that he knew his wife was attending Ernest's parties. But sweet God, I'd made so many mistakes in my life, how could I trust myself now? And yet . . . and yet . . . I did feel wise—well, wiser than I'd been a week before. That was for sure. Me from a week before seemed like a stupid baby (and as *The Simpsons* taught us, "Stupid babies need the *most* attention."). But who's to say next-week-me won't think this-week-me was stupid? See what I mean? But I also knew that this could just be an issue of follow-through. I've always had trouble muscling through to completion. At some point in every single task I've ever undertaken, I've simply wanted to quit—and often I did quit! I'd just say to myself, *Well, that's enough of that.* The truth? I love quitting things. I'm a great quitter! The relief of all that stress evaporating. The empty time opening up in front of you.

Lucky for me, I wasn't alone with my thoughts. I was speaking them out loud, expounding at length, to the stoic face of Detective Kurlansky. We were huddled together inside the abandoned attendant booth tucked inside a corner of the Jax's parking garage. Why was there an attendant booth at all down here? Maybe at some point it was going to be a public parking lot? Or at least open to the public? Maybe attendant booths just come as part of the deal when you build a garage? In any event, the tiny room we were crouching in was a dusty, disused box of concrete and plaster with cardboard taped up where a plexiglass window might have been.

"And honestly, any *plans* I have ever made? Trips, dinners out, concerts? The hour before it was time to go, I didn't want to. Every single thing I have ever planned, at some point, I just didn't want to do it. Do you relate to that at all?"

After a moment, during which perhaps Kurlansky was wondering if he should humor me, he simply said, "No."

Ten minutes before this rather one-sided conversation, Robin had opened the trunk of her BMW but demanded I stay put until she darted inside the Jax. Standing above me, she was suddenly full of nervous energy, like an actress on opening night. As soon as she was gone, I crept out of the trunk, opened the door to the Jax's basement, and slunk into the hallway. And there was Kurlansky. Pacing in my direction. In his signature outfit with his hands behind his back. As if he were going for a stroll in a garden. We stood there and looked at each other. I put my hands out for him to cuff me. But instead Kurlansky hastily ushered me to this abandoned half room where I was currently expressing my misgivings about . . . doing things.

"First of all," Kurlansky whispered, "you have the right guy."

"Patrick Backus?"

"Patrick Backus."

This unfinished room was *very* small. Kurlansky and I were facing each other in identical crouches, our foreheads practically pressed together. I'm not sure why we were crouching, as, like I've said, the opening was covered in cardboard, but we were, indeed, crouching.

"Last time I saw you," I said, "you thought *I* was the right guy!"

"Not true," insisted Kurlansky. "I never thought you murdered anyone. But you were acting insane, and you had a notebook with a kill list inside it!"

"It wasn't a kill list!"

"I had to at least tease you about it!"

"*That* was teasing?"

"I didn't expect you to go and confess in front of policemen and civilians!"

"Fair," I muttered.

My thighs were aching, so I stood up. Now it looked like Kurlansky was about to give me head, and of course that wouldn't do, so he stood up. We were still really close to each other, and I was grateful he was chewing gum. As if he read my mind, he handed me a piece. I've never been a big gum chewer, too gooey, but I didn't want to commit a social faux pas.

"Why didn't you just tell me you suspected Patrick Backus?"

"That would have been unethical," Kurlansky said.

"So you told me the building did it?"

"I was hedging," Kurlansky admitted. "And anyway, the building drove him to it. With its thin walls, huge rent increases, and unwillingness to address tenants' concerns."

"You are one hundred percent sure it's Patrick Backus?" I asked. My gut was suddenly telling me we were moving too fast, not that I trust my gut—I mean, it's only right half the time, and what use is that?

"Yes!" hissed Kurlansky. "Backus has a history of violence, no alibi for either death, and a long-standing feud with Ernest

Whitaker! Also, Patrick and his wife have refused to allow the police entry to their apartment."

"All right. Well, that's all very convincing!" I whisper-shouted.

"Why are we arguing if we're agreeing?" Kurlansky whisper-shouted back.

I took the gum out of my mouth and stuck it to the chipped plaster wall. "It was creating too much saliva in my mouth," I explained. "Why don't you just arrest him?"

"I need proof," Kurlansky said. "Especially since you've been doing everything in your power to make yourself look guilty to the deputy inspector and everyone else."

"What can I do?"

"Well, what did you come here to do?"

"I came here to drive Patrick Backus into a violent rage," I said.

Kurlansky considered. "Why don't you drive Backus into a violent rage and give me a reason to get him into an interrogation room?"

"Right, that's what I was saying. That was my idea."

"Why are you so defensive?"

"Because now you're making it sound like *your* idea!"

"There's no reason to be contentious!"

"I'm feeling insecure!"

"That's a natural way to feel as a human being! Most of us just have the good manners to hide it." Kurlansky put his hand on my shoulder. "Look, I need to arrest someone tonight. And if it's not going to be Patrick Backus, it's going to be you. Does that give you the motivation you need to follow through to completion?"

"Does that mean I might *not* be arrested tonight?"

"No promises."

Satisfied that the only way out was through, I gave Kurlansky the details of our plan as quickly as possible. Alina was supposed to make sure that Shaina attended the memorial. She was then going to make sure that Patrick knew Shaina was attending the memorial and then she would goad him into coming down. Once Patrick was in the basement, I'd be there to accuse Shaina of having sex with and then murdering Ernest. This would definitely make Patrick attack me. How could it not? And it would be in front of many people, not to mention officers of the law. And Zack would be there videotaping everything he could.

Said out loud, this plan seemed insane, but Kurlansky was nodding vigorously. He looked at his watch. "It's almost nine. The memorial is about to start."

"It's also a party," I reminded him.

"Let's go! Let's go! Let's go!"

I pulled my cap down over my face as Kurlansky hustled me through the garage. "Oh." I turned to him, both of us still in motion, and said, "Do you want to hear about the doggie downers? We haven't even talked about Dr. Laura Olander."

"Not now," Kurlansky said, making sure we maintained a quick pace. "People's lives are vast and complicated, sure, but let's stay focused."

"Focused. Right."

Kurlansky opened the door to the basement hallway, and we peered inside. A steady stream of young, attractive tenants was meandering down the passage and through an open door marked ELEVATOR MECHANICS.

Good turnout. Robin would be pleased.

"Think you can join that flow of people without causing a disturbance?" Kurlansky asked.

I put my head down and merged into the hallway traffic, only turning back to ask, "If you see a cup of coffee, could you grab it for me? I think caffeine will help keep me motivated." But Kurlansky just continued to survey the passing crowd.

I kept in step with the passably young and hip. Their jeans and summer dresses, accented with grays and blacks, nodding to grief and formality. Their everyday good looks conforming to the unstated dictates of their generation: Don't stand out; don't be inappropriate. I can honestly say I didn't recognize most of them. As we held the ELEVATOR MECHANICS door open for one another, I did notice Icon Hat a couple of people behind me. He was about to call out my name, that enthusiastic puppy dog of a man, but I held my finger to my lips.

The crowd was now carrying me along through an unlit, cinder-block hallway. As we reached a pitch-black set of downward stairs, everyone armed themselves with cell phone flashlights. *I wish I'd had time to tell Kurlansky about Dr. Laura Olander,* I thought. This is going too fast. I'm being led along by others. Literally. Dr. Laura Olander! Didn't she have every reason in the world to kill Ernest, since his misuse of prescription drugs threatened to ruin her career? And if my wife was somehow involved in the taking of or, God forbid, distribution of these pills, wasn't that a reason for Dr. Olander to kill her as well? Had Dr. Olander had sex with me to manipulate me into liking her? (Although it really wasn't that kind of sex.) Or, and this made my scalp burn like I'd just eaten a glob of wasabi, had Dr. Olander not been sex-strangling me but *actually* strangling me? Holy shit. Had she been trying to kill me, like, for real? *But* more and more people were coming down the steps into this dark subterranean hallway. And now I could hear the thud of electronic music ahead of us. I inhaled the dampness of the earth. Boy, this was a really narrow hallway, filled with lots of people. There was no way I could get back upstairs even if I tried. As we entered one final doorway, I counted my breaths so that I wouldn't panic.

Once inside this dead-end room, we all spread out. It was surprisingly . . . capacious. And it felt like we were breathing in cool drafts of air that had been stirring around since the Middle Ages. Robin stood at the far end, on a dais in her mind. She was lit by two vertical neon lights—one blue, one red. And I could now see that the walls were thick concrete slabs.

Robin still wore her slim purple blazer, dark hair newly slicked back with gel. Eyes wide on all of us. Counting how many of us had come? Planning her revenge on those who had not? I looked around, my fellow mourners turning off their flashlight apps one by one. Icon Hat, People Who Play Beyoncé by the Pool, Angry Gym Guy, Earbud Guy, oh, and the old folks from the jacuzzi. Wait. Was that Craig Finn of the Hold Steady? Holy shit. I'd say thirty or so people overall. Of course, most of them I'd never even seen before—Jesus, any of them could have killed Ernest Whitaker. But before panicky self-doubt set in again, I reminded myself that Kurlansky had assured me Patrick Backus was the killer, and Kurlansky was a crime-solving genius. And there Kurlansky stood, back by the entrance with two uniformed cops. I crept to one side of the room and huddled myself into the darkest shadow I could find. I had a very unpleasant image of all these memorial attendees tearing me inside out on Robin's command.

Robin, meanwhile, was preparing to speak. She lifted up her note cards, then rotated the blue neon light so that it shone more directly on her. In a steady low tone, she began to recite. "Thank you all for coming tonight. I'm so glad so many of you decided to join us. Ernest Whitaker did so much for this building. He trained our dogs. But more importantly, he brought us together when we were all alone." Robin's flat delivery in no way revealed the deeper feelings I knew she had for Ernest. Public speaking had somehow reduced her to a pale avatar of her actual self. "Ernest was one of those rare people who went out of his way to make plans that included others. When he started to have these get-togethers down here, he gave those of us who felt isolated a community. Yes, sometimes he would challenge our accepted social norms, but more often he just didn't want to be by himself. He wanted to converse and laugh and pet our dogs. He struggled with depression." She looked up from her cards. "You all knew that, right?" She stared blankly at us, and we stared blankly back at her. She went back to her cards. "He struggled with his need to be loved all the time by everyone. Indeed, when he excluded anyone, he did so because he was worried that you wouldn't be able to handle some of the things he was into . . . some of the things he made available . . ." When she said this, she looked squarely at the three geriatric vampires in the back of the room. "But he loved you all. And he loved this building. He really did. He didn't love it ironically or with an edge of cynicism. He just loved it here. Ernest Whitaker was just like the Jax." This was getting deep. I leaned in. "He was well meaning but overprivileged. A little bit boring but beautiful. And his time with us? Well, we rented it; we didn't own."

I glanced back at the doorway. It was worrisome that there was still no sign of Shaina. And no sign of Alina. The idea was that if Alina couldn't convince Shaina to come down here, she'd come down with Zack in tow. And then we'd . . . figure something else out. And if she got in trouble, she'd text Kurlansky. I looked back at Kurlansky questioningly. He glanced at his phone and shrugged.

"So tonight we celebrate Ernest Whitaker," Robin was saying. I wasn't the only one whose attention had wandered. My fellow mourners were checking their phones and whispering to one another. "So tonight"—Robin raised her voice a little desperately —"we're going to do the activity that Ernest Whitaker most loved to do with all of us!"

Oh boy, here it comes, I thought. This is going to get uncomfortable. This is where we all take off our clothes and have an orgy. Or take kinky pictures. Or sacrifice a newborn baby. I just hoped it wouldn't be an EDM dance party. I'd rather go to Rikers. Or maybe we were going to raise spirits from an ancient Native American burial ground? Maybe we should do a land acknowledgment ceremony first?

"Tonight, in honor of Ernest Whitaker, we play board games!" And with that jarringly joyful pronouncement, fluorescent lights popped up, and everyone, I kid you not, cheered. Tables were unfolded, blankets were unfurled. And everyone charged toward a cart behind Robin—why hadn't I noticed this cart before?—a cart that housed myriad board games: Sorry, Clue, Risk, Monopoly, Throw Throw Burrito, Exploding Kittens . . .

Indie rock played through speakers—where were these speakers? Maybe the music was Young Fathers? Or Vampire Weekend? Definitely wasn't the Hold Steady. I hoped Craig Finn wasn't offended.

It's not just that everyone was excited about the board games. It's that everyone was *expecting* the board games. In the depths of this building. In the depths of this community. In the depths of this man, Ernest Whitaker. Were . . . board games.

Now that I was no longer under the cover of darkness, the two cops next to Kurlansky pointed at me. Kurlansky motioned for them to stand down as he moseyed in my direction. I looked around at the chatting adults pulling out folding chairs and sitting on pillows. Most were opening their games and taking alcohol out of their bags, but a few were now looking askance at me and whispering nervously. My time down here was clearly limited. I darted up to Robin, but before I could ask her anything, she asked me, with manic energy shooting from her eyeballs, "How did I do? I think I did well. Do you think I could be the one to plan the parties now? Do you think *I* could be the glue?"

"Oh, um, sure. Absolutely. Hey, I thought you all were into drugs and sex and kinky shit?"

"That was just every once in a while," she said dismissively. "And frankly, it made everyone uncomfortable. We mostly did game night."

"Huh. Any word from Alina?"

"Who?" She clearly had more important things on her mind. "I'm going to make sure everyone has what they need. Sometimes dice and other spare parts go missing." Where were we? In a retirement community? As Robin scanned the crowd, looking for any hipster who might be in need of a tiny pencil, she noticed that a lot of the participants were now blatantly staring at us—staring at me. She whispered, "All right, you need to get the fuck out of here before you ruin the vibe."

A few people were actually getting panicky, and a couple of folks stood up. There was some loud muttering of the "Isn't that the man the police are looking for?" variety. Well, there was no way to get out of here, not with those two large officers, hands on holsters, guarding the only exit.

Clearly feeling the rising tension in the room, Kurlansky, who'd been hovering behind me, took a few steps forward and whispered in my ear, "I'm going to fake arrest you now." Then he loudly told me I was under arrest for the deaths of Ernest Whitaker and Laura Downing. He read me my rights and cuffed me. Boy, it was really hard to tell the difference between a fake arrest and a real arrest.

Then Robin told the jittery game players, "There's nothing to worry about. Everything has gone according to my plan!" Oh, she was now a mastermind of law enforcement. How nice for her. "How could we pay greater honor to Ernest Whitaker than by arresting his murderer?" Goddamn, they applauded. Goddamn. All these people looking at me as I was being escorted out of the room were applauding. Even Icon Hat! "Play on!" Robin commanded. And they did. Maybe Robin would be a good Ernest Whitaker replacement after all.

As Kurlansky frog-marched me roughly, too roughly, out of the room, he told the two cops to stay where they were. As we made our way up the dark stairway, I whispered to Kurlansky, "I'm worried about Alina."

"Me too. Let's go up to Patrick Backus's apartment."

"Are you going to uncuff me now?"

"No."

He opened the door to the main hallway, and we approached the elevator as it revealed a wiry young guy with messy dark hair whose neck comically protruded forward. He had all of this photography equipment hanging from his shoulders. "Paul?" he asked, somehow craning his neck out even farther. I swear for a minute I had no idea who this individual was. "It's me! Zack!"

"Oh, of course. Sorry. What are you doing in the elevator?" I asked. "Weren't you supposed to meet Alina in the lobby like an hour ago?"

"Dude! I was late! So I snuck in and rode the elevator looking for you! I don't know where I'm going!"

Kurlansky said, "Press floor seven," and Zack pressed it.

"He's got you handcuffed," Zack said in an ebullient stage whisper. "This is some down in Ohio shit!"

"A meme?" I asked, remembering that meme culture was Zack's whole thing.

"Damn right," he said with a toothy grin.

"He talks in memes," I told Kurlansky.

Kurlansky: "I'm aware of the down in Ohio meme."

"I'm just fake arrested," I said to Zack.

"Dope," replied Zack. "This whole place is dope as fuck! This is where I want to live when I grow up!"

With that, the elevator deposited us on the seventh floor.

"I feel like you're keeping these cuffs on me as a hedge," I muttered to Kurlansky.

"It goes against every instinct in my body to take them off," Kurlansky responded. "A bird in the hand so to speak."

"And you," I said to Zack. "Why did you bring all that equipment. I said just your phone."

"I got excited!" he shouted. "I am excited!"

The three of us were now standing outside apartment 725, home of the Backuses. First, we heard a crash from inside, then we heard barking, and finally we heard a stressed-out, high-pitched exclamation tear from the throat of Patrick Backus. "Goddamn you! Goddamn both of you!"

I looked over at Kurlansky. "Probable cause?"

Kurlansky nodded. "Probable cause."

Zack let all of his equipment drop from his shoulders while his left hand struggled to turn on his phone. "I'm recording! I'm recording!"

But before we move forward, I think it would be helpful to re-create, to the best of my ability, what Alina had been up to the previous hour. This is based entirely on Alina's recollection. She was recording audio on her cell phone, but that all turned out to be too muffled to be of much use.

Alina had arrived at the Jax at 8:00 p.m. She settled at the table in the Library and pretended to do some work on her laptop, but she was actually keeping an eye on the front door, waiting for Zack to show up. When eight thirty rolled around and Zack still hadn't arrived, she packed up her computer and took the elevator to the seventh floor.

I imagine Alina gathering her courage, straightening her posture, hitting record on her pocketed phone, and knocking on the Backuses' door.

Shaina answered in sweats. Behind Shaina, Patrick was sitting on the couch, petting their sleeping pit bull. Before Shaina could say anything, Patrick snarled, "What do you want?"

Alina played it real innocent. "Robin asked me to come up and see if Shaina was going to attend the memorial. It's about to start —the memorial."

"I told her I wasn't coming," Shaina said.

Alina pressed on. "It's important to her that everyone who knew Patrick intimately—I mean knew him *well*—come down."

Now Patrick approached the door. He said to Shaina, "I thought you barely knew him?"

"I did barely know him!" Shaina turned to Patrick, and Alina took this opportunity to step into the apartment.

"No one invited you in," growled Patrick, his face going purple.

"Look, why don't you both just come down for a minute and get Robin off my back," suggested Alina.

"The fuck do you care?" Patrick asked, having trouble making eye contact, already in a state of agitation.

"I-I'm just doing my job," Alina stuttered.

"Is harassing us part of your job?" Patrick asked, raising his voice but looking at his feet to maintain control of himself.

"Don't you need to keep your voices down?" Alina asked. "Aren't the kids asleep?"

"The kids are in Larchmont!" Patrick bellowed, as if to show how loud he was willing to get. "I would be there too, but the police want me to stay in town!"

"And why is that?" Shaina asked reprovingly.

"I don't know!"

"It's because of your temper," Shaina scolded him.

"It's because of my temper, is it?" Patrick laughed. "I had my life disrupted by that asshole upstairs, only to learn that his rent was raised a *fraction* of ours! He even had the nerve to rub it in my face when we both pulled our renewal notices from our mailboxes! Not to mention another tenant stole my anxiety pills, but you think this is all because of my temper!" Patrick stepped closer to Shaina. "*I'm* the victim!"

Alina was now in the middle of a full-blown domestic dispute. "Can we please continue this discussion as we go to the basement?" she tried lamely.

"Why would we go anywhere with you?" Patrick asked Alina through gritted teeth. "You're only trying to get us down there to antagonize me in front of people. I know that's what you're trying to do!"

"No!" Alina shouted back, matching his intensity to cover the fact that he'd guessed it in one. "I want your wife to come down to pay her respects to a man she liked—"

"She hardly knew him!" Patrick spat.

"—I don't give a good goddamn what *you* do!" Alina yelled over his words.

"*He* was gentle!" exclaimed Shaina, surprising them both. "At least Ernest Whitaker was gentle."

"Oh, fuck you," Patrick hurled in a quiet, hurt voice.

"And I'm going to his memorial," said Shaina, newly resolved. She went to open the door, but Patrick held it shut with his wide, bruised hand.

"The fuck you are."

At this point, Alina took out her phone to text Kurlansky, as she had promised she'd do if she found herself in trouble, but, with his free arm, Patrick whacked the phone out of her hand, and it flew across the room. "You're fucking recording me, aren't you? Fuck you!" Now that f-bombs had been introduced, they were flying around at will.

Alina was scared, but Patrick hadn't actually turned off the recording app on her phone. He was too busy holding the door shut, so she thought she might as well antagonize him into a confession. "You can't hold your wife here against her will," Alina said. "That's kidnapping."

Shaina was still pinned between Patrick and the door. "You see what's happening," he said an inch from his wife's face. "Don't you see what they're trying to do to me?"

"So what if Shaina liked to go to parties and take the occasional drug! It's her life!" Alina shouted as she backed up to the kitchen counter.

"What drug?" Patrick asked, taking his hand off the door and turning to Alina.

Shaina turned white and said to Alina, "You need to mind your own business."

Patrick was now between the two of them, looking from one to the other.

"I know what they were up to at those parties. Did he have you taking the fucking doggie downers too?" asked Patrick.

Shaina was pale and trembling. There was no use lying.

"That guy was trouble! He deserved to die!" Patrick yelled.

Alina instinctively looked over at her phone, but Patrick saw her, and he dashed to it, muttering, "Goddamn you." Then he picked it up and threw it at Alina, narrowly missing her head.

Alina let out a yelp as Shaina yelled at Patrick, "The pills were no big deal!"

"No big deal?" sputtered Patrick.

"You pop Xanax like M&M's!" Shaina stalked toward him, finding her strength, backing him up to the couch where the pit bull slept.

"I'm here taking care of this family," Patrick said, "and you're doing drugs and God knows what else with the dog trainer upstairs!"

"Taking care of this family?" Shaina laughed in his face. "You run away to the lobby constantly because you can't keep your cool!"

"I'm calling the police," Alina said. "This is a domestic situation and—" But as she went for her phone on the floor, Patrick grabbed her wrist and held it. Alina was shocked that his arm reached that far. Maybe the anger reverberating throughout the room had warped her sense of space.

Patrick was yelling, "That's the whole point of this! To find a reason to get the police in here!" And he said to Shaina once again, "Don't you see what they're doing to me?"

"It's your personality that keeps getting you in trouble, not me, not her!" Shaina yelled.

"I'm not nice like the loser dog trainer, right?" Patrick's voice was thick with malice. "He's only able to be *nice* because he doesn't have the stress of a real life!"

"That's not an excuse!" Shaina shouted.

"Let go of me!" Alina tried to pry Patrick's fingers from her wrist. "You're hurting me!"

Patrick did let go of Alina but not before flinging her backward. She fell into the all-purpose table, hitting her hip, and then tumbling to the floor. "Ow!" As she held her side, she noticed the pit bull was stirring. It was warily watching the three of them, emitting a low growl.

Then she looked up at Shaina, who was still right in Patrick's face, saying to him in a serious voice, "You need to stop this. You can't do that to people."

"You all torment me to no end, you constantly conspire to ruin my reputation, even with my own children, but the moment I give a tiny push—"

Then Shaina said, "I am calling the police—"

"Then stop talking about it and just do it already!" Patrick yelled. And with that, he gave Shaina his trademark tiny push, and she stumbled over her feet and fell on the laminate wood flooring.

"Patrick!" The alarm in Shaina's voice unexpectedly jolted their dog into action. Before anyone knew what had happened, the pit bull flew off the couch, barking viciously at Patrick, standing alert between him and the women, both of whom were still on the ground. Maybe it was the shame that he'd pushed two people in the span of a minute or maybe it was because even the dog had turned against him that Patrick screeched, nearly hysterical, "Goddamn you! Goddamn both of you!"

And that's when Kurlansky pounded on the door. "Police! Open up!"

Shaina pulled open the door, and Kurlansky, hand hovering over his holster, said, "Ma'am, are you in danger?"

"Come in. Please, come in." And I think it was the realization that she'd invited a police officer into her home that made Shaina break down, crying.

"Shaina, what the fuck?" Patrick shouted over the barking, yelping, salivating dog.

"Ma'am, do we have permission to search the premises?" Kurlansky asked.

"Yes, yes." And then to Patrick, she whimpered, "I only didn't want them to come in earlier because of the pills I have hidden." And that plain but beautiful woman wept.

Kurlansky meanwhile pulled a radio off his belt. "I need a full team on the seventh floor, please. And get animal control to deal with this fucking dog." Then he looked back at Zack. "Stop fucking filming."

"You're still not going to uncuff me?" I asked.

"Fuck no," Kurlansky said, with a harder edge than I'd ever heard from him. Before I had time to admire his grit, he was inside the apartment putting on rubber gloves.

Alina skittered out into the hallway with Zack and me.

"Are you okay?" I asked her. She nodded, but her eyes were unfocused.

A stream of cops flowed into the apartment, and we, the three of us, were mostly forgotten. I thought about running, but I was cuffed, and let's face it, that move was played out. I looked over at Alina. One minute she was cracking her knuckles. The next, she was biting her thumbnail. I tried to make small talk to put her at ease. "I can't help but remember this is the position we were in after we found Ernest. Just waiting in the hallway."

After a moment Alina's head turned toward me and she said apologetically, "That was just a lot." I nodded and looked at her sympathetically, but she couldn't hold my gaze. She was all tiny, jittery movements. It was as if she was blinking in and out like a malfunctioning hologram.

I turned my attention to the Backuses' apartment. The door was propped open wide. Patrick was standing in the entryway, with his back to me, watching the police search his home. A cop had leashed the dog, but it was still barking holy hell. And Shaina was on the floor. Still crying. Loudly. Messily. I saw Patrick look down at her. "How could you do this to me?" It seemed like he was trying to figure out a riddle. "How could you not defend me? The police have been by my work, they've asked me awful questions in front of my kids. Now they're in my apartment. How could you think I'd . . . kill?"

Shaina looked up at him and said in a clear, quiet voice, "Because I'm uncertain this, what you're saying right now, isn't an act."

I thought about how many assumptions we make to patch over all the uncertainties in our lives. For example, we assume that our spouses aren't deranged murderers. Shaina had probably long assumed the best about Patrick. Had I assumed the worst about Laura? How hard it is to square our assumptions about a person with the actual human being in front of us. Patrick and Laura were similar in one respect. They both had bad attitudes sometimes. But while Laura, under her bad attitude, had done nothing wrong as far as I could tell, Patrick was most likely a killer.

That phrase, *most likely*, started to play on repeat in my head.

Maybe Patrick felt my eyes on him because he turned to me in that moment. Had he not known I was there? He seemed disoriented by my presence. And in retrospect, I don't think he realized my hands were cuffed behind my back. He looked like he was about to ask me a question, but then we all heard an officer say, "I found something in here." And as the cadre of police officers gravitated toward the bedroom area behind the partition, Patrick, surrounded by Judases all, bolted out of the apartment and down the hallway toward the far stairwell. And for some reason, arms still cuffed behind me, I stagger-ran after him.

Alina called after me, "Paul! What are you doing?" And she and Zack were now on my heels.

"I'm worried he's going to hurt himself," I called back. And really, I was. I forced myself to pick up the pace.

Police officers were now yelling at us to freeze, but I also heard Kurlansky exclaim, "No one fires a shot!"

As I closed in on the stairwell, the door to apartment 706, my old temporary home, shot open, and there was Martin Stowell in a plush bathrobe (one that I thought suited me better), shouting in a British accent, "What is going on out here?"

"I'm so sorry about the mess I left in your apartment!" I yelled as I pushed past him and stumbled through the stairwell door. I heard Patrick slam the door to the roof, one floor above me.

"You!" Martin Stowell yelled. "You're wearing my purple Nikes!"

I tried to apologize again when I saw that Zack was recording with his phone. "Don't film that!" Behind Zack, police officers barreled closer to us, and I charged up the stairwell. I burst out onto the roof, suddenly subsumed by a surprisingly dense darkness. I dove behind some shrubbery and lay on my side, staying as still as I could, while half a dozen cops roamed the roof.

I tucked myself under a shrub, damp grass pressing against my shoulder and hip. Police flashlights shone above me and then moved on. Behind me I could hear the wooden gate that led to the pool area flapping in the wind. I rolled on my front and inch-wormed myself up onto my knees, no easy task with my arms behind my back. I started trudging along behind the hedge, keeping low, traversing the wet grass one soggy knee at a time. The topiary separated discrete areas of the lawn on this central section of the roof.

"Patrick," I whispered. "Where are you? Don't do anything stupid." I didn't understand why, and I wouldn't for a long time, but in those moments, trudging around, whispering his name, I felt a weird kinship with Patrick Backus.

I could see officers in the open lawn area on the northern end of the roof, pacing along the chest-high glass walls on the perimeter. But I was pretty sure Patrick was buried away with me somewhere in the middle of this hedge maze.

"Patrick," I hissed. "Where are you?" I heard shuffling on the other side of the bushes to my left. "I hear you over there. What's the plan, man?"

"Oh, I have a plan." Patrick slowly exhaled.

"I'd love to hear it." I sank lower to the ground, pressing my belly into the dirt, and peered under the bushes where, as expected, I saw Patrick lying prostrate. "That mud is going to play havoc with your plaid button-down."

Patrick's eyes somehow glinted in the darkness. He must have lost his glasses while running. "You thought you could steal my Xanax and what? Goad me into violence?" he asked.

"*More* violence."

"You're a liar, Paul. You know that, right? You pretend to be nice, but you're a self-involved oaf who really doesn't give a shit about anyone," Patrick said in a clear, soft voice. "My mistake is that I've always been honest about my true nature. I'm uptight and angry. That's right, that's who I am, I don't hide that, and so the world hates me for it."

"I like that you're really bringing your philosophical acumen to this," I said, "but we're kinda in the same boat here, wanted men, so I'm curious as to your *plan*."

"You already know my plan," Patrick said. "Because it's your plan but reversed. I'm going to goad you into violence in front of the police so they can see you for who you really are."

"Wait, are you stealing my idea?" I asked.

"You can't copyright ideas," Patrick countered. I made a mental note to fact-check that later.

I heard someone behind me. I turned and saw Zack crawling commando style on his arms and knees. I motioned for him to take out his phone. He gave me an enthusiastic thumbs-up.

"The cops will see you for what you are," Patrick continued. "And I'll be the victim once again."

I clocked Zack aiming his cell phone in my direction.

"How do you plan on goading me?" I asked. "I'm pretty incapable of violence. Well, except for that guy in the hardware store. I fucked up his leg, but it was an accident." I said this last part more to myself than to Patrick.

"We're all capable of violence," Patrick said.

"Not me, I swear. I'm just a super nice guy." I put a bit of aw-shucks in my voice to try to goad *him*. It was clear that we were in an old-fashioned goad-off. I motioned for Zack to stay put and film from under the shrubs. Then I crawled through the opening in the bushes so that Patrick and I could have this goad-off face-to-face, man-to-man.

"Nope. Your violence is just all bottled up," Patrick said, getting to his knees, looking me in the eye. We were both on our knees facing each other, greenery to my right, the glass-walled perimeter to my left. "Dude, your wife is dead," Patrick said.

"I do hate being called dude," I responded coolly. "And nice try, but I already know my wife is dead."

"But she's dead because of you." Patrick smiled. "My wife knew your wife a little, and she'd say, what an idiot that Paul guy is. He's so casually cruel to that talented, hardworking woman."

"Yeah, well, your wife was taking pills and partying!" I said, struggling to keep my voice quiet.

"You mean playing board games?" Patrick shrugged.

"In her skivvies!" Did that sound as desperate as I thought it did?

"I mean, really, Paul," Patrick patronized me. "If you could have seen yourself with your wife. Your eye-rolling, your dismissiveness—you looked like an asshole. And the blatant flirting with and leering at the front desk girl, someone who would never even look at you if she wasn't paid to? Do you know how pathetic you are?"

Okay, he was getting to me. He was the superior goader.

"Trust me," he pattered on, "you picture yourself twenty pounds lighter than you are in real life. You're a slouching overweight bore of a man. A loser."

Over Patrick's shoulder, I could see that officers had located us and were moving toward us. Four of their shadowy figures approached, Kurlansky in front warning them with a familiar gesture to go slow and lower their weapons.

Patrick, meanwhile, continued poking at me. "And you laugh too loud and your teeth are yellow, and your face—it's just disturbing the amount of forced energy that comes from your face."

"I mean, this is irritating," I said, "but it's hardly moving me to violence."

Patrick smiled wide. "That's because I'm just stalling until the cops get closer." Half a dozen cops were now indeed circling us on all three sides. I instinctively moved toward the glass fence, just to put space between me and the police. For his part, Patrick rose into a crouch and whispered into my face, barely audible, "I killed your wife, Paul. When she came back to the building that day, I knocked on the door. See, I'd been fucking her for a couple of months, on the sly, so she trusted me. She was upset, so I gave her a few of those pills she liked so much to calm her down. I left her alone for a few minutes, and when I came back, she was disoriented, and her breathing was labored. She was staring out the balcony window. I came up behind her and strangled her with the chain. Like I said, she was disoriented. She didn't know who was behind her, but in her last moment, do you know what she said? She said, 'Paul, how could you do this to me? Why are you killing me, Paul?' But she didn't even fight it. You'd made her life that miserable."

I stood to my full height. I wanted to attack Patrick. I wanted to hit Patrick. I wanted to kill him.

But there was one thing Patrick didn't know.

My hands were cuffed behind my back.

"What's wrong with you!" Patrick yelled. "Have you no honor, no pride!" Through gritted teeth, "Attack me." And then in a quiet voice, "I killed your whore wife, and she thought it was you doing it!" And then Patrick looked back and saw the cops closing in, and he realized they may even have heard him, and he was panicking, and he shoved me a little. "Hit me! Hit me!"

Patrick looked back again, and the police were closer, and his eyes were wild with fear. "Attack me! I murdered your whore wife!" And now he knew *that* was way too loud. He was fucked—he'd confessed, and the police had *heard*. He suddenly jerked into motion, charging at me—to attack me, to hit me, to kill me—and I just stepped aside on instinct.

And Patrick toppled over the glass partition and plummeted down nine stories to the parking lot, a concrete death. I could tell you what I saw as we all gawked over the ledge. But why keep you up at night? Suffice to say, it was no longer a man.

On either side of me, police officers lined the chest-high wall and looked down. Kurlansky was next to me, shaking his head. I looked behind me. Zack was still filming. And behind him, I saw Alina, her hand to her mouth.

Patrick had confessed. The police had heard it. Zack had recorded it. Apparently, there was evidence in Patrick's apartment. We'd won. I'd won. But I'll admit part of me was tempted to follow Patrick over the edge. Winning never felt all that comfortable to me.

CHAPTER 15
ROOMMATES

I went through the next few weeks like I was on a people mover in an airport, passively conveyed from scene to scene. Or more like I was on an airplane. Ears clogged. In-flight entertainment broken. No hope of landing.

Occasionally, in my apartment with the dog on my lap, I'd scroll the internet. Headlines were variations of "Aggrieved Tenant Kills Upstairs Neighbor." Laura's death was mostly a weight for paragraph three to bear. A few in-depth articles delved into Patrick Backus's final moments and questioned the police's tactics. Meanwhile, pertinent details trickled out. The public learned, for instance, that the murder weapon, the beaded chain, had been found attached to another chain on a window in the Backuses' apartment, hiding in plain sight. That these stainless steel balls had Ernest's DNA on them (but not Laura's, not that anyone seemed to care), made Patrick Backus seem less like a disgruntled apartment dweller and more like a serial killer, his murder weapon having served as a souvenir. And then finally the police released full tox reports. Both victims had used large quantities of acepromazine. This led to a series of investigative pieces on the recreational use of veterinarian drugs that in turn led to magazine articles comparing the ingestion of animal tranquilizers by hip wealthy Brooklynites to the use of the same drugs by fentanyl addicts in Philadelphia. Dr. Laura Olander was mentioned by name in a couple of these articles. But her practice had been shuttered. And Dr. Olander had disappeared.

True, on the night of Patrick's death, I'd been fixated on Dr. Laura as a potential murderer, but the more I thought about that scenario, the less sense it made. Hadn't Ernest's murder brought about the very scrutiny that Dr. Laura sought to avoid? I pictured her riding her motorcycle down to Mexico. Secure in her own conclusion that she was better off alone. But you know, a romantic kind of alone. The kind of alone that includes shots of tequila and seaside shacks and sunsets. Not the kind of alone that includes cavity searches and solitary confinement.

Alone was not a condition I had to endure very often the month following Patrick's fatal plunge. I found myself endlessly grateful to the people who held fast at my side (now that they were no longer worried I might murder them). Most touchingly, Alina offered to travel to New Hampshire with me for Laura's funeral. But I turned her down. Attending services in the company of an attractive young woman felt like it would be distracting and even inconsiderate to the other mourners. And so Alex drove me up in a rental car, Theo enjoying the breeze in the back seat. Our time together was amicable. We mostly talked about Alex's work and which galleries were showing it these days. Once we entered the un-air-conditioned A-frame Methodist church, I didn't say much of anything to anyone. I gave no eulogy. I left that to Alex and one of Laura's best friends from high school. Those speeches were moving portraits of an independent woman who fostered the arts in underprivileged communities. Curiously, I found myself in the role of support staff. I guided Laura's mother to the grave site. I helped Laura's dad find his glasses. I swept the living room and cleaned the dishes when her parents finally went to sleep at night. I acted like I was there to help those who truly deserved to mourn. This act of make believe made everything almost bearable.

My own parents didn't show up to the funeral. In all honesty, they rarely leave their sliver of New Jersey, an arid barrier island surrounded by the Atlantic Ocean. Their reclusive lifestyle is due to their trauma or their narcissism or both. But that's another story for another day.

When I returned to Brooklyn, I knew that Bob Shapiro would be waiting in my apartment. He'd offered to stay for a few weeks. Really, Bob Shapiro is a hell of a guy. A real mensch. Loves to have a good time, sure, but also regularly attends synagogue. He hangs out with his rabbi, like socially, can you imagine? They go to Broadway shows together, I swear to God. A super Jew, that Bob Shapiro. In the coming nights when Bob and I would drink Scotch on my balcony, dog at my feet, I'd fantasize that Bob Shapiro would take me in his big hairy arms and hold me tight forever. But since I have a lifelong aversion to body hair, I settled for listening to him talk about mystical Judaism. See, Bob Shapiro really digs Kabbalah. He'd drone on and on about how we're all broken shards that will be reunited with the Godhead in death. In death we will all shed our egos and come back together in a sort of eternal, universal, cosmic orgy. He'd opine about Maimonides and all sorts of other groovy mystic Jews until I could finally face bedtime, me and the dog. He deserves a book of his own, Bob Shapiro, he really does.

But here is what I did not expect that night when I returned to Brooklyn from New Hampshire. I did not expect that Alina Serrano would be, once again, against all odds, sitting behind the Jax's front desk. Her new look, a version of her old look. Still donning the white lacy shirt, but her hair was now pulled back severely and her makeup applied glossily. Contacts now replaced her signature large glasses. When I opened those double doors, Alina broke into a wide grin. It was surreal. It was as if I'd somehow gone back in time. Or as if the past two weeks had been a terrible dream.

"What are you doing here?" I asked as I dropped my duffel bag.

"Well," she said, resting her chin atop interlocked fingers, "my advance for the book was thirty thousand, paid out in two installments over one year. When you think about all the hours it took me to write that book, that's not even minimum wage. I found that to be . . . disconcerting. So I asked management if they'd just bring me back on as a temp, you know, to cover odd shifts here and there."

I didn't know what to say to that.

"And you know," she continued, now leaning back in her chair, probably taking in my puffy face and wrinkled clothes, "I could have taken a job somewhere else. But now I can keep an eye on you."

(Dear reader, for the first time in writing this, I'm worried that you are ahead of me. That you have figured out something crucial, about which I was still in the dark. Though, Jesus, maybe you've been ahead of me the whole time. Maybe you've been shaking your head impatiently as I doddered around, even screaming to your spouse, 'Jesus, it's so obvious!' If this is true, I am deeply ashamed.)

"Between you and me," she said, "I think I need some sort of stability in my life." She spread her arms out and grabbed both sides of the large granite desktop. "Maybe once my book is a bestseller and my publisher flies me to fancy conferences all over the world, maybe then I'll give up this grind." She looked up at me, smiled again, and crinkled her nose.

I'd like to say that during the next days and weeks my fellow tenants regarded me with sympathy or pulled me aside to say things like "I'm so sorry we ever thought you were capable of murder, let alone applauded when you were arrested," but they didn't. Here at the Jax, anonymity and apathy reigned once again.

How could these residents have lived through events of such enormity and then have gone back to normal life so easily? I remember feeling similarly surprised last spring when the pandemic seemed to have truly waned. I was left thinking, *Remember when we were all wearing masks? Remember when Broadway was shuttered? Remember when so many of our fellow New Yorkers died?* But no one knew how to process all of that, me least of all, so we just moved on. This time, however, I wasn't able to just move on.

After Bob Shapiro ended his residency in my apartment—he had to travel to Germany to recover some potentially stolen paintings from a European art dealer (his life is *fascinating*)—I struggled to fill my days. Walking Theo was a lifesaver. And chatting with Alina at the front desk was a highlight, though her schedule was erratic. About once a week, Robin invited me out to dinner. She'd pick a fancy restaurant, and I'd pick out some decent clothes. She'd spin a monologue, I assumed to entertain me, usually about how her coworkers were idiots or about how few of her fellow tenants attended her latest board game night. Her idea of conversation was usually a series of grievances, but I was grateful that at least she wasn't at all interested in me.

Unfortunately, even my legal troubles failed to keep me properly entertained. The police dropped the charges against me, most of which revolved around resisting arrest and reckless pursuit. All that remained were the charges resulting from the physical altercation I'd had with that dude in the hardware store, but we arrived at a civil settlement pretty quickly, for a sum of money that seemed quite reasonable, and those criminal charges were also dropped.

As for Martin Stowell and *his* threat to sue me, I guess he figured it wasn't worth the trouble, even though I was still blatantly parading around in his purple Nikes. It's too bad he didn't initiate any legal action because I really needed something to distract my mind.

My only other recourse from falling down ye olde endless pit of depression and despair was to constantly interrogate the veracity of Patrick Backus's confession, a line of inquiry that I could tell was getting on my front desk friend's nerves.

"All I'm asking," I said to Alina one humid morning on my way back in from walking Theo, "is are we *sure* Patrick Backus did it?"

"Paul," Alina said, closing her eyes to summon some inner strength, "the police found the murder weapon in his apartment."

"I know, I know," I said. "But you and I both know how easy it is to get into these apartments."

"But who would have planted it?" she asked.

At that moment, Stovan sauntered in from the sidewalk, redolent of cigarette smoke. With one hand he swung an unwieldy toolbox and with the other he fist-pounded me.

"What's up, brother?" he asked in nasal tones. "How you doin', pooch?" And off he trotted, looking very pleased with himself.

I leaned over the desk and whispered, "We never found out why Stovan was sneaking into people's apartments and moving things around. That's a loose end."

"True," Alina admitted, but she raised her eyebrows in the center, a sign that she was concerned for my mental well-being. "Why don't you ask him?"

———

"Hey, Stovan," I said, approaching him a few days later. He was sitting in a metal chair on the grass mound behind the building, smoking one of his tiny cigarettes. It was a weekend in August, but it felt like nature had already flipped the switch to fall. "Mind if I sit?" And I sat in the chair next to his. "If August stays this cool, maybe they'll have to close the pool early."

He smirked at me. "I wish. What a pain in the ass that pool is.

Why put a pool on a roof? You know, brother, in Asian cultures, it's bad luck to have water above your head."

"I didn't know that," I said, "but it explains a lot."

"Hmm."

I considered just sitting with Stovan in silence. But of course, I didn't. "Hey, I need to ask you a question."

"Okay. For you, whatever you want." The breeze playfully danced through his few strands of hair.

"Earlier in the summer, why were you moving people's things around in their apartments?"

"I don't know what you're talking about, brother."

"Come on," I said. "I saw you one night. When I was in Martin Stowell's apartment."

"And why were you in Martin Stowell's apartment?" he asked.

"The point is I woke up and you were letting yourself into that apartment in the middle of the night."

"You must have been dreaming, brother."

I thought that was as far as I was going to get with Stovan. But then one night, I woke up in bed to the pervasive smell of tobacco. I sat up and there he was, standing in my bedroom doorway, looking at me, drunk, slurring his words, barely able to grip his cigarette. "I am sorry."

"What for?" I tried not to cough.

"You seem like a nice guy," Stovan said to the floor. "You don't understand what it's like here. Money is good. Comfortable. I work with my hands. And Serbs, you know, we work a lot of these jobs in the nice apartment buildings. We hold these jobs for each other because they are good jobs." He ran his free hand back and forth over his stubble, not lifting his eyes. "You don't know. In the nineties what it was like in Bosnia . . . you don't know. You should never know."

He turned and started to slouch away, maybe feeling like he'd told me everything there was to tell.

"Wait, Stovan. I don't understand."

He looked back at me. "Sometimes I need to blow off a little steam, so I sneak into people's apartments and move things around. That's all." His bulky frame moved up and down in an all-encompassing shrug. "Don't tell Alina."

———

"I talked to Stovan," I told Alina one Friday night as various configurations of young people darted through the lobby to catch their Ubers, big nights in the city awaiting them all.

"And?" Alina pressed her lips together.

"I'm satisfied he had nothing to do with any of this."

Her lips relaxed into a smile. "Thank you." And then, as if we were turning the page, "When does your movie start shooting?"

"October," I answered. "But there's another loose end . . ." I wasn't turning shit.

"Paul, please."

"Do you have something more pressing to do right now?" I asked like a petulant child.

"No." Alina sighed and settled back into her chair.

A young woman giggled behind me as she skittered across the lobby and out the front door.

"The phone call bothers me," I said.

"What phone call?"

"The call that someone placed to Laura the day Ernest died," I said. "The one about the doggie downers."

"What about that bothers you?"

"We still don't know who made it."

"It was probably Patrick," Alina suggested.

"Alex was sure it was a woman."

I kept looking at Alina until she became exasperated. "I don't have the answer! I don't know! Go ask Kurlansky maybe?"

———

The esteemed detective and I met up at Temkin's Bar on Greenpoint Avenue. This bar, which had been silent when Alina and I shared a drink there a couple of months ago, was now jam-packed with people, music blaring.

"The call to your wife was made from Ernest Whitaker's phone!" Kurlansky answered, shouting over the din as he passed me a beer. His shirt was unbuttoned, showcasing the full flock of birds originating below his right pectoral and flying in formation up around his neck. He leaned his back against the bar and took in the scene of the young and not so young dancing cheek to jowl, pressed in close by tables and booths.

"That doesn't make sense!" I shouted back. "Ernest had died hours before my wife got that call."

"My guess? Patrick Backus stole Ernest's phone when he killed him!"

"So Patrick called Laura from Ernest's phone? Why? To lure her back to the building?"

"Maybe! I like that theory!" Kurlansky turned to me and slapped me on the back. "Patrick probably didn't want the call to be traced back to his phone."

"But wait, that doesn't make sense either," I said as Kurlansky ordered a shot of whiskey, bouncing his tush to the bass line. "See, Patrick got the idea to frame me only after he saw me in the elevator with that police officer," I persisted. "And that was a couple of hours after he'd killed Ernest. So there was no reason for him to take Ernest's cell phone at the time of the murder."

"You're right! That doesn't make a whole lot of sense!" Kurlansky laughed and downed his shot. "Who knows why he took the phone, that crazy fuck!"

"Okay, so answer me this."

"What?"

"Did you really know who killed Ernest the day we talked by the pool?"

Kurlansky broke into a goofy grin. "Fake it till you make it, bro!"

"So at what point did you know Patrick Backus was the killer?"

Kurlansky leaned low on the bar and gestured for me to come nearer. "Let me tell you a secret. I'd never been on a murder before. In fact, you probably know this, but there hadn't even been a murder in this district since 2017."

"I didn't know that."

"No wonder the rents are so high!" He laughed and boogied backward away from me, into the middle of the impromptu dance floor. "But I'll be seeing more action soon! Citywide homicide division, here I come! And I'm only twenty-six years old! Bruh!"

A song with a strong throbbing beat came on, and Kurlansky pulled a couple of middle-aged ladies toward him. I thought I heard him brag to one of them, "I extracted not one confession but two! One from that guy and one from the real murderer!"

Kurlansky, genius detective? Maybe not so much.

I plodded out to the middle of the revelers, feeling like a schoolmarm, and tugged Kurlansky back toward me by his elbow. "What if Patrick confessed sarcastically?" I asked, hoping the lack of expression on my face conveyed my seriousness.

And then with a nastiness I found alarming, Kurlansky spat, "You shut the fuck up."

"Detective Kurlansky is not a genius." I followed Alina around as she mopped the lobby floor on an obnoxiously bright weekend morning. Tenants I'd never seen before were coming in and out of the building with coffees, donuts, dogs. "He'd never even been on a murder before."

"Paul! Stop this!" These strangers traversing the lobby paused and stared. "I know this is hard!" she berated me (in front of strangers!). "But I'm telling you, stop it. Please!" And then recovering, "He confessed. Patrick Backus confessed."

Of course I had been waiting for her to say this very thing, so I could respond with, "But what if he confessed sarcastically?"

She gazed at the dirty water pooling at her feet. Then, after a moment, she looked up at me. "That was you. Not him."

———

That night, I called Zack up. He was still in preproduction for our film. I'd read the script and I liked it. I dare say I was looking forward to it. The plan was to film in October. Zack's parents had a house in New Jersey where we'd all stay. But I wasn't calling about that. I was calling about Patrick Backus's confession. The police had asked Zack to delete all copies of it, but of course he still had it.

I watched the scene over and over on my laptop that night in the Library. I didn't want to be in my apartment alone with this recording. It felt a little like those *Faces of Death* videos we'd watch as kids. Real crimes, real violence. There was something unholy about the whole enterprise.

"I killed your wife, Paul. When she came back to the building that day, I knocked on the door. See, I'd been fucking her for a couple of months, on the sly, so she trusted me. She was upset, so I gave her a few of those pills she liked so much to calm her down. I left her alone for a few minutes, and when I came back, she was disoriented, and her breathing was labored. She was staring out the balcony window. I came up behind her and strangled her with the chain. Like I said, she was disoriented. She didn't know who was behind her, but in her last moment, do you know what she said? She said, 'Paul, how could you do this to me? Why are you killing me, Paul?' But she didn't even fight it. You'd made her life that miserable."

Was he being sarcastic? Or was he just trying to goad me into violence, even if the truth was what it took? What stuck out the most to me this time, though, was his contention that he'd slept with Laura. I'd forgotten about that. And I almost laughed when I heard him say it. That more than anything made me sure something was very wrong here.

I looked up from my laptop at the sloppily stacked books on the shelves. Hardbacks, softbacks, kids' books, travel books. And there, sitting anonymously among them, I saw my red cloth notebook, which I'd lost in the chaos of that terrible week. Now it was one book among many on the Library shelves. I pulled it out and opened it up. And there were my notes. In my scrawl. Really only four or so pages. Not much. Nothing particularly witty. Nothing profound. Nothing of much value and certainly nothing worth keeping. I placed the notebook back on the shelf, between *The Artist's Way* and *The World According to Garp*. Then I considered that there was something depressing about how I'd just "put it away." And I swore to myself that I wouldn't do the same to Laura.

A few nights later, I was leaning over the front desk. "I know you're going to be annoyed with me," I said to Alina, "but I'm not convinced Patrick Backus did this. I want to talk to Shaina. I want to see what she thinks. I found Shaina's maiden name on Facebook and then I found her parents' address in Larchmont. My guess is that she and the kids are staying there."

Alina's head dipped into her hands. I looked at the pale white line created by the center part in her hair. She said, "This is over. You're only going to bring a lot of pain to her." She raised her head and put her hands on mine. Then her eyes filled with water. "Paul, go back to regular life."

I took this in. I considered what she was saying for what felt like a long time.

"I just didn't expect regular life to be this . . . awful," I finally said. "Not that I'm feeling sorry for myself." I wasn't sure why I said that last part.

"I think it's okay to feel sorry for yourself," Alina ventured.

"Whenever I start to feel sorry for myself," I tried to explain to both of us, "I see this whole thing from Laura's perspective and what she must have been thinking and feeling. And I don't know what to do with that . . ."

Alina's small hands were warm and moist on top of mine. And we just looked at her hands. How perfectly shaped they were. I was hoping she'd stay that way with me all night. I realized in the ensuing silence that it was raining outside, hard. The world felt wet all over.

But soon a few drunk revelers came sloppily prancing in, and we instinctively moved our hands away from each other. It was then I noticed a softbound copy of *The Crest* by Alina Serrano sitting on her desk behind the computer. The cover featured a picture of a building that looked very much like our own, at night, in the rain, faint light emanating from the lobby. In the lower right-hand corner, in a white circle, the words *Galley—Not for Resale*.

"Oh yeah," Alina said, following my eyes. "This is the advance copy of my book. It's started to go out for early reviews. Still doesn't publish for another three months." She sounded almost guilty—guilty about her own happiness, I guessed. She pushed the galley toward me. "Please, take this one. I want you to have it."

I held the softbound book. A far cry from the black plastic bag she'd given me in the beginning of the summer.

"Paul?" she said as I was about to get into the elevator. "Please don't go and bother Shaina Backus."

"All right," I said. "But I *am* going to work over everything one more time. I just . . . I can't let this feeling go that we got it all wrong." With more resignation than conviction, I concluded, "I won't stop." And the elevator doors closed me in.

I slogged into my apartment. Pulled my laptop off the counter and sat with it at the table. I put Alina's book next to me and ran my hand over the glossy cover. The dog hadn't stirred. I hadn't turned on any lights or closed any shades. Rain cascaded steadily down the floor-to-ceiling windows. The klieg lights from across the street shone through the water, creating black-and-white lava lamp patterns on the walls in front of me. And I started to write this. This. From beginning to end. As a way to examine all that had happened. As a way to find what I was certain I'd missed. I started with a simple sentence: "I woke up thinking it hadn't been much of a spring, rainy and cold." And I just kept going.

Alina's book served as a talisman. I used her style as a guide for my own prose. How do you decide when to start a new paragraph? When you say, "I passed by that building," do you use the word *passed* or the word *past*? And what about passive tense? How many times could I get away with it? And why do I like to use passive tense so much? Does the fact that I like to use passive tense mean that I am a passive person? And what does the world have against passive tense—and passive people for that matter?

On some level, I took solace in this project. Books, after all, whether you're writing them or reading them, are tiny time machines. As painful as the moments I revisited were, somehow they weren't as painful or, more precisely, as lonely as the present. So I wrote. While reporting what I'd gone through with half of my brain, the other half was considering what I'd missed along the way.

I wrote and I wrote and I wrote. I disconnected my computer from the internet. I discontinued the internet entirely. I wore a sleeveless undershirt. I'm not sure what was on my bottom half because I so rarely saw it, tucked under the table as it was. And it seemed that whenever I did look up from my computer, it was night, and the klieg lights had once again turned my body into a shadow on the wall.

One such night, there was a knock at my door. "It's open," I croaked, unaccustomed to using my voice.

The door briefly let weak light into the back half of the apartment. Robin sauntered down the dark passage between the bedroom and the kitchen, strolling into my field of vision. Pink tracksuit. White sneaks. Black hair slicked back. Roller board suitcase at her side. Small bulldog in the crook of her left arm. Theo roamed over lazily to investigate.

"I need a place to stay." Robin sighed. "Construction next door to my unit." I nodded and she wheeled her suitcase into the office space next to my bedroom.

As I went back to typing, I remember thinking that her company would probably be good for me. But then I instantly lost myself in the chapter where I confessed to Kurlansky and fled the police.

When I looked up again, Robin was sitting across from me, sipping tea. The kettle was steaming in the kitchen behind her, and she was leaning over, her white T-shirt hanging low at her neck. I could see her nipples. "I know you're doing me a favor, by letting me stay here," Robin whispered. "But I'm doing you a favor too. Alina tells me she barely sees you anymore. You hardly leave this apartment. You've hired a dog walker, and you have your food delivered. And look at yourself." I wasn't sure how to do that, so I just kept looking at her nipples. "You're a mess," she said. "What's that in your mouth?"

"Oh, that's my mouth guard," I answered through a surplus of saliva. "I realized I grind my teeth while I write, so now I wear my mouth guard all the time."

"Eat," Robin commanded. And then I noticed there were eggs and tea next to me.

The smell enticed me, so I took my mouth guard out and ate. Chewing, I noticed the dogs were curled up on the couch together.

Cute. I looked over at Robin and wondered if she envisioned us curled up together too. It was hard to tell. But really, I knew that Robin wasn't the cuddling type. I was alone. I was so alone. But I did have my book. And I had the Robin in my book. So I didn't have much use for this other Robin in front of me.

Sometimes at night, on subsequent nights, when I'd look up, I'd see Robin putting food and drink on the table. We didn't talk much, but I did notice that the apartment smelled better, even if I didn't. And it was nice to sense somebody's presence without having to interact with them. Sort of an ideal situation from that point of view.

One night, Robin was sitting across from me, watching me type. I couldn't tell you what she was wearing or not wearing. How long had she been staying here? "You're transfixed," she said.

"It's the book I'm writing. Sorry." But I wasn't sorry.

"I'll make you some more food," she said. Now I noticed her hair was messy. What time was it?

"Did I wake you?" I asked.

"You're a loud typer," she said as she pulled some leftover Chinese out of the refrigerator. "What's the point of what you're doing there? Art?"

"No, no. I mean, maybe," I said, resting my eyes as I spoke. I could feel them watering behind their lids. "But mostly I'm reconsidering who committed these murders."

"Why do you care? It's done."

My eyes still closed, I said, "I told Alina I wouldn't bother Shaina Backus, but I think I have to. I never properly talked to her. I think on some level I was more comfortable with a guy having done these killings. That was a narrative I understood. But . . . but . . ." I realized I was out of breath. I opened my eyes, startled.

"What's the matter?" Robin asked, her face close to mine, as she carefully placed a cup of coffee next to me.

"I'm just having trouble catching my breath," I managed to say.

"Drink up," Robin commanded. "And tomorrow get out of this apartment. You need some exercise."

"Yeah." I drank the coffee and ate the Chinese food. And next time I looked up, it was just me and the sleeping dogs. Those were the only sleeping dogs I'd let lie.

It must have been the next morning because the sun was impossibly bright and Robin was standing in the kitchen, dressed in her usual sleek black suit. "I have to go to work, but I want you to promise me, you'll get some exercise today," she said.

"I'm not feeling up to it. Maybe I have covid or the flu," I gasped.

She made me some tea. I drank it.

Later, I'm not sure how much later, I had to go to the bathroom. I huffed and puffed and held on to the walls. Only realizing once I was peeing that I hadn't quite made it to the toilet. What the hell was going on with me?

I stumbled back to my chair at the table, falling into it, struggling to take shallow breaths. I drank whatever was next to me. Maybe I was dehydrated? I pulled my computer closer and used my will to type one word at a time. I wanted to get this done. I wanted to finish one goddamn thing in my life. I was writing the scene in New Jersey where I was staying with Dr. Laura. Dr. Laura had just gone to the grocery store, and I was turning on Alina's laptop. Alina's manuscript was already open on the screen, and it happened to be at a page about Brent Dixon, a.k.a. Patrick Backus. In this passage, Brent is missing a package and threatens violence. That anecdote had strengthened my conviction that Patrick Backus was the guilty party. I wanted to re-create Alina's story about him correctly in my book, so I clumsily grasped for the galley of *The Crest*, which was still on the table. Now, true, my vision was blurry and I was still consciously sucking in each breath, but, oddly, I couldn't find any mention of Brent Dixon in the paperback. I skimmed again and again. It just wasn't there. I wondered why Alina had cut him out.

Feeling a bit of strength coming back, I staggered to the refrigerator and took a large swig of apple juice from the bottle. Maybe the sugar would rejuvenate me. But I just felt dizzier. I fought through it and got back to my chair and re-created that Brent Dixon section as best I could, from memory. But it was bothering me. Why had she taken that scene out of her novel? It could have just been excised in the editing process but then I remembered that I hadn't noticed it the first time I'd read her book.

I sensed the answers before I let myself acknowledge them.

Soon I was writing the conversation between Dr. Laura and myself where I'd asked her if we could take acepromazine. And I realized as I wrote that the sensation I had after I'd swallowed the doggie downer that night was very close to the feeling I was having now. That was my last thought before I truly lost consciousness.

When my eyes opened, Robin was force-feeding me a pill. Something for the flu, she said. It was natural, herbal. I was too disoriented to resist, but I very much knew the true nature of this medicine. I knew now that she had been crushing these chalky pills into my food and drink from the moment she'd started staying here. And I recognize, reader, that you were very likely ahead of me on this one because you, unlike me, are not a fucking idiot.

And now it is night again. And I have been finishing this manuscript when I'm able.

It's night again. I'm typing these words now. I am in and out of consciousness. Breathing is like trying to suck a thick milkshake through a straw.

I love milkshakes. I loved milkshakes.

My legs are bound to the legs of this chair and have been for a long while. Tie line? My arms are tied to the arms of the chair. Yeah, tie line. With cloth underneath so I don't bruise. I'm still able to type, though my wrists are angled up awkwardly. Good way to get carpal tunnel. Not that I'll live long enough to suffer that particular indignity.

She takes me to the bathroom once a day. She cleans up the best she can. I take pleasure in watching that. But she doesn't look disgusted when she wipes up the room or me. She looks like she's hiding deep inside herself.

I can only imagine she's killing me so slowly because she needs this to look like an accidental overdose. After all, the supposed murderer, Patrick Backus, is dead.

She was in here a few minutes ago . . . I think . . . and I asked her to please take good care of my dog. She said of course she would. "I'm not a monster. I let you type your nonsense, after all."

My eyes hurt.

My heart is loud in my ears.

Robin killed Ernest. Jealousy. She loved him. She told me she loved him. And he loved Dr. Olander.

"But, Robin, why did you kill my wife?" I think. But maybe I've managed to ask it out loud. Because she's standing in my kitchen, drinking my Nespresso, holding my tiny cup in her hands.

She takes a sip. "I killed her because I thought Ernest loved her. I just had my Lauras mixed up. Same as you."

So Laura hadn't been killed to frame me. That was a false assumption. My whole theory was based on a false assumption. So many false assumptions. That Laura had slept with Ernest. That Laura was killed to put the blame on me. That Kurlansky was some sort of genius. That Patrick Backus was capable of murder.

"That's why I went up to the pool every Saturday morning and got drunk. Because that was the morning Laura came to him."

Robin seems empty to me in this moment. Just a shell with

nothing underneath. I wonder if that's how I appear to her. How Laura appeared to her. How Ernest appeared to her.

"But how did you do it?" I ask. "You had an alibi. Alina was with you in the pool, then she watched you pass out in your bed." Idiot.

———

I look at the windows. All the shades are down. If I just rock my chair, maybe I can smack into a window. There's tuna fish salad next to me, but I know at least one of its ingredients. The smell makes me vomit.

I find myself resigned to my fate. Is that a sign of depression? Maybe I don't have ADHD. Maybe I suffer from depression. I'm thinking of how recklessly I ran away from the police just a couple of months ago. And now look at me. Unwilling to even try. Maybe I actually have bipolar disorder. That could be. What about narcissism? I bet I have narcissism. I'll have to try to unpack that later. Ha.

I find myself listing things in my head that I'll never have to do again.

I'll never have to go to the dentist again. That's a relief. I'll never have to be on an airplane with turbulence. Good. I'll never have to have chemo or Alzheimer's or see another Marvel movie.

Or remember a password.

I wake up because a liquid is being forced down my throat. I feel awful, dizzy, can't breathe, can barely type. Must type. Even though what I'm typing will be erased. Like my life. Like your life. Ha.

A voice brings me back to consciousness. Alina's voice.

Yes, Alina is here. Standing over me. "I didn't know she was doing this to you." And then, "Why are you typing what I'm saying?"

"Please go to the police." It takes great effort for my oxygen-deprived brain to form and speak those words. They come out as moans. But she's already shaking her head as I type.

Alina sits catercorner to me. She pleads into her hands. "I thought Robin was just keeping an eye on you to make sure you didn't continue prying. That's what she told me." And then Alina looks up to see if I'm buying it. I'm not buying it. So she resorts to anger. "Why couldn't you have just left things alone? I had it all figured out!" All those veins in her forehead—who knew? I suspect she's working herself up into a scene. Oh, that's one more thing I won't have to deal with when I'm dead—people working themselves up into scenes. "She wanted to put the blame on you all along! It's only because of *me* that we moved on to framing Patrick Backus."

Am I supposed to thank her?

"Stop typing!" Alina goes to grab my hands, but she stops herself. Maybe I'm too pitiful to touch. She starts making and releasing tiny fists. She stands up. She paces like a caged animal. Now she's crying. I'll admit, the fact that she's upset is making me feel better. It's like some sort of consolation prize. Sure, she's letting me die, but she likes me enough to feel bad about it. What does it say about my self-esteem that this feels like a win?

She tenses her entire body and focuses on me. I sense a monologue coming. I hope I have enough energy to type it.

"This isn't my fault. I didn't do anything," Alina whispers. "When I went up to the roof that morning, the morning you watched the front desk for me, Robin was in the pool, like I said. That ridiculous woman was in the pool every Saturday morning, drunk, because that was when Ernest had sex with the woman he truly loved—Laura. Robin talked about it all the time. How Ernest loved this woman whom he claimed didn't love him back and how it killed Robin inside, but she never said anything because she didn't want to lose Ernest altogether. Stop typing!" I keep typing. "I begged her that morning to stop making life hard for Stovan and to get her overprivileged ass out of the pool. She dried off and then yelled at me—screamed at me that I should have just let her be. That she was able to control herself as long as she was in the pool. That anything she did now would be my fault. Stop typing!" I keep typing. "Then she stormed off down the stairwell, and I stood up there with Stovan, both of us laughing at what a crazy bitch she is. On the way down, I stopped by her apartment to make sure she was all right. But her door was open and she wasn't there. So, oh shit, I knew something was wrong. I went up to Ernest's apartment, just to make sure she wasn't up there, but his door was open, and she was standing over him. She'd killed him. She'd already killed him. And she kept saying it was *my* fault, that I should have let her stay in the pool, if I had only let her stay in the pool. And then she told me to help her clean up. And I was so used to saying yes, I just . . . said yes. And I felt guilty, I guess? And part of me even felt bad for her? Why did I feel bad for her? And was she really as upset as she seemed, or was that just an act? But before I knew it, I was taking all of the sheets and the comforter from his bed down to her storage unit."

Oh, so that stuff from Robin's locker. That stuff she made us get rid of in the creek. Some of that was like actual evidence, like evidence evidence.

"And then we put a clean white sheet on the bed under Ernest. And she cleaned his bedroom and his body. That part was very weird. At some point someone knocked on the door. Robin said that was Ernest's lover, and as she looked around the room, I swear she was considering how she could murder her too. But the knocking stopped. And when we left, Robin kept Ernest's door ajar so that someone would find him. Before his body deteriorated."

She thinks for a moment. Shakes her head. "And then you wanted to go into that very same apartment. Remember you asked me why I was walking so slowly? I was walking like that because I knew what we'd find in there. It was like it was calling for me to come back . . . and that was freaking me out."

Yeah, I remember that.

"And then I guess Robin killed your wife, also out of jealousy. Jesus. I had no idea she was going to do that. I swear to God." Alina is crying, ugly crying. She runs to the bathroom to grab tissues to stop the endless streams of snot pouring from her nose. "But I realize now that shit was premeditated. She took Ernest's phone so she could find Laura's number and call her, and she lured her back to the building with the promise of commiseration and drugs. But of course, your Laura wasn't sleeping with Ernest. Ernest only had her number in his phone because he gave or, I don't know, sold her drugs. Imagine Robin's fury when Laura's only response to Ernest's death was, 'There go our doggie downers!'" The mucus keeps pouring out of her nose, like it was blood. "Oh Jesus." She goes back into the bathroom. I hear her voice. "But what was I going to do? I'd already become an accessory after the fact. I'd already lied to the cops." Alina started to laugh. "I would have lied to the cops for you too, but I was already trying to remember Robin's lies! How many lies can I remember for all you fucking tenants?"

Oh, Alina is back in the living room, becoming hysterical, wiping her nose with tissue after tissue. "I covered for her because I was scared of her!" Alina shouts, her eyes wide and terrified. Then her face darkens. "And Patrick Backus was an asshole. So when you started to think it was him, I kept leading you in that direction. I loosened his wife's photo in the album. I quickly typed that section in my manuscript about him and kept it open on my laptop so you'd see it. And Kurlansky had been looking at him too, so it was perfect. He'd already asked me if I'd seen Patrick in the Library that morning. And I honestly couldn't remember." Alina starts laughing. I'm worried she's losing her mind.

"Help me," I moan. I still have some sort of survival instinct buried under all this physical pain and depression.

"No," she says. "I never killed anyone." She's suddenly so calm. Her face is now clean and clear. "I'm not derailing my life.

Now that I'm closer to not working in a place like this but living in a place like this." She kisses my lips gently, but I don't feel it. "Thanks for your help with my book."

Alina turns to leave, and I know there is nothing I can say to change her mind. So I muster all of my energy and wheeze one last request.

"Will you play 'Time Has Told Me' by Nick Drake? I love that song." I'd like you to believe, dear reader, that I have some master plan, but I really just want to hear that song. She begrudgingly plays it on her phone. She's doing me this one kindness. We sit and listen to it. You should listen to it too.

The song is making me wistful for love, but whose love? My own love for myself? But I don't even like myself that much. The song makes me want to live, makes me want to feel love that's worthy of that melody, those words. Next time around I'll love with full faith, without reservation. Something is forming in my mind . . . an idea of what it all should have been about.

———

It's all been figured out. That's the thing about murder mysteries. There have to be answers. And answers are . . . disappointing. The not knowing is so much better.

———

Robin is forcing me to drink. Some of it has already gone down. She's trying to hold my mouth open, but gently, no bruising, and I'm fighting the best I can.

———

I try to say something. But nothing comes out. It's like my brain can no longer talk to my mouth.

———

I lay my head down on the table. Only typing when she's not looking. There's nothing fitting about me dying typing. It's not like I was a writer or wanted to be a writer. It's just a death. As my end gets closer, I feel more and more like a wounded animal.

———

I wish I had loved more fully.

———

Robin tries to get me to drink more liquid with the acepromazine crushed up inside. But I refuse. She's getting impatient. Why won't I die? I guess my organs are strong.

———

She's resorted to injecting it into my arm. Like the drug addicts in Philadelphia. I guess she assumes she can make it look like suicide by needle as easily as suicide by ingestion.

———

In my haze, through the blanket of pain that covers my body, I think about me fighting deranged Pineys in Zack's movie. Me killing the shit out of a bunch of murderous assholes in New Jersey. That brings brief moments of respite.

———

Oh, that thought I was having. Before. When the song was

playing. I try to follow that thought, that feeling, that feeling the Nick Drake song gave me.

I wish I had given myself over to love.

There it is.

I wish I'd had faith in love. I think I would have been happier, even if that faith turned out to be misplaced. The faith itself would have sustained me.

In my next life, I'll devote myself to something, to someone.

To Laura.

Laura.

She was a good friend. A good partner. I should have valued that above all else.

We can't know everything about anyone.

So faith.

Next time. Faith.

Faith. Not assumptions.

Faith in someone else.

Laura.

———

There are so many ways I didn't want to die. Tied to a computer in my own apartment wasn't one of them. I'm going to die typing. I'm going to die in an endless feedback loop with myself. Maybe this is an appropriate death after all.

———

You know something that annoys me? When people have all those unread emails in their inboxes. Like sometimes thousands. Just delete them. What's wrong with these people?

———

Why are commercials during *New York Times* podcasts so long and annoying? I've always wondered.

———

I'm wishing now that I'd written something beautiful and not this tale of lust and drugs. And pettiness.

———

One final confession.

When I started writing this book, I thought, oh, maybe this book will be the beginning of a series where I'm the hero. You know *Additional Attendee*. My series would be like Sue Grafton's but better because there are two *A*s, not one. And for the sequel there would have been two *B*s. Like *Battleship Buffet*. Or *Bellicose Boxer*. The *Blistered Butler*. You saw the subtitle? *A Paul Whatshis-name Mystery*? As if there would be more. More. More.

I remember now. I was going to call my next book *Bob Shapiro: Helluva Guy*. Wait. That's only one *B*. I need two. dksajfalijofh-wueajbjkn

THE END

PS. Don't worry. Paul will be back, resurrected, in *Bob Shapiro: Helluva Guy*. —*Ed.*

ABOUT THE AUTHOR

Josh Harper and his brilliant wife and brilliant son live in Brooklyn, where they act as emotional support people for their dog, whom they love very much.

ACKNOWLEDGMENTS

Michelle, Ben

Bernadette

Jonathan, Brigit

Fareeda, Nick, Danny, Sarah, Doug, Jeanine, Julie, Michael, Caroline

Ashley, Carolyn, Karen, Sarah